GONE THE NEXT

7/14
amazon

Reh

For Warren and Mirt Foster.

GONE THE NEXT

BEN REHDER

ACKNOWLEDGMENTS

I am very much indebted to the following people for their help with this novel: Becky Rehder, Helen Haught Fanick, Mary Summerall, Stacia Hernstrom, Marsha Moyer, Greg Rosen, John Grace, Tommy Blackwell, Don Gray, Juanita Pichler, and David Martinez.

GONE THE NEXT

1

The woman he was watching this time was in her early thirties. Thirty-five at the oldest. White. Well dressed. Upper middle class. Reasonably attractive. Probably drove a nice car, like a Lexus or a BMW. She was shopping at Nordstrom in Barton Creek Square mall. Her daughter — Alexis, if he'd overheard the name correctly — appeared to be about seven years old. Brown hair, like her mother's. The same cute nose. They were in the women's clothing department, looking at swimsuits. Alexis was bored. Fidgety. Ready to go to McDonald's, like Mom had promised. Amazing what you can hear if you keep your ears open.

He was across the aisle, in the men's department, looking at Hawaiian shirts. They were all ugly, and he had no intention of buying one. He stood on the far side of the rack and held up a green shirt with palm trees on it. But he was really looking past it, at the woman, who had several one-piece swimsuits draped over her arm. Not bikinis, though she still had the figure for it. Maybe she had stretch marks, or the beginnings of a belly.

He replaced the green shirt and grabbed a blue one covered with coconuts. Just browsing, like a regular shopper might do.

Mom was walking over to a changing room now. Alexis followed, walking stiff-legged, maybe pretending she was a monster. A zombie. Amusing herself.

He moved closer, to a table piled high with neatly folded cargo shorts. He pretended to look for a pair in his size. But he was watching in his peripheral vision.

"Wait right here," Mom said. She didn't look around. She was oblivious to his presence. He might as well have been a mannequin.

Alexis said something in reply, but he couldn't make it out.

"There isn't room, Lexy. I'll just be a minute."

And she shut the door, leaving Alexis all by herself.

When he first began his research, he'd been surprised by what he'd found. He had expected the average parent to be watchful. Wary. Downright suspicious. That's how he would be if he had a child. A little girl. He'd guard her like a priceless treasure. Every minute of the day. But his assumptions were wrong. Parents were sloppy. Careless. Just plain stupid.

He knew that now, because he'd watched hundreds of them. And their children. In restaurants. In shopping centers. Supermarkets. Playgrounds and parks. For three months he'd watched. Reconnaissance missions, like this one right now, with Alexis and her mom. Preparing. What he'd observed was encouraging. It wouldn't be as difficult as he'd assumed. When the time came.

But he had to use his head. Plan it out. Use what he'd learned. Doing it in a public place, especially a retail establishment, would be risky, because there were video surveillance systems everywhere nowadays. Some places, like this mall, even had security guards. Daycare centers were often fenced, and the front doors were locked. Schools were always on the lookout for strangers who —

"You need help with anything?"

He jumped, ever so slightly.

A salesgirl had come up behind him. Wanting to be helpful. Calling attention to him. Ruining the moment.

That was a good lesson to remember. Just because he was watching, that didn't mean he wasn't being watched, too.

2

The first time I ever heard the name Tracy Turner — on a hot, cloudless Tuesday in June — I was tailing an obese, pyorrheic degenerate named Wally Crouch. I was fairly certain about the "degenerate" part, because Crouch had visited two adult bookstores and three strip clubs since noon. Not that there's anything wrong with a little mature entertainment, but there's a point when it goes from bawdy boys-will-be-boys recreation to creepy pathological fixation. The pyorrhea was pure conjecture on my part, based solely on the number of Twinkie wrappers Crouch had tossed out the window during his travels.

Crouch was a driver for UPS and, according to my biggest client, he was also a fraud who was riding the workers' comp gravy train. In the course of a routine delivery seven weeks prior, Crouch had allegedly injured his lower back. A ruptured disk, the doctor said. Limited mobility and a twelve- to sixteen-week recovery period. In the meantime, Crouch couldn't lift more than ten pounds without searing pain shooting up his spinal cord. But this particular quack had a checkered past filled with questionable diagnoses and reprimands from the medical board. My job was fairly simple, at least on paper: Follow

Crouch discreetly until he proved himself a liar. Catch it on video. Testify, if necessary. Earn a nice paycheck. Continue to finance my sumptuous, razor's-edge lifestyle.

You'd think Crouch, having a choice in the matter, would've avoided rush-hour traffic and had a few more beers instead, but he left Sugar's Uptown Cabaret at ten after five and squeezed his way onto the interstate heading south. I followed in my seven-year-old Dodge Caravan. Beige. Try to find a vehicle less likely to catch someone's eye. The windows are deeply tinted and a scanner antenna is mounted on the roof, which are the only clues that the driver isn't a soccer mom toting her brats to practice.

Anyone whose vehicle doubles as a second home recognizes the value of a decent sound system. I'd installed a Blaupunkt, with Bose speakers front and rear. Total system set me back about two grand. Seems like overkill for talk radio, but that's what I was listening to when I heard the familiar alarm signal of the Emergency Alert System. I'd never known the system to be used for anything other than weather warnings, but not this time. It was an Amber Alert. A local girl had gone missing from her affluent West Austin neighborhood. Tracy Turner: six years old, blond hair, green eyes, three feet tall, forty-five pounds, wearing denim shorts and a pink shirt. My palms went sweaty just thinking about it. Then I heard she might be in the company of Howard Turner — her non-custodial father, a resident of Los Angeles — and I breathed a small sigh of relief. Listeners, they said, should keep an eye out for a green Honda with California plates.

Easy to read between the lines. Tracy's parents were divorced, and dad had decided he wanted to spend more time with his daughter, despite how the courts had ruled. Sad, but much better than a random abduction.

The announcer was repeating the message when my cell phone rang. I turned the radio volume down, answered, and my client — a senior claims adjuster at a big insurance company — said, "You nail him yet?"

"Christ, Heidi, it's only the third day."

"I thought you were good."

"That's a vicious rumor."

"Yeah, and I think you started it yourself. I'm starting to think you get by on your looks alone."

"That remark borders on sexual harassment, and you know how I feel about that."

"You're all for it."

"Exactly. Anyway, relax, okay? I'm on him twenty-four seven." Crouch had taken the Manor Road exit, and now he turned into his apartment complex, so I drove past, calling it a day. I didn't like lying to Heidi, but I had a meeting with a man named Harvey Blaylock in thirty minutes.

"Well, you'd better get something soon, because I've got another one waiting," Heidi said.

I didn't say anything, because a jerk in an F-150 was edging over into my lane.

"Roy?" she said.

"Yeah."

"I have another one for you."

"Have scientists come up with that device yet?"

"What device?"

"The one that allows you to be in two places at the same time."

"You really crack you up."

"Let me get this one squared away, then we'll talk, okay?"

"The quicker the better. Where are you? Has Crouch even left the house?"

"Oh, yeah. Been wandering all afternoon."

"Where to?"

"Uh, let's just say he seems to have an inordinate appreciation for the female form."

"Which means?"

"He's been visiting gentlemen's clubs."

A pause. "You mean tittie bars?"

"That's such a crass term. Oh, by the way, the Yellow Rose is looking for dancers. In case you decide to — "

She hung up on me.

I had the phone in my hands, so I went ahead and called my best friend Mia Madison, who works at an establishment I used to do business with on occasion. She tends bar at a tavern on North Lamar.

Boiling it down to one sentence, Mia is smart, funny, optimistic, and easy on the eyes. Expanding on the last part, because it's relevant, Mia stands about five ten and has long red hair that she likes to wear in a ponytail. Prominent cheekbones, with dimples beneath. The toned legs of a runner, though she doesn't run, but must walk ten miles a day during an eight-hour shift. When Mia gets dolled up — what she calls "bringing it" — she goes from being an attractive woman you'd certainly notice to a world-class head turner.

On one occasion, she revealed that she has a tattoo. Wouldn't show it to me, but she said — joking, I'm sure — that if I could guess what it was, and where it was, she'd let me have a look. Nearly a year later, I still hadn't given up.

"Is it Muttley?" I asked when she answered.

"Muttley? Who the hell is Muttley?"

"You know, that cartoon dog with the sarcastic laugh."

"You mean Scooby Doo?"

"No, the other one. Hangs with Dick Dastardly."

"I have no idea what you're talking about."

"Before your time, I guess. Are you at work?"

"Not till six. Just got out of the shower. I'm drying off."

"Need any help?"

"I think I can handle it," she said.

"Okay, next question. Want to earn a hundred bucks the easy way?" I said.

"Love to," she said. "When and where?"

3

Harvey Blaylock was maybe sixty, medium height, with neatly trimmed gray hair, black-framed glasses, a white short-sleeved shirt, and tan gabardine slacks. He looked like the kind of man who, if things had taken a slightly different turn, might've wound up as a forklift salesman, or, best case, a high-school principal in a small agrarian town.

In reality, however, Harvey Blaylock was a man who held tremendous sway over my future, near- and long-term. I intended to remain respectful and deferential.

Blaylock's necktie — green, with bucking horses printed on it — rested on his paunch as he leaned back in his chair, scanning the contents of a manila folder. I knew it was my file, because it said ROY W. BALLARD on the outside, typed neatly on a rectangular label. I'm quick to notice things like that.

Five minutes went by. His office smelled like cigarettes and Old Spice. Rays of sun slanted in through horizontal blinds on the windows facing west. As far as I could tell, we were the only people left in the building.

"I really appreciate you staying late for this," I said. "Would've been tough for me to make it earlier."

He grunted and continued reading, one hand drumming slowly on his metal desk. The digital clock on the wall above him read 6:03. On the bookshelf, tucked among a row of wire-bound notebooks, was a framed photo of a young boy holding up a small fish on a line.

"Boy, was I surprised to hear that Joyce retired," I said. "She seemed too young for that. So spry and youthful." Joyce being Blaylock's predecessor. My previous probation officer. A true bitch on wheels. Condescending. Domineering. No sense of humor. "I'll have to send her a card," I said, hoping it didn't sound sarcastic.

Blaylock didn't answer.

I was starting to wonder if he had a reading disability. I'm no angel — I wouldn't have been in this predicament if I were — but my file couldn't have been more than half a dozen pages long. I was surprised that a man in his position, with several hundred probationers in his charge, would spend more than thirty seconds on each.

Finally, Blaylock, still looking at the file, said, "Roy Wilson Ballard. Thirty-six years old. Divorced. Says you used to work as a news cameraman." He had a thick piney-woods accent. Pure east Texas. He peered up at me, without moving his head. Apparently, it was my turn to talk.

"Yes, sir. Until about three years ago."

"When you got fired."

"My boss and I had a personality conflict," I said, wondering how detailed my file was.

"Ernie Crenshaw."

"That's him."

"You broke his nose with a microphone stand."

Fairly detailed, apparently.

"Well, yeah, he, uh — "

"You got an attitude problem, Ballard?"

"No, sir."

"Temper?"

I started to lie, but decided against it. "Occasionally."

"That what happened in this instance? Temper got the best of you?"

"He was rude to one of the reporters. He called her a name."

"What name was that?"

"I'd rather not repeat it."

"I'm asking you to."

"Okay, then. He called her Doris. Her real name is Anne."

His expression remained frozen. Tough crowd.

I said, "Okay. He called her a cunt."

Blaylock's expression still didn't change. "To her face?"

"Behind her back. He was a coward. And she didn't deserve it. This guy was a world-class jerk. Little weasel."

"You heard him say it?"

"I was the one he was talking to. It set me off."

"So you busted his nose."

"I did, sir, yes."

Perhaps it was my imagination, but I thought Harvey Blaylock gave a nearly imperceptible nod of approval. He looked back at the file. "Now you're self-employed. A legal videographer. What is that exactly?"

"Well, uh, that means I record depositions, wills, scenes of accidents. Things like that. But proof of insurance fraud is my specialty. The majority of my business. Turns out I'm really good at it."

"Describe it for me."

"Sir?"

"Give me a typical day."

I recited my standard courtroom answer. "Basically, I keep a subject under surveillance and hope to videotape him engaging in an activity that's beyond his alleged physical limitations." Then I added, "Maybe lifting weights, or dancing. Playing golf. Doing the hokey-pokey."

No smile.

"Not a nine-to-five routine, then."

"No, sir. More like five to nine."

Blaylock mulled that over for a few seconds. "So you're out there, working long hours, sometimes through the night, and you start taking pills to keep up with the pace. That how it went?"

Until you've been there, you have no idea how powerless and naked you feel when someone like Harvey Blaylock is authorized to dig through your personal failings with a salad fork.

"That sums it up pretty well," I said.

"Did it work?"

"What, the pills?"

He nodded.

"Well, yeah. But coffee works pretty well, too."

"You were also drinking. That's why you got pulled over in the first place, and how they ended up finding the pills on you. You got a drinking problem?"

I thought of an old joke. *Yeah, I got a drinking problem. Can't pay my bar tab.* "I hope not," I said, which is about as honest as it gets. "At one point maybe I did, but I don't know for sure. Probably not. But that's what you'd expect someone with a drinking problem to say, right?"

"Had a drink since your court date?"

"No, sir. I'm not allowed to. Even though the Breathalyzer said I was legal."

"Not even one drink?"

"Not a drop. Joyce, gave me a piss te — I mean a urine test, last month, and three in the past year. I passed them all. That should be in the file."

"You miss it?" Blaylock asked. "The booze?"

I honestly thought about it for a moment.

"Sometimes, yeah," I said. "More than I would've guessed, but not enough to freak me out or anything. Sometimes, you know, I just crave a cold beer. Or three. But if I had to quit eating Mexican food, I'd miss that, too. Maybe more than beer."

Blaylock slowly sat forward in his chair and dropped my file, closed, on his desk. "Here's the deal, son. Ninety-five percent of the people I deal with are shitbags who think the world is their personal litter box. I can't do them any good, and they don't want me to. Most of 'em are locked up again within a year, and all I can say is good riddance. Then I see guys like you who make a stupid mistake and get caught up in the system. You probably have a decent life ahead of you, but you don't need me to tell you that, and it really doesn't matter what I think anyway. So I'll just say this: Follow the rules and you can put all this behind you. If you need any help, I'll do what I can. I really will. But if you fuck up just one time, it's like tipping over a row of dominoes. Then it's out of your control, and mine, too. You follow me?"

***

After the meeting, I swung by a Jack-In-The-Box, then sat outside Wally Crouch's place for a few hours, just in case. He stayed put.

I got home just as the ten o'clock news was coming on. Howard Turner had been located in a motel in Yuma City, Arizona, there on business. Police had verified his alibi. He had been nowhere near Texas, and the cops had no reason to believe he was involved.

So Tracy Turner was still missing, and that fact created a void in my chest that I hadn't felt in years.

4

Mia knocked on my apartment door at nine fifteen the next morning looking absolutely stunning. Black skirt that reached mid-thigh. A snug green top that gave a peek of cleavage. Medium heels. Hair loose and wavy and full of body. Not slutty, but sexy. Like she could be working as a receptionist at an advertising agency or a laid-back software company. Even her perfume was divine. It reminded me that I'd been contemplating making a particular proposition to her, but now was not the time. It could wait.

I was in jeans but still shirtless, so I waved her in and asked if she wanted coffee.

"Better not," she said. "It makes me pee all the time."

"Hey, good to know," I said, heading into my bedroom. "Gimme a sec. Make yourself comfortable."

"I'm not sure that's possible," she called out. I assumed she was referring to the piles of dirty laundry on the couch. A few seconds later, she said, "Jesus, Roy, what is that smell?"

Oops. I'd been meaning to take the garbage out. "The one like a bouquet of springtime flowers?"

"No, the one like a dead animal."

I slipped a T-shirt over my head, then looked around for my tennis shoes. "Oh, that's just my aunt in the guest bedroom. She came for a visit, and, well, I know it's sad, but she's in a better place now."

When I walked back into the living room, Mia was standing beside the bookcase, holding a picture frame in her hands. Laura. In a bikini. A shot from our honeymoon.

She looked at me. "You're fucking pathetic, you know that?"

"Don't mince words."

She shook her head.

"I found it in some old stuff. I wasn't going to leave it there."

"Right."

"Let's just go," I said.

You had to be clever about it. The subject couldn't think the incident was staged. That was the key.

Mia backed her 1968 Mustang into a space at the front of the complex, near the exit. I parked the Caravan in a spot near the corner of Wally Crouch's building, where I could see both his car and Mia's. The plan was to sit for an hour or so and wait for Crouch to emerge. In the previous three days, he hadn't left his apartment before ten o'clock. If he hadn't left his apartment by 10:30 or so, Mia would reposition her car closer to his apartment and actually knock on his door, which would be risky. He might get suspicious.

It didn't come to that. At nine-fifty, Crouch came waddling out to his Toyota. He climbed in and started it up.

I was sitting on the bench seat in the rear of the van, behind the tinted glass. I grabbed my cell phone — we had a line already open between us — and said, "The cow is leaving the barn."

A second later, I heard Mia's reply: "You are such a dork."

I watched as she stepped from her Mustang and raised the hood. The car was almost as eye-catching as she was. It was a fastback model that her dad had passed down to her a few years ago, mostly because he wasn't driving it much anymore. Same kind of car that Steve McQueen drove in *Bullitt*, with that famous chase, except Mia's was red, and her dad had insisted on some after-market safety improvements. But a girl like her driving around in a car like that? It was like something out of a Van Halen video.

Now Mia was bending over the engine, holding her hair back with one hand, her skirt riding up, showing a country mile of gorgeous thigh, and I knew right then that Crouch was dead meat. No warm-blooded heterosexual male in America could resist a damsel in distress who looked like that.

And here came Crouch, rounding the corner in his Tercel. I ducked as he passed the front of the van, then I raised back up and saw him slowing as he approached the Mustang. I lifted my handheld video camera and started recording.

I couldn't help smiling. Crouch had stopped and was leaning toward the passenger window, saying something to Mia. I could imagine the conversation.

You need some help?

Mia turned and looked at him. *Oh, God, yes. My battery is dead. You know anything about cars?*

You got jumper cables?

Mia gestured toward the Mustang. *Actually, I have a new battery in my trunk. I went to get it last night, but I don't know how to put it in. I bought a wrench, too, but I can't remember which thingy goes where.*

Right on cue, Crouch pulled into a parking spot beside her. I zoomed in a tad as he came around to Mia's car and proceeded toward the trunk. I noticed that she touched his arm — sort of a thank-you-so-much gesture — as he went by. *You are so sweet to stop and help.* He was grinning like a kid who'd found a twenty on the street.

Then Crouch bent over and came out of the trunk with a car battery weighing nearly forty pounds. His maximum was supposed to be ten. Searing pain? Nope. He hoisted the battery like it was made of Styrofoam.

Gotcha, you fat bastard.

"Damn, you *are* good," Heidi said an hour later, after we'd watched the recording twice.

"Thank you. Women often forget that I'm more than just a hot slab of beef."

The two of us were in a small conference room down the hall from her office. Heidi was sitting across from me, wearing a blue blouse, her blond hair cut in a pageboy. Cute as a button. Petite. Happily married, despite our occasional flirtations and innuendos. I'd seen the way her face glowed whenever she talked about her husband Jim, and I understood that, when it came down to it, our relationship was as inconsequential to her as that of a customer and a convenience-store clerk.

She pointed at the video screen. "That was all a set-up, right? The hottie in the Mustang?"

I shrugged. "Sometimes you have to get creative."

"Who is she?" Heidi asked. "Girlfriend?"

"Local prostitute."

She rolled her eyes. "Such a bullshitter. Hold on. I'll go get the other file."

She came back a minute later, holding a manila folder not unlike the one with my name on it in Harvey Blaylock's office. She handed it to me. I expected manila folders in a bureaucrat's office, but this was the private sector. I tended to tease her about it.

I said, "You know, they have these things called computer nowadays."

"Don't start with that again. We're getting there. Supposedly just days from pulling the trigger. Sadly, that means we will no longer be able to rendezvous like this."

"Sad is right."

Her office had been making the transition to a totally digital system, which meant thousands, or maybe millions, of documents had to be scanned and organized. From then forward, everything was to be electronic.

I made a show of blowing imaginary dust off the folder, and then I opened it.

Heidi said, "His name is Brian Pierce. Twenty-six years old. He's a dishwasher at a Mexican food joint near Lakeway."

Right up front was Pierce's photo, most likely from his driver's license. His hair was white-blond, sheared to a half-inch crew cut. Narrow jaw, not much of a chin. Small, wide-set blue eyes. Acne scars on his cheeks. Buck teeth. There was something about his bone structure that suggested Pierce hadn't gotten his fair share of chromosomes. The expression on his face — somewhere between a frown and a confused grimace — indicated he wasn't comfortable in front of the camera.

"This guy won't be modeling for GQ anytime soon," I said.

"Be nice."

"What's his story?"

"A week ago yesterday, he slipped on a wet floor and injured his wrist when he broke his fall. Supposedly. Nobody saw it happen. They heard glass break, but he could've tossed a stack of plates in the air."

"Which wrist is it?"

"Right."

"Is he right handed?"

"Yep."

"Seen a doctor?"

"Of course, but you know what that's worth. Even the legitimate docs can be fooled."

I nodded, continuing to scan the file. "Thomas Springs Road," I said, noting the street address.

"You know where that is?" she asked. "Out in the boonies, between Oak Hill and Bee Cave."

"Yeah, I know the area. My grandparents used to live on Thomas Springs."

"You had grandparents?" she said. "I figured you were hatched."

5

I went back to my apartment and took a two-hour nap. When I woke, I had a voicemail waiting.

Ballard, it's Spence. Just a heads-up that Wade Gruley is getting out tomorrow. Call me if you have any questions.

Duly noted.

Then I sat at my computer and began to do some research on Brian Pierce. In my line of work, Google is your friend.

Say, for example, a subject claims to have a foot injury. Say also that he's on a men's softball team, and you'd like to attend the next game, in case he decides he is miraculously healed and can run the bases after all. So you Google his name, sort through the results, and there you go. A complete schedule for the Austin Assassins. Just show up with your camera and hope the guy does something stupid.

Google Maps can also be helpful. When the subject lives out in the country — as did Brian Pierce — satellite shots of the property can tell you all sorts of things. The position of the house and any outbuildings. Is there a pool or a creek on the property? How about livestock, or farm and ranch equipment? Sounds irrelevant, but think about it. If a man is faking an injury, and he's sitting around the house all day, bored to tears, and he owns a horse, what's he going to do? Eventually, on a nice day, he's going to get cabin fever. He'll ride that horse, mow the back forty, or take a swim.

Maybe that's a bad example, because Pierce didn't own a horse. Or, if he did, I didn't see any evidence of it. What he did own was twenty acres of heavily wooded Hill Country land west of Austin, a good thirty-minute commute to downtown. The land had been deeded to him five years earlier, when he was twenty-one, so I was guessing it was an inheritance. Didn't matter. I didn't need to know.

The house was in the center of the property, ringed by cedar and oak trees. To the left of Pierce's property was a home on seven acres. To the right, a home on ten acres. Behind him, to the northwest, was nothing but raw land, with no buildings or paved roads for at least a solid mile. That chunk of land, I knew, was part of a nature conservancy. Four or five thousand acres of pristine beauty, free of man's clumsy footprint. Or, from a different viewpoint, filled with rocks, thorny things, and rattlesnakes.

Obviously, working a case in a sparsely populated area can be a challenge. The big question is: Where do you set up? How can you keep tabs on the subject without being obvious? Thomas Springs is a narrow two-lane blacktop with no shoulders. If you pull off the road, onto the grassy right-of-way, you look like you've broken down, and that's the furthest thing from being discreet. You can't park in a neighbor's driveway, even if the house is half a mile off the road, because eventually someone's going to wonder what you're doing there.

In this case, fortunately, there was a possible solution. About one hundred yards southwest of Pierce's driveway, on the other side of the road, was an old clapboard church with a caliche parking lot. I'd even set foot in that church on a couple of occasions, way back when, because my grandparents had been parishioners there.

I slapped together a couple of ham sandwiches, stuck them in an ice chest with three bottles of Gatorade, and headed out.

***

My grandfather, who'd been a professor at the University of Texas, had the foresight to buy fifty-seven acres off Thomas Springs Road in 1954. The tract included one of the highest points in Travis County, and at the top of that hill stood a home like a bomb shelter. Rock walls, concrete ceiling, a flat roof of tar and gravel. Back then, many of the locals lived in crude shacks tucked in the woods. Goat herders. Cedar choppers. Rednecks whose forebears had run whiskey during Prohibition.

The area west of Austin still had a rural feel to it — or parts of it did. But as I drove out Bee Cave Road, then waited for the light at Highway 71, I realized how much things had changed in the past decade. To my left was a strip center that included an HEB, a Starbucks, and a bunch of other chain shops. To my right was a retail shopping complex — massive in size — named the Hill Country Galleria. The developers called it a "lifestyle center," as if that would disguise its true nature. It had a Dillard's, a Barnes & Noble, a fourteen-screen movie theater. Yippee. Who needs trees and cattle when you can replace them with a Banana Republic? I suddenly felt guilty that I hadn't driven out this way in so long. My grandparents' old stomping grounds were being razed, paved, and homogenized.

The one bit of solace came five minutes later, four miles down the road, when I turned right on Thomas Springs and saw many of the same old homes that had been there since I was a kid.

Just out of curiosity, I drove the length of Thomas Springs Road — past the entrance to my grandparents' old place, past Pierce's driveway, with its No Trespassing sign on the locked gate, past the volunteer fire station, all the way down to Circle Drive, where I made a U and came back to the church, which hadn't changed a bit. I pulled into the parking lot, backed into a patch of shade, and killed the engine.

Sometimes I wonder about what happened next. Maybe it was fate.

Normally, when you start surveillance on a subject, you're prepared for the long haul. At least a day or two. Sometimes a week. Sometimes you have to cry uncle and give up. Hell, sometimes the subject really is injured, and the entire effort — watching him, and following him around — is a waste of time.

But considering where Pierce's house was located — and the privacy it afforded him — I figured it wouldn't hurt to at least see what I could see from the roadway. Take a quick walk along the shoulder and determine whether his house or even his yard was visible from the road. It was unlikely that would help me much, because it would be difficult to set up anywhere along the shoulder, but I wanted to know if it was even a possibility, in case Pierce didn't leave his property for several days.

So a quick wardrobe change was in order. I switched from jeans and a polo shirt to gym shorts and a ratty T-shirt. Put on some running shoes. Slipped an elastic iPod holder around my bicep. Now I looked like a guy out for a jog. The only giveaway would be the very small pair of binoculars I'd carry along.

I left the Caravan where it was and walked along the edge of road as if I belonged there, past mailboxes and gravel driveways. At one point, a truck drove past; the driver raised two fingers off the steering wheel, and I gave him a nod in return, hands on my hips, like I was catching my breath in the middle of my jog.

I came to the near corner of Pierce's acreage and it didn't look promising. Thick cedar all along the property line formed a natural barrier. I kept going, and after about thirty yards, I caught a glimpse of blue — probably the siding on his house, well over a hundred yards away. I raised the binoculars and took a quick peek, but I couldn't see much. I needed a bigger gap in the tree line. I kept walking, hoping there wasn't a neighbor somewhere watching me through a window, wondering what I was doing. Maybe this was a stupid move.

I was thinking about retreating to the van, but I'm glad I didn't, because I took a few more steps and suddenly I had it. A small but very useful gap in the brush. A sliver of unobstructed view to Pierce's house. I could even see a white truck parked in front.

And movement.

Someone was beside the truck, with the door open. There was no traffic coming from either direction, so I quickly raised the binoculars again and took a look. I saw the person leaning into the truck, as if he'd just come outside to grab something from the vehicle. When he emerged, I saw him in profile, and I was fairly sure it was Pierce. No bandage around his right wrist, but that didn't mean anything.

He closed the door to the truck and bounded up the porch steps to his house — and there, behind a screen door, like an apparition, was a little blond girl wearing denim shorts and a pink top.

6

The girl was scared at first, he could tell, but she didn't cry. That was a good sign. If she'd been a crier, he wasn't sure what he would've done about it. But she was quiet. Meek. Shy.

"When am I going home?"

Barely loud enough for him to hear.

"First thing in the morning."

A lie.

"I don't want to stay here. I want to see my mommy."

"I know you do, honey, but you'll have to wait until tomorrow. You can do that, can't you? Spend the night away from home? Like a big girl?"

And tomorrow he'd tell her the same thing. Just one more day. Tell her that her parents wanted it this way. In fact, it was their idea. Because they needed some time to themselves. So they'd asked him to watch her. See, he was a friend of the family. Like an uncle. Eventually, she would trust him. Even start to like him. Baby steps. Much better to build a relationship on affection rather than fear.

"Are you hungry? I've got a pizza in the freezer. We could make a pizza together. How about that? Wouldn't that be fun?" Trying to make

it sound like a big adventure. "Do you like pepperoni, Emily?"

"I already told you, that's not my name."

"Oh, I know. But that's what I'm going to call you, okay? It's a little game we'll play. Emily is a pretty name, don't you think?"

She shook her head.

"I'll make a deal with you. If you'll let me call you Emily, I'll let you make up a name for me. That's fair, isn't it? Anything at all. Steve, Ted, Henry, Albert. I don't care. You pick one. You can even call me Spongebob Squarepants if you want."

And finally, he saw the faintest trace of a smile on her face. Like she wanted to pout, or to continue being homesick, but she couldn't resist this silliness, the very idea that a grown man would let her make up a name for him.

"I bet you have a name in mind, don't you?"

She nodded.

"Tell me," he said.

"Jimmy."

"Oh, that's a good name. I like it. From now on, I am officially Jimmy. And you're Emily. That's the deal. Okay?"

"Okay."

"Now, back to the original question. Do you like pepperoni?"

Emily nodded her head again. She had an appetite. Another good sign.

"Well, then, let's go make a pizza!"

He took her by the hand and led her into the kitchen. There were windows on either side of the door to the backyard, but he'd closed the curtains and safety-pinned them together, like all of the curtains in the house. He'd disconnected the telephone line, out at the box. He'd also installed deadbolt locks on all the doors — the kind that need a key even from the inside. He'd done that when he was still in the planning stages. The same day he nailed the windows into place. He had a computer on a table in the bedroom, but he'd changed the settings so nobody could log on without his password. Couldn't be too careful. Kids her age knew how to use computers nowadays. And cell phones. That's why he was keeping his cell phone on top of the refrigerator, out of reach. Just in case she wanted to call mommy.

He pulled the pizza from the freezer and showed it to her. "Looks pretty good, huh? You want to unwrap it and put it in the oven?"

She appeared confused. "I'm not supposed to touch the oven. Mommy says I'll hurt myself."

He smiled at her. "You just have to be careful, that's all. Here, I'll show you how to do it."

7

Lieutenant Paul Holland was a big man, maybe six-two, two-twenty. Short, sandy hair and a pale complexion. Possibly a Scandinavian background. Early forties. The other one, the detective, was Hispanic. Built like a baseball player. About my age. Last name Ruelas. I'd missed the first name. Both men wore suits. We were in a small interview room in a substation of the Travis County Sheriff's Office on Hudson Bend Road, about fifteen minutes from Brian Pierce's place.

It had been more than an hour since I'd spotted Tracy Turner and I didn't know what the hell we were doing. As far as I knew, no action had been taken, other than requesting I come here for an interview.

I'd called 911 immediately, of course, then waited for a deputy. He had come quickly, I'll give him that. Pulled in next to me in the church parking lot and asked me to repeat everything I'd told the dispatcher. Ten minutes later, another cruiser showed up, and I was thinking these guys were idiots. Talk about tipping your hand.

Then the first deputy asked me to follow him here, to the substation. It appeared the other deputy was going to stay put.

"Can you get an unmarked unit over here?" I said at the time, nodding toward the second patrol car. "Instead of this guy?"

"What's the problem?"

Christ.

"Well, it seems like you ought to keep a low profile."

He gave me a patronizing smile. "We run radar along this road all the time. People are used to seeing us."

So I went with him. And now I'd just finished telling my story for a third time, to Holland and Ruelas. My heart rate was still elevated. My palms were sweaty. I could hardly sit still.

Why, then, were Holland and Ruelas so calm? They appeared underwhelmed. Something wasn't right.

Ruelas had a notebook on the table in front of him — he'd been taking notes — and now he closed it, saying, "Thanks for coming in, Mr. Ballard. We appreciate it."

And that was all. Both men rose from their chairs. Evidently, we were done. But I didn't get up. Instead, I said, "Can you tell me what's going to happen now?"

Holland checked his watch.

Ruelas said, "Uh, well..."

Pithy guy.

And just like that, I knew what was happening. And I knew what was *going* to happen. Nothing. "Consider the source, huh?" I said.

"Pardon?"

"You know who I am. You know my history. You think I'm a flake. Am I correct?"

Ruelas hesitated, shifting his notebook from one hand to the other. Yeah, he knew exactly who I was. Holland had already opened the door, ready to move on.

"Please sit down and talk to me," I said.

"Mr. Ballard, I — "

"Just give me a few more minutes. Hear me out."

He looked at Holland, who said, "I'm going to get some coffee."

Ruelas nodded, and Holland left. I knew I wouldn't be seeing him again.

Ruelas turned back to me, and before he could speak, I said, "It was a little blond girl. Pink top and denim shorts. That's what I saw. I'm not mistaken."

He placed his notebook on the table, slowly pulled out a chair, and sat back down. He seemed to be weighing exactly what to say.

I continued. "I saw a photo of Tracy Turner on the news last night. I know what she looks like. I'm almost certain it was her."

But I could be wrong. I knew that from experience. I had to admit it to myself. I wasn't one hundred percent sure.

Ruelas said, "She's been missing for eighteen hours. In that time, since the Amber Alert was issued, do you know how many people have called in, claiming they've seen her?"

"I know how it works."

"Fifty-six. All of them positive of what they saw. Just like you."

"Brian Pierce doesn't have any kids. He has no siblings, which means no nieces."

"Maybe he's babysitting a friend's kid."

"Okay, maybe he is. So why not check it out?"

"How would you propose we do that? Just walk right up and knock on his door?"

"Well, why not?"

"What if he doesn't answer?"

I sat silently. I knew where he was going.

He said, "Then...what? We can't just bust the door down, not without a warrant, which we can't get, not without probable cause, and we're not even close to having that. And now — let's just assume that you correctly identified the girl from more than a hundred yards away through a pair of binoculars, which is a damn big assumption — now we've tipped him off. If we knock on his door and he doesn't answer, we gain nothing and he gains a lot."

The door was still open and two deputies in uniform passed by, talking loudly, on their way to the break room.

"Are you going to set up on him?" I asked.

Again, a hesitation, and I knew the answer. Then he said, "Mr. Ballard, I can't tell you what we are or are not going to do. Let me say that I do believe you saw a girl. I do. But the odds of that girl being Tracy Turner...you know how many little blond girls are running around Austin right now wearing pink tops?"

"And denim shorts," I said.

He didn't reply. He was done talking.

I'd already told him what I did for a living, and that Pierce was my latest subject, so now I said, "I still have a job to do. Pierce is suspected of insurance fraud."

It was a clever way to force Ruelas's hand. If he was planning to put Pierce under surveillance, he wouldn't want me doing the same thing.

But all he said was, "I understand, Mr. Ballard. Thanks again for coming in."

I've made plenty of mistakes in my life. The mullet I sported in high school. Getting married at twenty-one. Betting on the Astros.

All of those things are nothing — absolutely meaningless — compared to what I did on a cool spring day nine years ago. A Saturday. Laura had gone to an aerobics class, with plans to stop by the grocery store afterward, so I decided to take Hannah to the dog park near our house. We'd been talking about getting a Labrador, and I wanted to see how Hannah would handle herself around large dogs. Would she be nervous? Excited? Frightened?

The park was crowded. Maybe thirty or forty owners and their dogs in two fenced acres. No leashes were required inside the fence, so dogs of all sizes and shapes were sprinting and bounding and leaping all over the place. Plenty of barking, too, of course, but no growling, because a sign said that dogs who caused problems weren't allowed to come back. These were all friendly, playful dogs, and most of the owners were, too.

Hannah and I sat on one of the many shaded benches away from everybody else and simply watched. She seemed a bit nervous when some of the larger dogs came near us, but she also seemed intrigued.

When a tan-and-white pit bull came up and nuzzled her leg, Hannah giggled hysterically.

"That's Belle," said the owner, a woman I had seen a few times in the neighborhood before. A jogger. Slender and very pretty. Great legs. Medium-length blond hair. About my age. Not the stereotypical pit bull owner, that's for sure.

"Say hi to Belle, Hannah," I said. I'll admit I was a little hesitant about it. "Is Belle friendly?" I asked.

"Oh, God, yes," the woman said. "She's a sixty-pound lap dog."

"Can I pet her?" Hannah asked. That was a great sign.

"You bet. She'd love it," the woman replied. Then, to me, she said, "I'm Susan Tate."

"Roy Ballard," I said, "and my daughter Hannah."

Hannah was petting Belle's head cautiously, and I may be wrong, but Belle appeared to be smiling.

"What a cutie," Susan said. "How old are you, Hannah? Wait, let me guess. Are you five?"

Hannah was too busy with Belle to pay any attention to Susan.

"She'll be five next month," I said.

"I know this sounds like a standard comment from a parent, but wow, she is really pretty."

I'd heard it dozens of times, but I still beamed when anybody said it. Hey, it was true. Hannah was an exceptionally beautiful child. Who was I to argue?

"We ordered her from a catalog," I said.

"You did not," Hannah said automatically, without looking up, because she'd heard me use that line before.

"Must be quite a catalog," Susan said, smiling. Great smile. "Where can I get a copy?"

"Well, I'm afraid the factory closed down. They ran out of perfect little girls."

"Darn it. I would've ordered three."

Hannah looked up at us both, just for a second, and the look on her face said she thought both of us were as silly as could be.

"How old is Belle?" I asked.

"Eight. Got her from my brother. He raises Staffordshire terriers."

"Oh, I thought she was a pit bull."

"Well...they're closely related. Some people say they're basically the same breed."

"We're getting a dog soon!" Hannah said.

"Oh, you are? What kind?"

"I want one just like this."

Susan looked at me. I'm sure she saw a certain look on my face. No, I did not want a pit bull — or a Staffordshire terrier — but I didn't want to offend her. "We're thinking maybe a Lab," I said.

"A Lab, huh?"

"Yeah."

"Can't blame you for that. A good ol' Lab."

"Yep."

"A good ol' predictable Lab."

Was she teasing me? She plainly was.

"I like to push the envelope," I said. "Set trends. When other men zig, I zag."

"Oh, I can tell. You're a trailblazer."

"Absolutely."

There was some flirting going on. No doubt about it. Laura had complained in the past about my tendency to flirt, but I never understood the problem. Flirting is fun, and basically harmless, because I never acted on it. I was faithful. Always had been, always would be.

Meanwhile, Hannah had slid down from the bench and was making herself more comfortable with Belle, who was obviously enjoying the attention.

"I want a dog just like this, Daddy," Hannah announced.

"You know..." Susan began.

I laughed. I knew what she was going to say.

"My brother does have some puppies available at the moment."

Again, here came the smile. But now there was something more. Something in that smile said *Go for it. Don't be a boring married guy with a Lab and a minivan.*

Then I thought of Laura. A pit bull? Wasn't going to happen. Not in a million years.

"Uh, I'll keep that in mind," I said. "Very nice of you."

She knew I was ducking the offer, but she simply smiled, then she and Belle wandered back into the throng of people and their dogs.

A few minutes later, Hannah and I returned to my Nissan Sentra — which is most certainly not a minivan, by the way — and then I began to think, *Maybe I should get her number. Just in case.* I could at least talk to Laura about it, right? It wasn't fair for me to assume that she would say no, was it?

Hannah was in the back seat, already buckled in, so I hurried to speak to Susan. I'd make it quick. Except I couldn't find her. It appeared she'd already left. So I gave up and returned to the Nissan. I opened the driver's side door — and then I froze. A panic gripped me so suddenly that I could feel my heart lurch in my chest.

The car was empty.

Hannah was nowhere to be seen.

I left the sheriff's department substation and headed back toward my apartment. I was tempted to go directly back to Thomas Springs Road and set up on Brian Pierce, but I had to be realistic. It was almost sundown and there would be nothing to see. I'd be sitting on the side of the road in the dark. Better to go home, think it through, and come up with some options. I needed to talk to someone, so I called Mia while I was driving and told her the full story.

"What are they going to do?" she asked, meaning the cops.

"Far as I can tell, nothing."

"Why not?" She truly sounded surprised. Then she added, "Oh." So much meaning in that one soft little word.

See, Mia and I have no secrets. That's because not only is she a bartender — and there was a time when I spent many hours in her presence, well lubricated, with loose lips and all that — but she has since become a close friend. So we share stuff. She knows virtually everything about me. Probably more than Laura ever knew.

For instance, Mia knows that, after Hannah disappeared, I more or less came unglued. Aimlessly wandering the street, day and night, just searching. Pointless rambling with no hope of success. Yet there were several times when I was certain I saw Hannah. Saw her in a car passing in front of me at a red light. Saw her in an elevator with the doors just closing. Saw her in a shot of the crowd on a televised baseball game. Situations like that. Called the cops four different times to report these sightings. Made them think I was losing my shit. That's almost certainly what made Ruelas and Holland so dismissive of me earlier today. They typed my name into a computer, saw my history, and thought, *Okay, this guy is a bit of a nut.*

Hence the reason for Mia's "Oh." She'd connected the dots.

Now she said, "How sure are you of what you saw?"

A fair question. I didn't answer right away. Being completely honest, I was starting to question myself. That's what happens. You lose confidence in your judgment. After being wrong so many times, you think you'll never be right again. "Ninety percent," I said.

She didn't say anything. All I could hear was the background noise. She was at work and it sounded like the tavern was busy for a Wednesday night.

"You think I'm crazy, right?" I asked.

"Of course not. I mean, it's not like you're claiming you saw Amelia Earhart. You saw a girl and you think it might be Tracy Turner. You did see a girl? Not a shadow or a dog or something?"

"Are you friggin' kidding me? It was a girl."

"Hey, don't get all defensive. The eyes can play tricks. Did you shoot any video?"

"I didn't have a camera on me."

"Hang on." I could hear Mia talking to a customer. Then she said, "So what's your plan?"

"Ha. Plan."

"So...no plan yet."

"Doesn't help that his house is stuck in the middle of the woods. I can't get close enough. Not without being obvious."

Now I could tell she was talking to another customer. Then she said, "You want to meet me later and talk about it?" Code for, "I'm too busy to talk right now."

"That's okay. I think I'm in for the night."

"Call me tomorrow. My day off."

***

It's difficult to understand why one missing-person case catches the nation's heart and soul while thousands more hardly get thirty seconds on the local news. You know the type of high-profile case I'm talking about. The one that gets near-constant play on CNN, Fox, MSNBC, and every other national media outlet hungry for ratings.

Polly Klaas.

Elizabeth Smart.

Natalee Holloway.

Laci Peterson.

Caylee Anthony.

Nancy Grace will yack about one particular case for an hour without telling the viewer anything new. Looping the same video over and over. There's something salacious about it. It seems to be more about entertainment — and ratings — than about offering information that may somehow help solve the case.

Something else bothers me, too. The cases that receive mega-airtime almost exclusively involve a white victim. An upper middle-class white victim. An attractive, upper middle-class white victim. I'm not sure if that says something about the value we place on various members of society, but I hope not.

Regardless, for whatever reason, Tracy Turner quickly became one of those high-profile cases. When I got home and turned on the TV, there she was on the screen, hair in pigtails, and I could feel a hole open up in my chest. The news anchor was talking to an expert who was delivering statistics that I knew, unfortunately, by heart.

Roughly 800,000 children are reported missing in the United States every year. Two thousand *every day*. Many of them are runaways, some are abducted (usually by a family member), and some are lost or injured.

Child abductions leading to murder are relatively rare. One hundred cases a year. Most are "average" kids leading "normal" lives with "typical" families. Three quarters of the victims are female. Eighty percent of the time, the initial contact between victim and killer takes place within a quarter-mile of the child's home.

The average abductor-killer is twenty-seven years old, unmarried, and has at least one prior arrest for a violent crime. He lives alone or with his parents. He's unemployed or working in an unskilled or semi-skilled occupation. He's what cops and psychologists and criminal profilers call a "social marginal."

When a child goes missing — listen up, mom and dad; listen up, small-town deputy who thinks the kid might've just wandered off — you'd better get your ass in gear, regardless of what the statistics say. More than three quarters of children who are abducted and murdered are dead within the first three hours. Yes, the odds are overwhelming that a missing kid won't be killed, but if he or she is in the hands of a killer, time is absolutely of the essence. Three hours. That's how small the window is.

Tracy Turner had been missing for 36 hours. When — okay, if — I had seen her this afternoon, she'd been missing for about 32 hours. I wasn't sure what that meant. I had to hope that since she'd made it past the first three hours, that she'd make it for many more.

Brian Pierce had a Facebook page.

I'll admit that I was a little surprised. A lot of lowlifes don't bother with Facebook because they don't have many friends to begin with, or because they aren't social animals. They value their privacy. They don't want to share anything with anybody. More often than not, they are hiders, not sharers.

Even bigger surprise, Pierce had 359 friends. That's a pretty big number. I couldn't see his wall, so I wasn't able to gauge how many of those were real friends versus online friends. If I could see some of his status updates and the resulting comments, I could learn a lot about him. But he had his privacy locked down fairly tight. Facebook users can still hide most of their content, despite gripes to the contrary.

I couldn't see Pierce's photos, either, or even his friends list.

What I sometimes do in this situation, in the course of an investigation, is send a friend request to the suspect. Not from my own account, of course, but from either "Linda Peterson" or "Robert Tyler." They are fictitious identities that I had created in the past couple of years. Both of them have been online long enough to collect more than one hundred friends. Both of them are above average on the attractiveness scale, but their profile photos aren't such ridiculous come-ons as to look like spam. Beyond that, both of them are average people with average tastes in music, film, and literature. They don't post often, but when they do, it's never about politics or religion. Examine either page more closely and you'll notice that there is hardly any identifying information. No high school listed, no college, no job history. Just a hometown and some favorite musicians, books, and movies.

But it works, especially when Linda Peterson contacts a young, single guy. You'd be surprised how many men will accept a friend request from a strange woman if she is a pretty redhead. Sometimes I have to pretend I'm a forgotten classmate, or a former co-worker, or whatever works. Sometimes I'll get a "Do I know you?" in response, but I can usually make up something that gets me in, especially if their wall is visible.

Did I want to do that now? I had a hard time thinking of a reason not to, so I went ahead and sent Brian Pierce a request. I mean Linda Peterson did.

10

It took me several hours to fall asleep, but I was finally snoozing soundly when my cell phone rang at 7:17 the next morning. Mia calling.

"What?" I croaked.

"Love you, too."

"What are you doing up this early?"

"You watching CNN?"

"No, I'm busy organizing my stamp collection."

"They're talking about Tracy Turner's parents. Her mom and her stepdad. You need to turn it on."

I grabbed the remote off my nightstand and powered up the small flat-screen mounted on the wall opposite my bed. Punched in the numbers for CNN. One of their anchors was speaking with one of their crime reporters.

The reporter was saying, " — with Kathleen Hanrahan last night, until she refused to answer any more questions and walked out of the interview."

Kathleen Hanrahan was the mom. Remarried, so she had a different last name than Tracy Turner. I sat up in bed.

The anchor asked, "At this point, do the investigators think she had anything to do with the disappearance of her daughter?"

"No, they are saying that they were asking routine questions, but Kathleen Hanrahan was no longer willing to speak with them. They did acknowledge that Mrs. Hanrahan has spent more than twenty hours in interviews so far, and she has been a willing participant."

"Interesting, huh?" Mia said in my ear.

"What is this I hear about witness fatigue?" the anchor said. "Isn't it true that even the most agreeable witness can reach a point where she's simply had enough and needs a break?"

"Oh, absolutely, Roger."

"Could that be what's happening here?"

"There's no real way to know for sure."

"Oh, come on," I said. "This is all bullshit."

"What? Why?" Mia said.

"Hold on."

The anchor asked, "Has she brought in an attorney?"

"Not yet, no, but that might be the next step."

The reporter was on audio only, because now they were showing photos of Kathleen Hanrahan. Photos of her alone, with Tracy, with her husband, all three of them together. She was an attractive and well-put-together woman. Maybe forty years old. Impeccable clothes, precise makeup, expensive jewelry. Your garden-variety affluent white woman with good taste. The headline at the bottom of the screen said: MISSING TOT'S MOM ENDS INTERVIEW.

"What about Patrick Hanrahan?" the anchor said. "Where does he stand in this? Is he still speaking with the police?"

"That's a good question, and we're looking into it. The interview last night took place in the Hanrahan home and it's unclear if Patrick, Tracy's stepdad, took part. However, he has been interviewed at length several times already and we've seen no sign that there has been any sort of problem as it relates to him. I also understand that he has offered a one million dollar reward for information that leads to her safe return."

"Are the investigators making any comment about the possibility of kidnapping?"

Good question, I thought. A lot of people lump kidnapping and abduction into the same category. They are a world apart.

The reporter: "Nobody is raising that possibility at the moment, but nobody has ruled it out, either. The fact is, Patrick Hanrahan is worth upwards of fifty million dollars — "

"Jeez," Mia said.

" — and it's only natural to wonder if that played a role in this situation. There is one other adult with regular access to the Hanrahan house — a nanny — but she has been interviewed and cleared."

They continued to talk, speculating on this or that, but nothing substantial or factual came up. I turned the TV off.

"Why did you say it was bullshit?" Mia asked.

"About the mom ending the interview?"

"Yeah? Doesn't that seem weird to you?"

"Not even a little bit," I said. "First of all, we don't even know if that report is accurate. She might have said, 'Guys, look, I'm beat, and I need to take a break.' By the time it gets to the reporters, it sounds like she's got something to hide. But even if she *is* refusing to talk anymore, let me tell you, sometimes there are good reasons."

"Such as?" She wasn't being snotty. It was an honest question.

"The parents are always the first suspects. Always. Everybody knows that. When you're the parent, you want to answer their questions as quickly as possible and get them moving on to other things, to the real investigation. But sometimes they don't move on. They keep asking you questions — totally irrelevant questions — and the clock is ticking, and you start to lose your patience. *You* know they are wasting their time, but they won't let it go. Just a few more questions. One more interview. Finally you just want to throw your hands up and say, 'Enough!' You want to make them move on. They're used to that kind of behavior, the stonewalling. They know it might mean nothing at all. But the public — well, they're ready to believe just about anything. You're guilty until proven innocent. Worse than that, you're probably a goddamn murderer. You killed your kid and dumped her in a lake, or you chopped her into pieces and flushed her down the toilet. Doesn't matter how whacked out the theory is. And the media? Hell, they'll keep pimping whatever draws the ratings." I realized my voice had been rising and my fists were clenched. I took a deep breath. "Do I sound cynical?"

Mia didn't say anything.

"You there?"

"Yeah, I'm here." A pause. Then: "I don't know if I've ever said this, but I'm really sorry for everything you went through."

By now — again, being totally honest — my ninety percent certainty from last night had dropped even further. Had I really seen a little girl in Brian Pierce's doorway? I had been a long ways away, looking through binoculars. Sometimes light can play off a screen door in odd ways. The eyes can do tricky things. For instance, who hasn't heard of a hunter mistaking a stump or a shadow or a fellow human being for a deer? Happens with alarming regularity. People "see" Bigfoot, leprechauns, and UFOs. Your brain tricks you into seeing what you want to see.

So I did what I would have done anyway if I hadn't possibly spotted a missing girl: I loaded up all of my regular supplies — my laptop and an ice chest full of food and drink — and headed out to conduct surveillance on Brian Pierce. It was, after all, my job.

But as I drove down Thomas Springs Road toward Pierce's place, I saw something unexpected. A marked deputy's cruiser was parked in the church parking lot, shaded, and fairly well concealed by the canopy of a towering oak tree. Almost exactly where I had parked yesterday. In that position, the deputy would be able to see Pierce's driveway where it met the road.

I had to wonder — was this cop simply running radar, just like the deputies had said yesterday? Or had Ruelas perhaps changed his mind and decided to keep tabs on Pierce after all? That could make sense. Hide in plain sight with a marked unit. As I passed, I gave a little wave. The deputy — one of the deputies from yesterday, I think — glared at me, stonefaced, and didn't wave back. He probably recognized my minivan.

I continued down Thomas Springs until it teed into Circle Drive, where I pulled into the empty parking lot of the Circle Country Club, a modest little beer joint I had visited once or twice in years past. It wasn't open this early, so there wasn't a soul around. I let the engine idle.

What now? I hadn't planned on this at all.

If the cops were watching Pierce, by all means, I should leave them to it and stay out of their way. On the other hand, I wasn't going to lay off if the deputy was in fact on traffic patrol and had no interest in

Pierce. If I pulled up beside the deputy and simply asked him what he was doing, what would he say? Well, he sure wouldn't admit that he was watching a suspect. But I could think of one good way to find out.

I pulled out of the parking lot and went back the way I had come. But this time, instead of observing the posted speed limit of 35 miles per hour, I floored the gas and held it there. The deputy saw me coming from at least fifty yards away. Blew past him at about seventy, and then watched in my rearview, fully expecting him to come after me. Maybe I could talk my way out of a ticket by explaining what I had just done and why.

But the cruiser didn't budge.

Interesting.

I continued down Thomas Springs, hit Highway 71, and stopped at the light. Then I continued straight across the highway, onto Old Bee Cave Road, simply driving, pondering what I was going to do next.

Should I call Ruelas? Couldn't see how that would do much good. He wouldn't tell me anything.

Should I call Heidi and tell her that Pierce might be a suspect in the abduction of a child, in which case his workers' comp claim might very soon be rendered moot? Bad idea. Heidi might be as skeptical as the cops, and she might even think I'm a little nutty, and I didn't need my best client thinking I was a space case. Especially when I was starting to have doubts myself.

What, then?

I found another spot to pull over and killed the engine. Climbed into the back seat and opened my laptop. Thanks to a USB modem, I had a broadband connection nearly everywhere I went. Worth every cent.

First, I checked CNN, just to make sure Kathleen Hanrahan hadn't broken down and confessed in the last hour. Of course she hadn't. I knew that.

Then I checked Facebook. Brian Pierce hadn't responded to Linda Peterson's friend request yet.

Next I opened my folder on Pierce. I had scanned all the documents Heidi had given me, so everything I needed was right at my fingertips, including the name of the restaurant where he worked.

I checked the restaurant's web site to see if they were open for breakfast. As luck would have it, they were.

11

The name of the place was La Tolteca which, if I recall correctly, means "The Rabid Squirrel," but I'll admit my Spanish isn't so great. It was in a shopping center in the posh little village of Lakeway, on the western outskirts of Austin.

The hostess was waiting there to greet me as soon as I walked in, and she led me through the sparse breakfast crowd to a two-top against one of the walls, under a neon sign for Corona beer. It was your typical Mexican food joint — lots of pastel colors, framed bullfighting posters and velvet paintings, a large mural of a man in a sombrero taking a siesta beneath a stucco archway. Colorful woven blankets acted as curtains in the windows up front. Mexican music — with plenty of accordion, of course — played softly over the sound system.

"Good morning." A waitress had slipped up beside me. Not Mexican at all. Probably Scandinavian. Her ancestry, I mean. Fair-skinned. Blond hair pulled back. Cute. Very cute. Mid-twenties. "My name is Jessica and I'll be your server today. Can I start you off with something to drink?"

"Yes, I'll have a 1979 Château Lafite Rothschild Pauillac. Bring the whole bottle. I'm celebrating my expulsion from the priesthood."

She knitted her brow for a second. Grinned just a little.

I said, "No? Okay, let's go with iced tea, please."

She handed me a menu and came back a few minutes later with a large plastic tumbler full of tea. "Have you decided?"

I was still looking at the menu. "How are the migas?"

"Really good. They taste a lot like eggs."

I like a waitress with a sense of humor. "That's what I'll have, then."

She started to write on her little pad. Now that I was getting a longer look, I could tell that she was in her late twenties or maybe even early thirties.

"With or without chorizo?" she asked.

"Don't be ridiculous. With."

"Cheese?"

"Please."

"Refried beans?"

"Absolutely."

"Tortillas?"

"Of course."

"Flour or corn?"

"Both."

"Potatoes?"

"You bet."

"Salsa?"

"No, I'm watching my figure."

"I'll have that right out."

While she was gone, I pulled out my cell phone and checked the news on the Internet. Still nothing new about Tracy Turner or her parents. No emails for me. No texts. Fine. I had other things to do.

About seven minutes later, the lovely Jessica returned with a large platter of food. It smelled great. Then she refilled my tea and said, "Anything else I can get you right now?"

"Yeah, I was wondering — is Brian Pierce working today?"

"No, he hasn't been in for about a week."

"Vacation?"

"No, he hurt his arm."

"Bummer. Please tell me it didn't involve some sort of high-powered kitchen implement."

"No, he slipped on a wet floor, I think. I wasn't here."

"Did he break it?"

"What, the floor?"

I laughed. I liked this girl.

She said, "I think he tore the ligaments or something."

"Oh, well. Guess I'll catch him next time. Haven't seen him in like forever."

"How do you know Brian?"

"We went to the same high school." I could see her checking me out, looking slightly puzzled, wondering why, if I was the same age as Pierce, I looked ten years older. "I was several years ahead of him, though. He hung around with my youngest brother."

"Oh, yeah?"

"I saw on Facebook that he worked here, so I thought I'd drop by and see if he was around. Surprise him, if he even remembers me. No big deal." I tried to get an amused, sort of gossipy look on my face — one that said: *This is just between you and me.* "How did ol' Brian turn out, anyway? He was sort of a strange little kid."

She grinned. "I don't really know him that well."

"Yeah? But you're smiling. Is he like a major loser or something?"

Her grin got even larger, though I could tell she was trying to suppress it. "That's mean. Brian is fine."

"Big hit with the ladies? You and him are an item?"

"No!" Boy, did she say that quickly.

"Well, I guess that answers my question."

"No, Brian is just a little quiet, that's all."

"You mean creepy."

"I didn't say that." She was keeping her voice low, glancing around, worried about being overheard.

"So, deep down, he's a rock-solid, salt-of-the-earth type, huh?"

"You got me. He's a good dishwasher."

"Wow. A good dishwasher. High praise. So he is absolutely, without question, not creepy?"

She squinted her eyes at me, playful, like, *Why are you trying to get me in trouble?* "I'll be back to check on you later," she said.

She was true to her word, and when she returned, midway through my meal, I changed courses. "Listen. I wasn't totally honest with you earlier."

"Oh, yeah? About what?"

I handed her one of my cards. "I've never met Brian Pierce in my life. I'm a fraud investigator. Kind of. I was hired by the restaurant's insurance company to double-check on him. To make sure he really did injure his arm."

It was a gamble — she might get pissed that I'd misled her, and she could even alert Pierce that I'd been there. I was hoping I'd sized her up right.

"You're a pretty good liar," she said.

"Well, I prefer *actor* or even performance artist."

"No, I think *liar* sums it up pretty well." But she seemed like she was teasing me, rather than being spiteful.

"The truth is, sometimes I have to be less than honest about who I am. Like a cop working undercover."

"Wait a sec. You're trying to catch a guy who might be scoring a paid vacation by faking a wrist injury, and you're comparing yourself to a policeman who might catch a murderer or bust a major drug ring. Really?"

"I know. It almost makes the cops sound a little silly, doesn't it?"

Finally, she laughed. A small laugh, but a laugh nonetheless.

I said, "Here's what I'd like to do. Let me take you out to dinner. My way of apologizing for unleashing my powers of deception on you."

She didn't say anything. Just set my card down on the table and walked away. But when she gave me the check, she'd written her phone number on it.

12

What he hadn't expected was how paranoid he became after he had the girl. Emily. That was her new name. He had been nervous in the planning stages, and terrified during the actual execution of his plan, but he had assumed he would be calm and collected afterward. He wasn't. If anything, he was even more on edge, because now he had so much more to lose. Especially now that Emily was adjusting. Asking about her parents less often. Starting to seek his attention. His approval. Settling in. It was all working exactly as he had hoped, and the thought of losing it now made him frantic.

So he became anxious.

Suspicious.

And eventually he began to feel that he was being watched.

Every car that passed was a cop, in plain clothes, trying to catch him during a moment of carelessness.

Neighbors were spying on him from a distance through binoculars, or attempting to peek through the fence.

The mail carrier had been tipped off. Same with the UPS driver. The meter reader. They had all been told to keep their eyes open and report what they saw.

Every incoming phone call was a test, with the caller hoping to hear the babblings of a little girl in the background.

It wasn't true, though. It couldn't be. He knew he was letting his imagination run away with him. He took Xanax, and that helped. Besides — even if it was true, which it wasn't — what could they do if they did in fact suspect him?

Absolutely nothing.

They'd need evidence to do anything more than watch, and he hadn't given them any. No matter how anxious he became, that was one thing he never doubted. He had left no evidence. And without evidence, they couldn't get a search warrant. All they could do is put him under surveillance.

He could handle that. It was important to go about his usual routine. Do the things he normally did. Don't cut off contact with the outside world. Pretend that nothing had changed.

And if worse came to worst, he was well prepared for virtually any scenario. He had a range of options and alternatives that nobody could imagine. Some were simple and pragmatic, while others were more drastic and potentially heartbreaking.

But he was prepared to use any of them.

13

"So you picked up the waitress?" Mia asked. "Wow. You don't ever give it a rest, do you?"

"I wouldn't say 'picked up.'"

"Close enough. She gave you her number. Not exactly playing hard to get, either of you."

We were on her apartment patio, kicked back in lounge chairs, enjoying the relatively cool afternoon. She was drinking a beer in a frosty mug. I was drinking a Dr Pepper in an attractive aluminum can.

"Hard for any mortal to resist my charms," I said. Mia and I frequently shared the details of our dating lives. Okay, maybe I did a little more sharing than she did.

"You gonna call her?"

"Well, yeah, that's the idea. I want to ask her some more questions about Pierce."

"I thought she hardly knew him."

"Doesn't mean she can't be useful. She might overhear something one of the other employees says. Or she might agree to do some digging around. Maybe I can sucker her into helping me out the way you do."

I knew immediately that I'd crossed a line. Just a little, but enough.

Something in Mia's face changed.

"Hey, I was just kidding," I said.

"Yeah, I know. You jerk." She was playing it cool. Acting like I hadn't just hurt her feelings.

"My idea of a little humor. Very little."

"Relax, Roy. It's okay. I'm used to your swipes."

That made me feel worse. I took a big swig of cold Dr Pepper. Sat quietly for a few minutes, trying to enjoy the warmth of the sun.

"I think I'm going to take a nap," Mia announced.

"Can I take photos?"

She didn't say anything.

"You work later?" I asked.

"My day off, remember?"

"That's right."

"Can I give you a little friendly advice?"

"Sure."

"You might try paying attention to what other people say once in awhile."

Whoa. My earlier remark had definitely pissed her off. I was about to respond when my cell phone vibrated in my pocket. Incoming email. I pulled it out and checked the screen.

Brian Pierce had just accepted my friend request.

What I hope to find, when I first gain access to someone's Facebook page, is immediate and undeniable evidence that that person is committing insurance fraud. It's nice when the proof just falls into your lap. Does this mean I'm lazy? Possibly.

For instance, I had a case involving a woman who was a personal trainer for wealthy folks in Austin. (If I mentioned the names of her celebrity clients, you'd recognize them, as well as their highly toned buttocks.) Early last year, she claimed to have injured her back when her Jaguar was hit from behind by a Miata going about ten miles an hour. She said she couldn't work, so she couldn't haul in the two hundred dollars an hour that was her usual rate. The doctors said she might have a disc injury, hard to tell. Of course, in her line of work, making connections and being visible is important. Privacy is not a priority, as evidenced by her 3,672 friends. So she granted my friend request within hours. After all, I might be someone important, right? Everything looked legit on her page, including status updates in which she complained about her sore back. But eleven days later, someone posted a video from a party on a houseboat. It wasn't even her own video, but someone had tagged her in it, so it showed up in the newsfeed for all her friends to see. In the video, she dove off the side of the boat several times, and she even slid down the water slide, letting out an excited whoop in the process. Perfect. The video disappeared less than an hour after it was posted (I can imagine the frantic phone call she made to the friend who had posted it), but I had already used some handy specialty software to download a copy. Slam dunk. Case closed.

Unfortunately, Brian Pierce had not been invited to any houseboat parties, at least not recently. While Mia napped, I hung out on her patio with my laptop and explored Pierce's Facebook profile.

He appeared frustratingly normal. Boring, even.

Music he liked: Foo Fighters, Rolling Stones, Green Day, George Strait, Katy Perry.

Television shows: Tosh.0, Modern Family, NCIS, Breaking Bad.

Books he liked: Well, like a lot of people on Facebook, he hadn't listed any.

I could go on, but you get the idea. No help at all. His most recent status update, from just yesterday afternoon, said, "We sure could use some rain." I kid you not. Weather talk. We were in a drought, but come on. Three people had given him a thumbs up, but nobody had commented.

I scrolled downward, and thus backward in time. The day after his alleged accident at the restaurant, Pierce had written, "tore some ligaments in my wrist, typing with one hand is no fun."

Some guy had responded, "Wait till you have to go to the bathroom."

Another guy had said, "at least it won't affect your relationship with rosie palm."

Witty bastards with their high-brow banter.

A young girl had said, "Ouch. What happened?"

Pierce: "slipped on a wet floor at work and landed wrong"

The girl had responded with a sad face icon. The empathy was palpable.

I scrolled back further and saw that Pierce didn't post often, but when he did, it was about as banal as it gets. Lines from movies. Quotes from famous people. Comments about sports. Lots of re-postings of other people's posts. Very little substance. In other words, Pierce's page was about like everyone else's.

Most of his photos weren't original; they were things he'd lifted from around the web. No help there, either.

I closed my laptop and went inside Mia's apartment. Her bedroom door was closed. I scribbled a quick note: *Sorry. Sometimes I am a horse's ass.*

Then I changed my mind and crossed through the word "sometimes."

As I approached my van, I noticed that I had a flat tire. Then I came to a full stop. It wasn't just one tire. All four were flat.

Son of a bitch. That was my first thought.

Wade Gruley. That was my second thought, remembering the voicemail Spence had left me yesterday. Spence works in the Travis County jail system and he warns me when certain inmates are going to be released. He does it out of the goodness of his heart, and because I give him a bottle of Johnny Walker Blue for each heads-up.

See, one small problem with my line of work is that, on occasion, one of the scumbags who commits fraud gets upset with me. And they know exactly who I am, because my work isn't always complete after I get the cheater on video. Sometimes I have to show up in court to testify. I'm not wild about it — I'd much rather remain anonymous — but some of my clients insist. That's because video is great, but nothing beats a real, live person, as far as evidence goes. And I'll admit, I'm persuasive, charismatic, and, let's face it, ruggedly handsome up on the witness stand. I'm good with the jurors and the judge. Together, my eyewitness testimony and the video evidence can deliver a one-two punch: The cheater not only loses a monthly income, he might end up going to jail for six months or a year. Most of the cheaters spend that time coming to the realization that crime doesn't pay, but a few of them spend the time daydreaming about ways to seek revenge.

Wade Gruley was one of those people. During the first few weeks of his government-sponsored vacation, he'd called me up a couple of times and made veiled threats. How dumb is that, calling from jail? Those calls were recorded. He said things like, "When I get out of here,

I'm going to look you up and let you know how much I appreciate what you did for me." Very stupid to make the calls, but not quite stupid enough to say anything that would result in additional charges.

The good thing is, these people are insurance cheats, not murderers or gangbangers, so none of them have ever come after me directly. Instead, they go after my vehicle. Flat tires are always popular. Sugar in the gas tank. Acid on the paint job. A hammer to the windshield. It doesn't happen often, but it does happen. The van has a high-dollar alarm and security system, which prevents anyone from stealing it or its contents, but it doesn't prevent this sort of petty vandalism.

Most of the time, I suspect who the culprit is, but I never know for sure. That's because they usually strike once and that's it. For most of these losers, that's enough. Sure, in jail, they might've vowed to themselves that they would hound me to my dying day, but after they're released, their keen sense of focus wanes. They key my car door or snap my antenna and that seems to fulfill their need for payback. Their anger fades, then they get distracted and move on to other things, like, you know, day-to-day life.

Doesn't mean I'm not careful.

I looked all around the parking lot, making sure Wade Gruley — who was a pretty big guy, if memory serves — wasn't lurking behind a vehicle, and then I approached the van for a closer inspection. The left front tire had an inch-long slit in the sidewall. Someone had plunged a knife into it. Same with the other three. That kind of damage can't be repaired, so I'd need four new tires.

Know who pays for it? My insurance company, of course. So, assuming the vandalism had indeed been committed by Gruley or one of my other past targets, once again an insurance company would be coughing up cash to pay for his illegal transgressions.

I called the non-emergency number for the Austin Police Department and asked them to send a unit. My insurance company would want a police report. Then I called to arrange a tow truck. I'd be good to go in a couple of hours. Which was just as well, because I was going to need my van quite a bit in the coming days.

14

The deputy wasn't on Thomas Springs Road at seven o'clock the next morning. This was getting confusing. Were they checking Pierce out or not? I didn't really *need* to know, but I sure wanted to know. I pulled over and placed a call that was answered by an actual live human being.

"This is Ruelas."

"Good morning, Detective, this is Roy Ballard."

Silence.

I said, "Remember? Tall, good-looking guy with a staggering intellect?"

"You need something?"

"Absolutely. A minute with the lieutenant. Holland?"

"He's on vacation."

"You mean, like, literally?"

"Florida. Left this morning."

"Okay, then I'll ask you instead. Yesterday morning there was a deputy parked at the church on Thomas Springs Road. Today he's not there — at least, not right now. I know better than to ask what he was doing there, but you know what I do for a living, and I need to go about my business without interfering with *your* business. I'm sure you understand what I'm getting at."

He let out a heavy sigh. "I didn't hear the question."

"Fair enough. My question is, do I need to stay away from the Thomas Springs Road area?"

My assumption was that he wouldn't tell me if they were watching Pierce, but he would tip me off if they *weren't*, just as he had at the substation.

What he said was, "Do whatever the hell you want. Makes no difference to me at all."

Good enough.

"Thank you. So the deputy yesterday was simply running radar?"

"Mr. Ballard, let me make a suggestion. Assume that everyone at the sheriff's department knows exactly what they are doing. That way, you won't have to lay awake at night wondering if we need your help."

"Good tip. Are you a Capricorn, by chance?"

"What?"

"With Mars in retrograde, that might explain your current irritability."

Dial tone.

I saw an interesting newspaper ad once for one of the local news outfits. They liked to take credit for always getting the big scoop, no matter how hard the digging might be. The ad featured neatly arranged rows of ten-digit numbers — hundreds of them, or maybe thousands. The headline said something like, "If you want to know how exciting investigative reporting is, find the number listed twice on this page."

Same thing is true in my line of work. People think it's a non-stop thrill ride, or that it's at least mildly entertaining.

Silly, silly fools.

Sure, there are moments. But the rest of the time, it's just a job, like any other. Repetitive. Not particularly challenging. Sometimes downright boring. More about grunt work than brain work. Show up, be persistent, and wait for your long hours to pay off.

So that's what I did. Had no choice, really, considering where Brian Pierce lived, way back in the woods. I couldn't trespass, so I had to stake him out and hope he left the property.

Friday morning passed slowly. I was tempted to park along the shoulder of the road, where I could see Pierce's house through the small gap in the trees, but I couldn't run the risk that he'd notice me. So I parked in the church parking lot again. Sat. Waited. Got bored, so I checked Pierce's Facebook page, but didn't see any activity. It's times like this when your confidence begins to drop. You start to doubt that your subject is even in the house. Last thing you want is for him or her to suddenly come home, after having been out and about for hours without you knowing it. But it happens sometimes, because you can't conduct surveillance 24 hours a day, by yourself, for a prolonged stretch.

So. You sit and wait. If you're like me, there are times when you desperately want to take a nap, but you can't do that. But you can surf the web. You can listen to the radio. You can read. You can also talk on the phone, so by mid-afternoon I decided to call the number Jessica had given me. It went straight to voicemail, so I said, "Hi, Jessica, this is Roy Ballard, your customer from yesterday. Well, just one of many customers, I assume, unless you had a really bad shift. Anyway, I forgot to mention that I represent the Texas Restaurant and Innkeepers Association and you have won a major award for your superior hospitality and luminescent smile. It is my responsibility to bestow the award upon you, so it only seems fitting that we conduct the ceremony over dinner, where we can critique the performance of our waiter and/ or waitress. At your convenience, but without any undue delay, why don't you give me a call? I don't want to spoil the surprise, but I will say that this award is in the form of a trophy, not some cheesy plaque. Plaques are passé, and the association is well aware of that fact. Hope to hear from you soon."

You can also simply sit and think, but that's not always a good idea. I did that for awhile, later in the afternoon, and unpleasant memories began to fight for my attention. This Tracy Turner thing had brought them to the forefront. I didn't need the assistance of a therapist to arrive at that conclusion.

Painful.

The dog park. Walking back to my Nissan and discovering that Hannah was missing...

Panic set in quickly, of course. I looked in every direction. Shouted her name. *Screamed* her name. Tried to remain calm, but that was impossible. My heart was thundering. Breathing as hard as a sprinter after a race. I started babbling at passersby, pleading for their help, seeing in their faces that they thought I had lost it. Then seeing that they finally understood. My daughter is missing! Please help me!

I called Laura first. Don't know why. Should've called the cops, but I called Laura. She couldn't believe what I was saying. Hannah couldn't be missing. She must have just wandered off. Now I was wandering with the cell phone in my hand, searching in a wooded area not far from the parking lot. Finally Laura began to understand the seriousness of the situation.

"Please come right now," I said.

"I will. But you find her, Roy!"

"I'm looking."

"Don't you lose our daughter!"

That's when it really sank in. If I didn't find Hannah...I didn't want to even think about it, but if I didn't find Hannah, not only would she be gone, which was the worst nightmare I could imagine, but I'd be to blame. It would've been horrible enough if Hannah had gone missing under someone else's watch, but it had happened under mine. I couldn't imagine shouldering that guilt.

Laura and the first cop car arrived at the same time. We gathered in a tight circle and I immediately began telling them both what had happened. A small crowd clustered around us — people who had been looking for Hannah but had now given up. There was nowhere else to look, really.

"I left her — I left her for just a minute," I said.

"You left Hannah?" Laura asked. I've never seen a more grotesque look on her face. "Left her where?"

"In the car. It wasn't more than a minute."

"Where did you go? Why did you leave her?"

"There was a woman. I had to talk to her." I told them about Susan Tate, and the conversation about dogs, and about the pit bull puppies that her brother had. It came out in a disjointed jumble and I didn't know if any of it was making sense.

The cop said, "So you had had an earlier conversation with this woman and you went back to speak to her again?"

"That's what I'm saying!" I looked around for Susan Tate in the crowd, hoping she might appear, but I didn't see her. Not that it would have mattered.

"What did you need to talk to her about?" the cop asked.

"I wanted to get her phone number."

Laura looked like I had slapped her. "You wanted to get her phone number? Are you fucking kidding me?"

I knew what she was thinking. She had complained about my flirting in the past. Never quite trusted me.

"It wasn't like that, Laura."

She turned and walked rapidly toward the wooded area, which I had already searched, calling Hannah's name.

The cop told me that a detective who specialized in missing children would be here shortly.

Obviously, it was far and away the worst day I'd ever experienced, and I was pretty sure it would remain crystal clear and sharp as glass in my head for the rest of my life.

But now, years later, I was given a temporary reprieve. A distraction. Something important was happening. A car on Thomas Springs Road had slowed and was pulling into Brian Pierce's driveway.

15

The car, a white Volkswagen Jetta, stopped at the locked gate. I already had the video camera zoomed in and recording, so I would get a decent shot of whoever emerged from the car. Unfortunately, from this angle, one hundreds yards down the road from the driveway, I wouldn't get video of the license plate. The windows of the Jetta were tinted too dark to see how many people were inside.

The driver's door opened and a person stepped out. A female. The view through the binoculars revealed that it was a middle-aged woman. Pierce's mom? No, probably not, unless she'd had him when she was a teenager. A sister? Maybe. The woman was fairly attractive. Brown hair. Slim. Dressed casually in jeans and a sleeveless top. She went straight to the gate and began to unlock the combination lock on the chain that kept the gate closed. She seemed to open it very quickly, which meant she had likely unlocked it before. That might be helpful information later, or it might not. She swung the gate open wide, drove through, hopped out, closed the gate, locked it, got back in the car, and drove onto the property, until the car was obscured by the cedar trees.

Interesting that she locked the gate. Planning to stay awhile? Or just wanting to ensure that nobody could wander onto the property?

Either way, I was glad *something* was happening. It had always been a possibility that I might have sat out here for several days with no activity at all.

Thirty minutes passed. The Jetta did not come back down the driveway. It was nearly five o'clock, so I was wondering if the woman was here for the evening.

I transferred the video from my camera to my laptop. I reviewed the video frame by frame and saved a decent still shot of the woman's face. Then I began to scroll through Brian Pierce's friends on Facebook, to see if I could find her. Didn't know what I hoped to learn, but learning anything would be better than learning nothing.

Here's something I discovered early on in this business: Guys don't change their appearance much, even over a period of years. Easy to recognize ol' Joe, time after time, unless he puts on or drops an amazing amount of weight. Women, on the other hand, might look very different from one day to the next. A woman is much more likely to change the color or the length of her hair, for instance. Brown one day, blond the next. Long, flowing hair becomes an updo, or maybe even a bob. New make-up, new eyeglasses, new clothes, and suddenly the girl from yesterday has a dramatically different appearance. So it didn't surprise me that I couldn't positively identify the Jetta driver on Pierce's friends list. There were about four women she *might* have been, but I couldn't say for sure. Or maybe none of them were her.

I was studying each profile closely, completely focused on what I was doing, when there was a loud rapping on my passenger-side window and I almost had a stroke.

A woman was standing beside the van. Maybe seventy years old. And she was scowling. I regained my composure long enough to use the button in the driver's door to lower the power window on her side. I gave her a broad smile. She elected to continue scowling. Her short gray hair was covered by a visor to keep the late-afternoon sun out of her eyes. Her cheeks were rosy from the exertion of a brisk walk.

"Boy, you sure startled me," I said.

"May I ask what you are doing here?"

I avoided the question. "Well, not much. Is there a problem?" Trying my best to sound friendly.

"I live right down the street. I drove by this morning and noticed you parked here. And now I see that you're still here."

"Yes, ma'am, I am."

"Is your van broken down?"

She came across as a retired high school principal, or the stereotype of one, anyway. Stern. Had heard every excuse in the book. Won't be fooled.

"No, ma'am, fortunately, it isn't."

"We had a break-in earlier this spring, you know. One of my neighbors. That's why we're all keeping our eyes peeled."

"I understand, but I can assure you that — "

"Anybody parked here all day like this is going to get noticed. You have business at the church?"

"No, ma'am."

"You're on church property, you know. I came very close to writing down your license plate number and calling the sheriff."

"I don't blame you at all. It's wise of you to be cautious. Feel free to ask for Detective Ruelas. Tell him Roy Ballard says hello."

Her attitude changed by precisely one nanometer. "What exactly are you doing here?"

I knew better than to lie to a sharp old woman like her. "I'm conducting an investigation."

"You're a police officer?"

"No, I'm working for an insurance company."

Her nose wrinkled at those words. *Insurance company.* Now I noticed her eyes scanning over everything inside my van. Well, everything that was in plain sight. Some of my most valuable items were kept in a concealed compartment underneath the rear passenger bench. That includes a Glock nine-millimeter handgun, which I am not licensed to carry, because a guy with my criminal history can't get a license.

"You normally conduct an investigation this way? Park in the same spot all day?"

This woman wasn't bashful, I'll give her that. Downright pushy, really. She turned and looked one way down the road, then the other, as if attempting to puzzle out who or what I was investigating. Her gaze came to rest on Pierce's gate. Damn, she was good. Then again, my van was facing in that direction, and there was nothing else down that way that I would be watching. Process of elimination. Simple logic.

She pointed. "I know the young man who lives there. I knew his grandparents well."

She was feeling me out. Wanting to see if her deduction was correct.

"Is that right?" I said. "You know, my own grandparents used to live along this road."

She looked at me. "What were their names?"

"Jim and Beulah."

Her eyes lit up. "Oh, you're kidding me. Jim and Beulah Ballard. They had the rock house on the hill, way back near the conservancy."

"That's the one."

"Lovely people. Salt of the earth." Just that quickly, she was a different woman. Friendly. Not suspicious.

"Yes, they were."

"Had dinner with them many times. What a smart, engaging couple."

"Unfortunately, I didn't inherit that gene."

"Oh, go on. I remember them bragging about all their grandchildren. Which one are you?"

"Roy."

"Roy Ballard! That's what you said a minute ago but I didn't make the connection. Roy, I'm Emma Webster."

I was worried that she might have recognized my name when it appeared in the newspapers way back when, and that she would remember that now, but I didn't see any indication of it.

"Nice to meet you, Mrs. Webster."

"Please, it's Emma."

"I remember my grandparents mentioning your name, but you seem way too young to have been one of their friends."

She ate that up. "Well, they were several years ahead of Tom and me, but that didn't stop us from forming a friendship. I only wish we'd known them longer. By the time we moved here, well, we only had the pleasure of knowing them for a handful of years."

In other words, they died. Why did people avoid stating that simple fact? Everybody dies eventually. Some people die sooner than others. No need to use euphemisms or sugarcoat it.

"They had a lot of good friends out here," I said, just to say something, because I was starting to feel a little awkward about having a conversation through my van window. What was the proper etiquette?

Was I a host of sorts? Should I offer her a Coke and some potato chips? Also, I was a little worried that the woman in the Jetta might choose this particular moment to leave Pierce's place, and I'd have to say a quick and possibly rude goodbye to ol' Emma.

"This area just isn't the same anymore," Emma Webster said. "This used to be out in the country — you know that — but there's been so much growth, all these new subdivisions, and nobody knows their neighbors like they used to. Like this Pierce boy. Brian Pierce. As I said, I knew his grandparents, Larry and Faye, but they're gone now. Things change, I guess. I've run into Brian a couple of times when I was out on one of my walks — sometimes I catch him when he's out checking his mail — but he doesn't have any interest in talking to an old woman. Or maybe talking to anyone. I think he's a bit of a loner."

I nodded toward Pierce's driveway. "That guy is? Pierce?"

"He's young and single, so when he first inherited the place, we were worried there'd be some late-night parties. Lot of distance between our houses, but you'd be surprised how sound carries. Not to mention drunk drivers. Young people don't always use common sense. But we rarely hear a peep from his direction. Hardly ever see any strange cars coming and going from his driveway. Just his truck, a big white thing."

I realized now that Emma Webster didn't fit the role of a retired principal after all; she was, instead, an enthusiastic neighborhood gossip. Mrs. Kravitz from *Bewitched*. I was starting to wonder how long she'd go on.

"Sounds like a recluse to me," I said.

"Yes, that's exactly right. He does have a very nice home, with a large back patio that would be perfect for entertaining, but, well, I guess it's really none of my business. I just know that when I was his age I was a lot more sociable. My friends and I were *always* doing something. Always getting together for this or that."

"I can imagine."

"But I've never even seen Brian with another person. Always by himself. I'd get lonely living like that. Although there was the one time I saw Brian with a little girl in his truck."

16

A couple of years ago, I was having trouble catching one particular fraudster, so I wore a wire into a bar and struck up a conversation with the guy. I posed as a house painter — same profession as him — and we hit it off well. I was drinking ginger ale, pretending it was something stronger, and pretty soon we got around to bitching about our jobs. Damn hard work, wasn't it? Long hours. Crappy benefits. Dangerous. Fumes that could slowly damage your brain. Sure didn't want to be doing this when we were sixty years old. Then, after about his eighth beer, the guy grins and tells me he's on workers' comp at the moment because of a back injury. Fell off a scaffold — but not really. He was faking it. Taking some paid time off. He deserved it, didn't he? *Perfect.* That's all I needed. I was literally seconds from sliding off my bar stool and walking out the door when he said, "Something else I haven't told anybody..." Hard to resist a line like that. So I said, "Yeah?" and he leaned in closer and said, "I'm not proud of this, but one night last fall, I was a little bit buzzed, but driving anyway, and I hit a guy on a bike."

Whoa.

That moment was similar to this one with Emma Webster, in that both of them had blurted out something big and unexpected. Hell, this wasn't just big, this was enormous. I wanted to say, "Wait a sec, Emma, what did you just say?" But I played it cool, even though my heart rate immediately jumped up a notch.

"That's weird," I said. "A little girl?"

Emma Webster said, "I was walking by just as he was pulling into his driveway. I could see her on the passenger side. Probably five or six years old. Little blond girl. No car seat, and that's what bothered me."

"This was recently?"

"Oh, let's see. Probably February or March. A few weeks later, I saw him again out by his mailbox. So I stopped and casually mentioned the little girl. I said something about a child that young needing a car seat. You know what he did?"

"What?"

She rolled her eyes. "He denied having that little girl in his truck. Said I must have been mistaken. I mean, I can understand him being embarrassed or feeling guilty for not having a car seat, but there's no reason to lie about the situation. Just own up to the mistake and have a car seat the next time. If there is a next time. I never did figure out who that little girl was. Brian has never been married, and he doesn't have any brothers or sisters, so it wouldn't have been a niece."

By now, I could hardly control my expression or even sit still. The growing doubts I'd had about seeing Tracy Turner at Pierce's house were quickly receding. "Maybe he was babysitting for someone," I said. Did my voice sound odd? It did to me, but she didn't seem to notice.

"I wouldn't know who, but I suppose that's possible. Anyway, I don't mean to go on and on — you probably think I'm a terrible busybody — but I saw you parked here and I wanted to be on the safe side. I didn't mean to come on so strongly. But it's been wonderful to meet Jim and Beulah's grandson."

She was preparing to leave, but before she left, I needed to make sure she wouldn't blab to her neighbors about what I was doing down here. Word might eventually get to Pierce, and now, more the ever, it was important that he not know I was watching him. I figured the best way to keep Emma quiet was the actual truth.

So I said, "Emma, I'll tell you a secret, if you want to hear it."

Hook, line, and sinker, all rolled into one.

"What's that?"

"It *is* Brian Pierce I'm investigating. See, he claims he injured his arm at the restaurant where he works — and he probably did — but my clients hire me to check those kinds of things out. Make sure everything is on the up and up."

To me, this was boring, everyday stuff, but I could tell she thought it was juicy.

I continued. "What I normally do is follow the person around discreetly and see what they do. See if they take part in some activity that they shouldn't be able to do because of their injury."

She was intrigued, probably because she considered us to be kindred spirits. We both kept tabs on other people. "So you sneak around after them," she said. There was definitely some amusement in her voice.

"Well, yeah, but I'm sure you can understand why. When a guy like Pierce commits insurance fraud, the rest of us pay higher costs. Anyway, I felt like you deserved to know what I was doing out here, and why I might be here tomorrow, and maybe for several more days."

"Interesting," she said. "And here I thought you might be a burglar."

"No, ma'am."

"Glad I didn't call the sheriff."

"Me, too. And I really need you to do me a favor. I need you to promise that you won't tell anyone why I'm parked here."

Emma Webster made the familiar my-mouth-is-zipped motion and didn't say another word. I figure, for her, that would be a monumental undertaking. I hoped she could live up to it.

After she continued on her walk, I stayed parked where I was. The sun fell and the woman in the Jetta never left, and if she had, it probably would have taken me a minute to snap to, because my mind was racing.

Brian Pierce had been seen with a little blond girl a few months ago. Then he denied it. This was, to put it mildly, a cause for alarm, at least it was for me. Who was the little girl? Where had she come from? I hated to even wonder it, but was Pierce a serial child abductor with a predilection for blond girls?

I tried to remember any headlines from February or March about a missing girl, but I didn't recall any. So I jumped online and started searching various news sites. Didn't take me long to determine that there hadn't been a case like that in the Austin area. Of course, Pierce could've made a road trip, so I cast my net wider and searched a public database of missing children on the website for the Texas Department of Public Safety. They operate a very user-friendly site that allows you to narrow your search by age, gender, height, weight, date of birth, race, and so on. Which means it's easy to get quick results. As far as I could tell, there wasn't a missing girl in the entire state that matched up with this blond girl Emma Webster had seen.

I visited Pierce's Facebook page again and began to scroll downward, back in time. I paid particular attention to his status updates from late winter and early spring. I'd reviewed these postings before, but I wanted to check them again in light of this new information.

There was only one comment that interested me, but it would be a stretch to say that it was significant. On March 3, Pierce had simply written: *Love comes from a lot of unexpected places.*

Kind of odd, considering that none of his other posts were in the least bit philosophical, and considering that he didn't appear to have a girlfriend or boyfriend, nor did he seem to date regularly.

Could mean anything. On the other hand, it could be disturbingly creepy. It would be nice to have some context, but none of his updates before or after that one seemed to relate, and none of his friends had commented.

There weren't many times when I'd stay on a stakeout all night, but I decided this would be one of those times. I ate a cold ham sandwich, drank a Coke to keep me awake, and along about midnight, my tenacity paid off. No, I didn't learn anything about Brian Pierce, the blond girl, or the woman in the Jetta.

What I learned came once again from the media. This time, a talk radio program was reporting that Patrick Hanrahan — Tracy Turner's stepdad — had agreed to, and failed, a lie-detector test.

Twice.

17

"I feel like I'm on a seesaw," I said. "One minute I'm sure Brian Pierce had something to do with Tracy Turner's disappearance, the next minute some strange development happens with the parents."

"What about what you said the other day?" Mia asked.

"My rant about the parents always being the first suspects? Well, the mom ending the interview was one thing, but this...I guess there comes a point when you have to start to wonder."

"I'll be honest. My money's on the parents. At least one of them, but maybe both."

"One covering for the other?"

"Exactly."

"You could be right."

"The mom won't talk and the stepdad is lying to the cops. *Something* is happening there."

We were having brunch in a little café called Cypress Grill in South Austin. Sort of a Louisiana type of place. Saturday morning at eleven. I had managed to remain in the church parking lot on Thomas Springs overnight, until about two hours ago. Nothing had happened. Never saw Pierce. Or the woman in the Jetta. Or a deputy. Or even Emma

Webster. Eventually you have to give up and try again later. That's when you wish you weren't working solo and that you could trade shifts with someone, because it was easy to feel that I'd wasted the better part of a full day. There were also a couple of times when I dozed off in the wee hours, but I was clever enough to point my video camera at Pierce's driveway and leave it running, just for those occasions. If someone had come or gone — which, as I said, nobody did — at least I'd have known about it, even if I would've missed the chance to follow them.

"The most likely scenario," I said, "if we're speculating wildly with no solid evidence at all, is that the stepdad killed Tracy and the mom is in denial. She suspects what happened, but since she didn't see it with her own eyes..."

We were both keeping our voices low, because the tables were fairly close together and there were plenty of families scattered around the café. I had caught several of the dads sneaking glances at Mia when they could. I didn't blame them. I was glad I didn't have to sneak my glances. I could look all I wanted.

"Or maybe she knows exactly what happened," Mia said, "but doesn't want him to get in trouble. You hear all kinds of twisted stories."

That was an understatement. Parents murdering their kids. Or selling them. Locking them in basements for years and using them as breeding stock. Just about any scenario was possible, no matter how horrid and nightmarish. Accidentally or intentionally killing a child, then covering it up — with the full cooperation and participation of the other parent — was becoming an all-too-common phenomenon. But, as much as I wanted to defend the parents, based solely on what I went through myself, it was looking more and more like something along those lines had happened in this case. This morning, the cable news networks were buzzing that Patrick Hanrahan had hired a lawyer, and the lawyer was claiming that Hanrahan hadn't failed the polygraph tests, but that the results were simply inconclusive. Happens all the time. Doesn't mean anything. But Mr. Hanrahan didn't appreciate the insinuations, no sir, so he was joining his wife in no longer speaking to the authorities."Either way, it wasn't Pierce," I said. I took a big bite of my bacon, lettuce, and avocado sandwich. It was what I usually had, and it was always excellent, but it wasn't quite hitting the spot this morning. Don't know why. Mia was having French toast, which looked pretty tasty.

"You sound like you're trying to convince yourself," she said.

"I do?"

"Yep."

Our waiter came by, refilled our mugs, then scooted away.

I said, "Well, I mean, it *is* weird, what Emma Webster told me. But it obviously doesn't have anything to do with Tracy Turner. Maybe Emma didn't see what she thought she saw."

Mia paused with her fork in mid-air. "Wait, now come on. What are the odds that both of you thought you saw Pierce with a little girl, but you're both mistaken?"

I groaned. "Don't do this to me. I'm tired of going back and forth on this."

"No, that's not what I'm saying."

"What are you saying?"

"Well, I'm *not* saying there's anything going on with Pierce, other than maybe he's committing fraud. As far as the little girl, there could be a logical explanation for that. In fact, I'd say there probably is. Probably the little girl you saw is the same one Emma Webster saw. The descriptions match."

"Some other little girl. Not Tracy Turner."

"Right."

"Who, then?"

"Got me. Doesn't matter. A friend's daughter or something. I realize that young, single men don't usually do a lot of babysitting, but it's possible. Seems a lot more likely than Pierce being a sicko who has never gotten caught."

"I am definitely paying attention to what you are saying," I said. An intentionally clumsy reference to her remark from Thursday afternoon, since she hadn't mentioned the apologetic note I'd left for her.

She rolled her eyes. "Point is, you can follow the process of elimination, right? It doesn't matter whether Emma Webster saw Pierce with a little girl or not. If there wasn't a missing little girl matching that description back in February or March, well, that gives you your answer, doesn't it?"

"Makes sense to me."

"But you still seem like you're waffling."

"Waffles, damn it. That's what I should've ordered."

"You want the rest of this?" She slid her plate forward. "I'm done anyway."

"You sure?"

"Yeah, go ahead."

So I did. We sat in silence for several moments as I scarfed down the rest of her French toast.

"I have to be at work in one hour," she announced.

She didn't know it, but I was about to spring something on her — a proposition prompted by what she'd just said. Something that had been running through my mind for quite some time.

"I have an idea I want to run past you."

"What?"

"It's a big idea, so brace yourself."

"Oh, I'm always braced when I talk to you."

"I'll take that as a compliment. First, let me ask you something. You want to work in that bar all your life?"

She frowned, puzzled, wondering why I was asking. "As a matter of fact, yes. I want to be serving drinks to horny, drunk guys when I'm sixty years old. That's my life's dream. By then, my ass will have been groped roughly ten thousand times, so how could I not be fulfilled?"

"I'll take that as a no. So here's a thought. Ready? Come work with me."

That definitely caught her off guard. She hadn't been expecting it. Her eyes widened, and she opened her mouth to say something, but nothing came out. Then finally she said, "Work with you?"

"That's what I'm thinking. I need some help."

"Really? But — I'm not qualified at all. I can't do what you do."

"Sure you can. You're a fast learner. I can teach you a lot of stuff. You'll pick up the rest."

"Don't you have to be licensed or certified or something?"

"Nope. Private investigators do, but legal videographers don't. Any nutcase like me can do it."

I was having a tough time gauging her expression, but she appeared to be intrigued — at least a little bit. What I was hoping for.

She said, "Okay, the first thing that pops into my head: I'm not sure I could handle being your employee. We're friends, Roy, and I don't want to — "

"Partners, Mia. That's what I'm talking about. Fifty-fifty. I don't want to be your boss. Hell, you're smarter than I am. I *couldn't* be your boss."

She was too surprised to even offer a snappy comeback agreeing with my assessment. "What brings this on? The Pierce case?"

"Well, yes and no. I've been thinking about this for a couple of months, actually. Business has been really good and I don't see why it won't continue. I'm spread thin. I need a partner. Someone who is competent and smart. Also, it doesn't hurt that you have the attributes to make guys like Wally Crouch lift car batteries out of trunks. But that's just a bonus."

She smirked. "Attributes?"

"Your ankles. Ankles like that can drive a man wild."

She already knew the details of the job: The long hours. The boredom, punctuated by occasional excitement. The risk that one of your targets might get angry and flatten your tires. She'd heard it all.

The waiter brought the check and I handed him a credit card. I said to Mia, "Even better, we'll be able to write these meals off. Think of the satisfaction of dodging the IRS. Legally, of course."

"When would I start?"

"Whenever you're ready. Tomorrow. Next week. A month from now."

"Full time?"

"That's what I'm looking for, but hey, if you want to try it part-time for awhile, that's fine with me. We can work something out. However you want to arrange it, I'm up for it."

"What about all your gear? Your laptop, your cameras, all that stuff? I don't have any of that equipment."

"We'll share at first, and then we'll buy some more stuff. The van can be our rolling office. We can just pass the keys off and everything you need would be inside. I'll buy another car for myself."

"I don't know how to use any of the equipment."

"You'll learn. It's easy."

She shook her head. "You *have* put some thought into this, haven't you?"

"A lot."

She was quiet for a minute.

I said, "You don't have to decide right now, obviously. Mull it over.

Ponder it. Ruminate. I'm sure you'll have other questions, and I'm fully prepared to make up bullshit answers."

"What I said earlier, about being friends. I meant that. You know what they say about doing business with friends. If we were to do this, and if it began to affect our friendship — "

"The friendship is way more important. No question."

"I'm glad you think so."

"Mia, I'm going to say this without getting all sappy. You're the best person I know. My best friend. I mean that."

She didn't exactly roll her eyes, but she did have a look of skepticism on her face. "Roy, that's very sweet, but if that's the case, you really need to expand your circle of friends."

18

On the third day, his nerves began to settle. He was not being watched. He had overreacted. That was obvious now. So he let himself begin to relax. To let his guard down occasionally, as he knew he'd have to eventually. But then a new source of anxiety arose.

"I don't feel good."

That's what Emily said when he went to get her out of bed. He felt her forehead and she was burning up. Out came the thermometer. Her temperature was one hundred and two. This was a cause for concern. He let her sleep for an hour, then he checked on her again. Her fever was unchanged. He hadn't planned on this sort of problem. He gave her half an aspirin, but beyond that, there wasn't much he could do.

By mid-morning, she began to throw up. Not just once, but multiple times. Violently, and with great force. He kept a trash can beside the bed, but she couldn't always reach it in time, because her nausea would come on so suddenly. The bed linens were a mess very quickly. Now he began to wonder if giving her the aspirin was a mistake. Was she allergic? Well, too late now.

He knew he had to keep her hydrated, to replenish the fluids she was losing, but should he feed her? He didn't know. He asked if she was hungry, and she said she wasn't, not even a little bit. How about some soup? Just a little? She shook her head. But she did want the Gatorade — the fruit punch flavor — and she quickly drank a very large glass of it. Moments later, it all came right back up. Red vomit that would almost certainly stain the bedspread.

His worry grew. Taking her to a doctor, even one of those minor emergency clinics, was out of the question, of course. So he went online to do some research. Found a useful page written by a pediatrician.

The first thing he learned was that he shouldn't have given her the Gatorade so quickly, because a sick child would simply vomit it right back up, as Emily had done. Better to wait thirty minutes, or even an hour, then start giving it in small sips. Slow and steady. Not all at once, even if they ask for it.

The web page said that it was probably a virus that was making her sick. There was no cure for it, but it would pass in time. This doctor didn't say anything about a fever. That was stupid. The information was incomplete. Worthless.

He kept surfing and found another page on the site of a major hospital. According to this page, the vomiting could be caused by a virus, motion sickness, overeating, or food poisoning. It could also be the result of a concussion, encephalitis, meningitis, intestinal blockage, appendicitis...

He began to investigate meningitis, which was a mistake, because now he became convinced that Emily had it. She had many of the symptoms. Yes, the vomiting and the fever, as well as agitation, irritability, rapid breathing, fast heart rate. Meningitis could be viral, bacterial, or fungal, with the bacterial kind — the most dangerous kind — requiring antibiotics. As quickly as possible. The text said treatment with antibiotics should reduce the risk of dying to less than 15%. Without the antibiotics, Emily could be facing a buildup of fluid between the skull and the brain, possibly resulting in neurological damage or death.

That didn't sound pleasant at all, especially since she wouldn't be in a hospital setting. It would be slow. Painful.

But, again, what could he do? He'd known from the start that there could be unforeseen challenges. Unexpected complications.

Silly. Once again, he was overreacting. The odds that she had meningitis were small. Tiny. This was likely just a stomach bug, or even food poisoning, but it would pass.

By eight o'clock that evening, Emily's temperature was one hundred and four.

19

Mia had brought up a good point about the equipment I relied on in my line of work. I use quite a few gadgets, and some of them are damn expensive.

Start with the laptop. Top of the line Macintosh. Three grand right there.

Video cameras? Seems like I buy a new one every two or three years, because the technology is always changing. Each new camera is smaller, lighter, more powerful, more functional. The only brand I'll own is Canon. My opinion, they make the best cameras around. Same for my still cameras and zoom lenses. It's easy to spend a bunch of money very quickly on this stuff, so I have to remind myself I'm not shooting a feature motion picture. But I do insist on one of their pro-level high-definition camcorders, which cost a cool four thousand bucks. I also own one of their 35mm SLRs, which shoots pretty decent video, too, in a pinch, along with a pocket-sized point-and-shoot.

It's important to be intimately familiar with the operation of each camera and all the accessories so you can flip it on and start shooting in just a few seconds. You don't want to be fumbling around while your supposedly injured target is hoisting a barbell or running to catch a bus.

You have to practice regularly. And it goes without saying that you want to put freshly charged batteries in your cameras every time you go out. I keep a charger and back-up batteries in the van.

Other gear includes a couple of kick-ass sets of binoculars, a police scanner, and plenty of high-quality flashlights. I also keep pepper spray handy — one of those big-ass canisters designed to ward off a bear attack — because, well, you never know. It's not implausible that a target might spot me trailing him — "getting burned" is the phrase for it — and decide to get hostile. Hadn't happened yet, but I was prepared. Better to use pepper spray than a Glock, that was my attitude.

Then there are the devices that people tend to think of as spy equipment. A tiny video camera built into a baseball cap. Another one that looks like an electrical outlet. Another one that's built into a teddy bear. Yeah, I have a lot of cameras. I also have a motion-activated GPS device that feeds real-time tracking information to my laptop or iPhone. And I have various listening devices, including one with a parabolic sound-collecting dish that lets me pick up and record conversations at up to one hundred yards. For more intimate conversations, I have another audio recorder that looks like a remote control for a vehicle. And another one that looks like a wristwatch.

All told, I probably have twenty thousand dollars worth of high-tech toys, not counting the van itself. None of it is illegal. Your average Joe can hop online and order all of these things himself, or get them at a retail store. On the other hand, *how* you use some of this equipment — that's what can be illegal. Or legal, but unethical. Which doesn't necessarily stop me. Remember, I'm not a cop. And I'm not a private investigator, either, so I'm not bound by any particular professional code of ethics, except my own.

After brunch, I checked Craigslist and found a non-working dryer being given away in South Austin. It was waiting at the curb, first come, first served. I drove to the address and there it was, ready to load.

Then I returned to Thomas Springs Road, because now it was time to get serious. Instead of sitting and waiting, I was going to take action.

Okay, actually, I would have to sit and wait at first, which is what I did, in the same old spot in the church parking lot. Another eight hours in the van, in the summer heat, watching Brian Pierce's gate. And nothing happened, except for an occasional vehicle passing by. No county deputies. No Jetta. No Emma Webster.

The sun set, but I waited another thirty minutes for good measure. Then I stepped out of the van and began walking toward Pierce's place. There was just enough moonlight to make the landscape easy to navigate. I covered one hundred yards in just over a minute.

I stepped over to a cedar tree about twelve yards from the driveway itself. Perfect. There, at the base of the trunk, I placed my rock camera. That's right, a camera that looks like a rock. Not a fancy rock, just a rock. About eight inches tall. Totally self-contained. Records up to eighty hours of video on a 32 gig SD memory card. The battery can last up to a solid year. Is technology great or what?

There were other rocks in the area, and this "rock" looked enough like those rocks to make it virtually invisible. Which was good, because if someone walked off with it, that was a loss of seven hundred bucks, not to mention whatever was on the memory card.

I would have preferred to place the camera across the road — for a better chance of capturing license plates of any vehicles coming or going — but the camera was motion-activated, meaning every vehicle passing on the road would have set it off. This way, the camera would only activate when someone was coming or going from Pierce's place.

I walked back to my van, started it up, and pulled onto Thomas Springs. Drove the hundred yards to Pierce's driveway, plus a few yards past. Then I backed into Pierce's driveway.

No traffic coming from either direction.

So I hopped out, popped open the back of the van, and wrestled my recently acquired non-working dryer out onto the ground. Better a dryer than a washer. Dryers are much lighter, but this one was still heavy enough for my purposes.

Had to move quick. You never know when a car might come along. Every second counts. Which is why I had situated the camera before unloading the dryer. Even those extra few seconds, with my van sitting there as plain as day, could've screwed me.

I maneuvered the dryer close to the gate, so that a vehicle couldn't squeeze around it. Then I jumped back into my van and took off. Total time spent in Pierce's driveway: about thirty seconds.

Here's something most people know if they've driven enough rural county roads: Every now and then, some pinhead who needs to get rid of a large item will simply abandon it on the side of the road. A worn-out couch. A busted refrigerator. A soiled mattress. An old stainless steel sink. Rather than taking it to the dump or a recycling facility, or giving it away, the idiot just pulls over and leaves it. Now it's not his problem. Eventually, someone from the county comes and removes it. Not quickly, though. So it would be up to Pierce to move the dryer himself, with my rock camera recording the action. Would be difficult for him to do it if his wrist was really injured.

I felt pretty good about the arrangement, so I went home, went to bed, and crashed for a solid nine hours.

The next morning, I slept late, had a big breakfast, then went out to my van, where I saw that all four tires were flat again.

Gruley. That son of a bitch.

This was getting old fast.

20

"This is the second time this has happened?"

I said, "Well, it's the second time recently. The first time was on Thursday."

"Three days ago?"

"Yes. Thursday."

"Same thing then? Flat tires?"

"Yep."

"All four?"

"Yes. All four."

This particular Austin cop — who had shown up an hour and a half after I called — couldn't have been more than 25 years old. Probably a rookie. But what do you expect for a call about a vandalized van? Not like they're going to send detectives and a forensics squad.

"Any idea who might have done it? This time or the one three days ago?" He had that expression that I had seen before on other cops' faces. The one, semi-amused, that said, *What did you do to piss someone off?*

Patience. This happened every time. I had to repeat myself. So, just as I had done with the cop on Thursday, I proceeded to tell him the abridged version. What I did for a living. Why some people were prone to get angry with me. How the van was a regular target. Then I gave him the name Wade Gruley, and told him why Gruley had just spent three months in the county jail.

"So he got out, when, middle of last week?" he asked, as he made detailed notes. The funny thing about rookies is that they aren't all jaded and cynical. They still think they might actually make a difference in the world. They write paragraphs when a veteran would write a few words.

"Pretty sure it was Thursday. Same day my tires were flattened the first time."

"Can you spell his name for me?"

"W-A-D-E," I said. He didn't get the joke at first. Too intent on his note-taking. Then he got it and smiled. I spelled 'Gruley' for him. "Might be easier to check the report from Thursday," I said. "It's all in there. I was hoping someone from the department might've spoken to Mr. Gruley, but I haven't heard from the responding officer."

It was a subtle jab. Not that I really expected anyone from APD to track Gruley down and give him a lecture on the evils of vandalism or to even question him. Hundreds of incidents like this happened every single day. The cops were way overloaded. Some scumbag went on a shopping spree with my credit card number a few years ago, and the investigator on that case said she had more then four hundred open files. That was her way of saying, *Don't expect to hear from me again. Ever.*

The cop said, "I'll make a note that you think the two incidents are related." He glanced around the apartment complex's parking lot, inspecting the light poles.

"No video," I said, before he asked.

"Any cameras at the front entrances?"

"Nope."

"Maybe this will inspire the management to install cameras. You should tell them what happened."

"I'll do that," I said. I would not do that.

"Do you know if any of your neighbors saw anything?"

"Haven't heard from anybody." *But you are free to ask them.*

"Has this guy Gruley contacted you?"

"Not since he got out."

"Before that?"

"Yeah, he called a couple of times when he was a guest of the county. Made some vague promises to come see me."

"But no outright threats."

"No, he's just this side of being that dumb."

"Did he say he was gonna flatten all your tires?"

"Nope."

"So there is no actual evidence that he did this."

"Well, it's just a hunch, but my hunches are so eerily accurate, they are admissible as evidence in most courts of law. Except in Arkansas. Those guys are really strict."

He got the joke this time and gave me a halfhearted grin. "You know, without a witness..."

"Yeah, I know. And I know you have better things to do. I really do. I just need the report for the insurance company."

So he finished it up, handed me a copy, then whipped out a business card with his numbers on it. "If you hear from Gruley or see him hanging around, give me a call."

It was like bad dialogue from a cable-channel cop show.

"You can count on it," I said, because that would've been the next line from the script.

I went back inside and planted myself on the couch. The tow truck driver would call my cell when he pulled up outside. I'd been going at it pretty hard for the past week, so I figured it was time to just take a break, even for a few minutes. I tuned the TV to a Texas Longhorns baseball game.

But my break didn't last long.

A newsflash — in the form of a crawl across the bottom of the screen — caught my eye in the bottom of the third. The disappearance of Tracy Turner had grabbed the nation's attention so absolutely, every new detail was disseminated via every possible media outlet as quickly as possible. The crawl said that a source in the case had revealed that, just last week, Kathleen Hanrahan had met with a divorce attorney.

Whoa.

That was big. Another bombshell, really. The circumstantial evidence continued to look really bad for Patrick Hanrahan. First he failed two polygraph tests, or at least he hadn't passed them, then he cut off communications with police, and now this. His wife had been planning to leave him, or had been considering it.

I flipped to CNN, knowing they'd be on it, which was an understatement. At this point, the Turner case was probably eating up half of their broadcast day. At the moment, one of their legal experts was conjecturing on the implications of the latest news.

"...can only imagine how Patrick Hanrahan might've reacted upon hearing that his wife was thinking about a divorce. He has a lot to lose, because even though he is not Tracy's biological father, as we've learned in the past few days, he is as close to her as if she were his own flesh and blood. He has been in her life, acting as her father, since she was one year old. One can only guess what — "

I flipped to MSNBC. They were interviewing one of Kathleen Hanrahan's friends, but they were concealing her face and altering her voice for anonymity. The woman — at least, it sounded like a woman — was saying that Kathleen had been unhappy for several years and had spoken about divorce on many different occasions. Then the woman said that Kathleen had recently seemed even more troubled than before — like something traumatic had happened. I listened for a few minutes, but the woman never gave any actual reasons why Kathleen was unhappy, and it became obvious that there were no hard facts beyond what I already knew.

I flipped to Fox News. They were doing a segment on how the secular left was taking God out of school and simultaneously pushing the radical homosexual socialist agenda.

I went back to the baseball game just as my cell phone rang. I didn't recognize the number. I answered anyway, expecting the tow truck driver, but what I got instead was a woman with a very nice voice asking, "Is this the Texas Restaurant and Innkeepers Association?"

I'll admit that, for maybe a full second, I had no idea who it was. Too distracted. But I recovered before it became obvious.

"It is indeed. This is Roy Ballard, assistant vice president of the hospitality appreciation division. Who's calling, please?"

"Jessica Klein."

"Let's see. Klein, Klein, Klein. Oh, Klein! As in the award winner."

"That's me."

"Are you calling to schedule your acceptance dinner?"

"Uh, that sort of depends."

"Oh? Depends on what, Miss Klein?"

"Well, Mr. Ballard, let me ask you something. Are you asking me to dinner because you actually want to go out with me, or are you asking because you want me to snoop around about Brian Pierce?"

"Wow. You cut right to it, don't you?"

"I think it's a legitimate question."

"You know what? I do, too. The bottom line is I'd love to go to dinner with you, regardless of this thing with Brian Pierce. If you don't want to talk about him, we won't talk about him."

"Good answer."

"Honest answer."

"Okay, but if I *had* heard something about Brian, you'd want to hear it?"

"Well, sure, yeah, I'm not gonna lie."

There was a pause, then she said, "I'm off today. Why don't we meet for a drink later and I'll tell you what I know. We can get that out of the way, and then, if you really do want to go out — "

"I do."

"One step at a time. A drink first. And don't forget my trophy."

21

"Brian Pierce did not want to apply for workers' comp," Jessica Klein said.

I took a sip of my iced tea and let that sink in, wondering if my case had just come to an end. It was a little past six in the evening. We were sitting on the patio of a restaurant called the Iron Cactus in the shopping center — oh, excuse me, the "lifestyle center" — called the Hill Country Galleria. Not far from Pierce's house, and not far from La Tolteca, the restaurant where he and Jessica worked. Maybe she lived nearby, too, but I hadn't asked her that yet.

"He didn't?" I asked, because my interview techniques are honed to a razor's edge.

She shook her head. "It sounds like he didn't even know what workers' comp was, or at least he didn't know that it would apply to his situation."

Jessica looked even prettier than the previous time I'd seen her. Her blond hair, which had been pulled back the other day, was now loose and flowing past her shoulders. I was fairly sure she was wearing more makeup. The baby-blue V-neck tank top hugging her torso was a hell of a lot more flattering than her waitress outfit. It wasn't easy to remain totally focused.

"How do you know this?" I asked.

"Manager told me. He said he had to twist Brian's arm" — she grinned — "ha, no pun intended, but he had to twist Brian's arm to get him to take workers' comp. I didn't really understand why, but Terry — that's the manager — he said that the higher-ups would *want* Brian to apply for it. It was better if he did."

"Yeah, workers' comp is a trade-off," I said. "In exchange for benefits, you agree not to sue for negligence."

"Oh, is that how it works?"

"Pretty much."

"Well, Terry said that Brian didn't even tell anybody he got injured. I mean, some of the other people working that night heard what happened. He started to fall, so he reached out for the nearest thing, which was a stack of dishes. A couple of people came in to see if he was okay, and he said he was. But later on it was obvious that he was hurt because he couldn't keep up with the work. By the end of the night he couldn't even use that hand anymore."

"So he finally admitted he was hurt?"

"Yeah, Terry talked to him. Brian said he'd probably need to take the next day off, and Terry insisted that he go see a doctor. Brian wouldn't have to pay for it, the restaurant's insurance policy would. Brian resisted at first, because he thought the whole thing was his own fault."

"Why would he think that?"

"Apparently he had hosed off one of the rubber floor mats and left it out back. He knew he wasn't supposed to work without that mat in place, but he did anyway, and he slipped on the wet tile."

"Sounds like maybe it *was* his fault, but workers' comp still applies. It's a no-fault type of insurance."

"Well, regardless, even when the doctor said Brian had a pretty bad injury and wouldn't be able to work for at least a month or two, Brian still resisted the insurance benefits at first. But Terry talked some sense into him. Anyway, my point is, isn't the fact that Brian didn't want workers' comp a pretty good sign that he's probably not faking his injury?"

"Almost certainly."

"So this is useful information?"

"You bet it is. Very useful. I really appreciate it."

"Did I earn my margarita?"

"I'd say two, if you're up for another one." Her first one was almost gone.

"Maybe." She looked at my iced tea. "Do you not drink?"

Dates — or whatever this was — inevitably arrived at this topic. I always gave an honest answer. "Oh, I would if I could," I said. "I'd love a cold beer right now. But it would violate my probation."

She laughed, as they usually do, until she realized I wasn't joking. Then she frowned. "Whoa."

"Yeah, I know."

"Really?"

"Here's the story," I said slowly, "assuming you want to hear it..."

"I do, if you want to share it."

"Okay, about three years ago, I broke my boss's nose. He called one of my female coworkers a really vile name and I lost my temper. I ended up pleading to a lesser charge and getting probation because, well, he didn't want to push it too hard. He was a misogynist who routinely harassed women and all of that would've been brought up in my trial. Anyway, I had just finished my probation for that when I got pulled over for suspicion of DWI."

Her eyebrows went up.

"The Breathalyzer proved I was legal," I said. "Not even halfway to point oh eight. But they found a small bottle of pills in my van. Stimulants. There were a couple of occasions when I took them to stay awake on stakeouts. I think maybe I did that eight or ten times total. No more than that. Cross my heart. Anyway, I can't drink. That's one of the terms." I took a sip of tea and gave an exaggerated sigh of refreshment. "Ah. Good stuff."

She was studying me, and I don't blame her. There are a lot of liars out there. Many of them downplay their problems. Gloss over their shortcomings.

"Questions?" I said. A lot of women are done at this point. Not just done asking questions, done with me.

"How much longer is your probation?"

"Eight months, three weeks."

"Popped any pills lately?

"Ha. No. I'm done with that."

"Any other arrests I should know about?"

"Not a one. Haven't even had a speeding ticket in fourteen years."

"What was the name the guy called your coworker?"

"You really want to hear it?"

"I'm a big girl."

"But man, I really hate this particular word. It rhymes with *runt*."

She nodded. "Gotcha. That *is* the worst one. So you decked the guy?"

"I had a microphone stand in my hand at the time. I popped him with that. It was just a reaction, to be honest. If I'd known it was gonna break his nose, I probably wouldn't have done it."

"You seem like a pretty mellow guy."

"Hey, I really am. It just — I don't like guys talking that way. It's ugly."

The waiter came just then and asked if she would like another margarita. The moment of truth. Had I totally freaked her out? She looked at me. Grinned. Finally said, "Yes, please."

An hour and a half later, sitting in the van before I left the Galleria, I called Heidi's cell. She answered by saying, "Calling on a Sunday evening must mean you have an update on Brian Pierce."

"I do. He didn't want workers' comp. It had to be practically forced on him."

"Come again?"

"A source says the manager of the restaurant had to poke him with a sharp stick just to get him to make a claim."

"How reliable is this source?"

"I'd say very reliable." Heidi didn't reply right away. I could hear kitchen sounds — dishes clanking in the background. "Sorry if I interrupted your dinner."

"Oh, I'm done. That's Jim cleaning up. Like a good husband should."

I waited.

She said, "Okay, I guess we close the file on Pierce."

"That's what I figured. Got another one for me?"

"At the moment, no, but I have one I'll probably send your way in a day or two. End of the week at the latest."

"You're a peach."

"And you know what? No more manila folders. Our new system went live on Friday. We have joined the electronic age."

"So I won't get to see you as much?"

"Only through binoculars from the parking lot."

"Okay, good. As long as that part hasn't changed."

I took a left out of the parking lot and came very close to taking a left on Bee Cave Road to head home. Wish I would have. Instead, I remembered my rock camera. It was still at the base of that cedar tree, aimed at Pierce's driveway. Didn't want to leave a seven-hundred-dollar gizmo on the side of the road longer than I had to. So I continued east on Highway 71 for several minutes, then turned right on Thomas Springs Road. Dusk had settled in good and tight.

As soon as my headlights reached Pierce's driveway, I could see that the dryer was gone. I was glad, because although I might be a conniving bastard, I'm not a litterbug, so if the dryer had still been there, I would've felt obligated to haul it away.

I drove past the driveway and continued down the road to the church parking lot, where I stopped and waited for a few seconds. No traffic from either direction. So I drove back to Pierce's place and pulled over on the shoulder. This would be quick. Hop out, grab my rock camera, and be on my merry way.

Except it didn't turn out like that at all.

I should say that there are times when I am wary and maybe even on edge, because my line of work might actually put me in danger. I've talked about the subjects who get angry after I've documented evidence of their fraud. Likewise, there are times when they'd get upset if they caught me in the process of trying to document that evidence. Nobody wants to be exposed as a cheater.

This didn't seem like one of those times. The case was closed. It appeared that Pierce was not committing fraud, so he would have nothing to be jumpy about. And on top of that, he was a skinny little guy. He didn't seem like the type that would present any sort of danger, even if he caught me red-handed watching him.

So I wasn't being particularly careful. I wasn't sneaking around or trying to be discreet. I wasn't watching my back, or my front. No subtlety at all. Hell, I was even using a flashlight to make my way to the cedar tree where I'd hidden the camera.

And then — in the instant before the trouble began — I thought I heard something. Very faint. A rustling sound. A small limb rubbing against fabric. But I didn't have time to react. Because then I heard a much louder sound — *pop!* — followed by an intense stabbing pain in my upper back that quickly spread all over my body. My motor skills evaporated instantly. My muscles contracted and I went as stiff as a board. I knew I was falling but I couldn't do anything to stop it. I hit the ground hard.

Getting Tasered. I knew that. And whoever was doing it hadn't released the trigger yet. The juice was still flowing. I wanted so badly to scream, but I didn't have the capability. I was totally helpless. Somebody was making some strange grunts and moans. Took me a second to realize it was me.

Then I heard a voice. Low. Commanding. Right above me.

"Don't you fucking move. Not even an inch."

22

Apparently the guy released the trigger at that point, because the electricity coursing through my body came to an immediate end. I can't tell you how happy that made me.

"You hear what I said?"

I nodded.

"I'll repeat it anyway: Don't fucking move. And don't say a word."

I couldn't speak yet even if I wanted to. He grabbed my right arm and pulled it behind my back. Then the left. I could feel handcuffs clicking into place.

Now there was cold steel alongside my temple. Easy to identify.

"Feel that?"

Nod.

"Know what it is?"

Nod again.

"I'll use it if I have to. Not a threat, just a fact."

The gun went away. I was doing my best to memorize the man's voice, for later. Assuming there was a later.

"Lift your head."

I raised my chin off the ground and a hood was pulled roughly over my head. Now I couldn't see a thing. I really did not like where this was going. With just the handcuffs, it had still been feasible that this man, whoever he was, was going to call the cops. But a hood over my head? That meant he didn't want me to see his face, which meant he definitely wasn't calling the cops. On the bright side, it could also mean he wasn't going to pump a slug into my skull, because in that case, it wouldn't matter if I saw his face beforehand.

"On your feet," he said, and he hoisted me up by my handcuffed arms. Powerful grip. He was using his right hand. Brian Pierce's right hand was injured. Or supposed to be. I had no idea what to think at this point. Was this Pierce? Somebody else?

He spun me around and we started walking, with him guiding me along the uneven shoulder of the road. Toward my van. Of course. He couldn't very well leave my van sitting there, not if he was going to haul me away cuffed and hooded.

"Step up."

Ever try climbing into a tall vehicle when you can't see where the hell you're going? Not easy. But he steered me and turned me and flat-out manhandled me into place, and suddenly I was sitting in the passenger seat. I pulled my feet in after me.

"Watch your elbow."

I leaned slightly toward the center of the vehicle and he closed the door. Maybe another good sign. Would he be concerned about smacking my elbow with the door if he was planning to take me into the woods and execute me?

It was obvious that this was a well-planned operation, with a purpose. It wasn't as if he'd randomly found me on the roadside and decided to abduct me. That meant this guy had found my camera. He knew I had been watching Pierce's place, so he had responded by waiting for me to show up, knowing in advance how he would proceed if he got his paws on me.

The driver's door was still open from when I had climbed out less than two minutes earlier, and now I felt the van dip slightly as he climbed in and took a seat. The door closed and he shifted into drive. Then he proceeded northeast on Thomas Springs Road, toward Highway 71.

I said, "Aren't you going to buckle me in?"

No reply. I was taking a risk, talking, even though he'd told me not to.

"I didn't hear the click of your seatbelt either," I said. "Are you aware that driving without a seatbelt is a misdemeanor punishable by a fine of up to two hundred dollars?"

"Shut up. You will not get another warning."

It's probably no surprise that I didn't want to get Tasered again, so I did shut up. Besides, it was a better use of my time to try to figure out where we were going. I could tell that he turned right on Highway 71, but after that, he took several more turns quickly, and it was hard to follow it in my mind's eye. I think that was his intention. Then we drove for about ten minutes at highway speeds. No turns, no stopping at traffic lights. We had to be on either Highway 290 or Highway 71, heading west.

Eventually, we took a left and went much slower for a short distance. Several more turns followed, and then we finally came to a stop. He killed the engine immediately.

"What's your name?" he asked.

"Johnny."

"Johnny what?"

"Johnny Hungwell."

"That's a bad start. I'm telling you right now that I'm not a patient man."

I was thinking about the nine-millimeter Glock hidden in the secret compartment beneath the rear passenger bench. Wasn't doing me much good there, was it? Hell, it could be in the glove compartment, right in front of me, and it still wouldn't matter until he uncuffed me.

"Roy Ballard," I said.

I felt an arm brush my leg as he leaned toward the glove compartment and popped it open. He was checking my name against various documents. He found what he was looking for and closed the glove compartment.

"What were you doing on the side of the road tonight?"

"Looking for a place to take a leak. I've been drinking these new diet shakes and my bladder is the size of a — "

Bam!

He zapped me again, this time on the left biceps. God damn, did it hurt. Must have been a handheld stun gun this time, rather than a Taser. Either way, it lit me up like a squirrel on a transformer. Fortunately, it lasted no more than a few seconds.

He gave me a moment to recover, then said, "I told you there would be no more warnings. What were you doing on the side of the road tonight?"

I was beginning to have revenge fantasies. The things I would do to this asshole if I got the chance. But, for now, I had to just get through this. I figured I should tell the truth. Hard to make up good lies on the fly.

"I was wrapping up surveillance on a man named Brian Pierce. He lives right there on Thomas Springs Road, but I guess you already know that."

"Why were you watching him?" The guy didn't sound like a local. More of a northeastern accent, but softened by being in the South for at least a little while. My guess, anyway.

"He filed a workers' comp claim for a job-related injury. I get hired by insurance companies to make sure guys like Pierce aren't committing fraud. That's why I have all this equipment in here."

Now he got up and went into the rear of the van. I could hear him looking into various zippered bags and plastic bins, going through all my stuff. Double-checking my story. Or maybe looking for stuff to steal.

I said, "Do I get my camera back at some point?"

"Shut up."

He rustled around back there for another minute or so, then returned to the driver's seat. "You put the dryer in his driveway?"

"I did. Hoping he'd move it with his injured hand and I'd catch it on video."

I noticed that he didn't stumble or hesitate when he said "his driveway," as opposed to "my driveway."

"How long have you been watching him?"

"Couple of days."

"Be specific."

I definitely did not want to get blasted a third time, but something told me to lie. Gut instinct. I went with it. "Since Thursday afternoon." The truth was, it had been Wednesday, the day I thought I had seen a little girl at Pierce's place.

"You sure?"

"Yes. Thursday afternoon."

"Learn anything?"

"Nothing. Hard to see his house past all those trees. And if I were to trespass, any evidence I got would be worthless. He never went anywhere, so I couldn't trail him."

"Did he have any visitors?"

I'm betting he already knew the answer to this question and was testing to see if I would answer it honestly.

I said, "Only one that I saw. A woman in a Jetta. I never got the plate number so I have no idea who she was."

"So now you're giving up?"

"I have other reasons to believe he isn't committing fraud."

"What reasons?"

I didn't want to answer. If I did, I'd be revealing that someone from the restaurant had spoken to me. Again, my gut was telling me to keep that to myself. If there was any chance at all that I might be putting Jessica in danger, I was going to keep her name to myself.

I still hadn't answered when I sensed movement near my left ear. I flinched. Couldn't help myself. Then I heard the crackle of the stun gun just inches from my head. I flinched even bigger this time. I was making a vow to myself at that moment. I was going to put this son of a bitch through the same damn torment. Nothing greater, nothing less, just the same.

I said, "I was going through the paperwork last night and I saw something that my client had overlooked, which was that the manager of the restaurant said that Pierce had originally declined to file a claim. He didn't want the benefits, but the manager encouraged him to take them. That means there is basically zero chance that he is committing fraud, hence no need to investigate him."

A long silence followed. The man was weighing my answer. Either believing it, and contemplating it for reasons I didn't understand, or trying to decide whether I was lying or not. No way to know.

I realized then how quiet it was. Wherever we were parked, there was no traffic noise at all. No other suburban sounds, either, such as a dog barking or the hum of a streetlight. Nothing but the buzz of crickets.

"Here's the situation," the man said. "I don't give a flying fuck about Pierce. Don't know him and don't care whether he's committing fraud or not. That's none of my business. But I work security for someone else in that area and I needed to know why you were hanging around. Now that your work is done, it would be best if you stayed the hell away from Thomas Springs Road. You understand me? Don't go anywhere near there."

This was good news. Not the bullshit about him not knowing Pierce, but the fact that he wasn't going to shoot me. All I had to do was be cool.

"I hadn't been on that stretch of road for years," I said. "And I sure don't have any reason to go back. My client has already closed the case."

"If you go back there, I can promise that you will regret it. Immediately."

"I won't be going back."

Long pause. He was trying to think of any other questions he should ask or threats he should make. Evidently he decided that he wasn't quite done.

"You report this and you're gonna wish you hadn't. Got me? But if you let it go — look at it as a learning experience — then you and I won't have any further problems. Sound reasonable?"

"Hey, that's fine by me. You're just doing your job."

"Okay, in the back, on the floor."

I didn't have much choice. Again, he steered me with a rough hand on my arm. I went to my knees in the rear of the van, behind the bench seat.

"All the way down."

He laid me flat, my arms still cuffed behind me.

"I'm going to remove the mask. If you want to make the biggest mistake of your life, try to get a look at me. You understand what I'm saying?"

"I do."

He pulled the mask off my head and it felt good. I hadn't realized how sweaty my head had gotten. It was dark enough in the van that I couldn't have gotten a good look at the guy even if I'd tried. But I didn't try. I kept my nose to the carpet. Why blow it now?

"Now I'm gonna take the cuffs off. Do not move. Do not get off the floor. I want you to stay right where you are for ten minutes. If you move before that, there's a real good chance I'll be standing right outside watching you. Then again I might be gone. Much better for you if you wait the ten minutes. *Comprende?*"

"Yep."

He popped the cuffs off and that felt even better than having the hood removed. By then, my arms and shoulders were throbbing.

"Ten minutes," he repeated. "Your keys will be a hundred yards down the road."

I felt the van shifting as he made his way to the open door and exited. Then it was still again. I'm not positive, but now I thought I could hear an engine idling somewhere not too far away. His ride, waiting for him. Somebody had followed us out here. Which meant there was at least one other person working with him. Assuming I really was hearing an engine, and now I wasn't so sure.

I waited one minute, then pushed myself off the floor of the van. I didn't get shot, Tasered, clubbed, smacked, or otherwise assaulted.

Looking out the rear window, I got my bearings quickly. There was just enough fading light to see that the van was parked in a cul-de-sac. No houses to be seen anywhere. Just oak and cedar trees, and faraway hills turning gray in the twilight. Ten feet from the van, a wooden stake with bright-orange surveyor's tape tied around the top was driven into the dirt. Smart. He had driven us down into an empty neighborhood. The roads had been put in, but nothing had been built yet. Nobody would be poking around here after dark.

I quickly checked all my gear, and it appeared that nothing was missing. My Glock was still in the hidden compartment. I exited the van and started walking, using a flashlight as I went. The keys were right in the middle of the road, about one hundred yards away. The man was a damn humanitarian.

23

First thing the next morning, Mia called to say she'd put a great deal of thought into it, and she had decided that she'd like to be my partner. I literally had to laugh.

"What's so funny?" she asked.

"Well, you might change your mind in a minute."

"Why?"

I gave her a quick summary of what had happened to me last night. Just the highlights.

"Jesus, Roy, that's nuts. Did you report him?"

"Nope."

"Why the hell not?"

I could tell she was angry that someone had treated me that way, which made me feel sort of good.

"Think about it. First I reported that I saw Tracy Turner, or some other little girl, at Pierce's place. The cops plainly didn't believe me, and given my history, I'm not sure I would've believed me either, and, in fact, I'm not sure I *did* see anything. Okay, so now I'm going to report that an unknown assailant blasted me with a Taser, threatened to shoot me, then hauled me off to the boondocks for questioning? But I have no evidence? And I can't describe the guy? Man, they would think I've totally lost it, or that I'm still trying to make them believe my first report. No way I'm putting myself through that. Waste of time."

She said nothing for a few seconds. Then: "You know what?"

"What?"

"I'm coming over. We need to talk about this."

She arrived thirty minutes later with hot coffee and a fresh bag of glazed donuts, which reaffirmed her potential as an excellent partner.

She set them on the coffee table and gave me a concerned stare. "You okay?"

"I'm fine. It wasn't like he beat me with a rubber hose."

"Yeah, but a Taser..."

"Thanks, really, but I'm fine."

"Let me see where he got you."

"It's no big deal."

"Stand up, Roy. Let me see."

I stood, as I was told, and rolled up my left sleeve to show her my biceps. "I'm sure you'll notice that I've been working out."

She studied my upper arm.

I said, "If you can find a mark, I'll give you a hundred bucks."

"You're right. I don't see anything. You said he zapped you twice."

I turned my back and pulled my t-shirt up and over my head. "Control yourself," I said.

She placed one hand against my lower back — sort of a "stay right there" gesture. Truth is, it felt nice. Really nice. Was that because it was Mia? Or would I have liked the touch of any beautiful woman's hand at that moment?

"Yeah, okay," she said. "Nothing back here either. I figured it would leave a burn mark or a pair of red welts or something."

I realized that I wasn't making a move to pull my shirt back on. And Mia's hand was still on my back. She slid it around on my skin for a bit, as if feeling for a lump or a bump. It felt warm and smooth and believe me when I say I could imagine it running over other parts of my anatomy.

"You have goose bumps," she said, almost in a whisper.

I still didn't move. Her hand didn't either.

"What man wouldn't?" I said.

Something was happening. I wondered if we were about to cross a self-imposed boundary I'm pretty sure we both have considered crossing at some point. Or was I imagining it? Mia was the type to express concern by touching you.

Regardless, she pulled her hand away, and the moment — if there was one — was broken.

"I need a donut," she said.

"So where had he taken you?"

I was on one end of the couch now. Mia was on the other end, sitting cross-legged, facing me. She was eating a donut, as promised, which included occasionally licking her fingers. I could charge admission for that show.

"Out 290, past Nutty Brown Road. A new neighborhood off to the left. No homes yet."

"Why there?"

"Good a place as any."

"You think he knows the area?" She finished her donut and wiped her hands with a paper napkin.

"More likely he scouted for a spot in advance, just for that purpose. Him or the person working with him. I'm almost positive I heard an engine idling somewhere nearby."

"Yeah, I can't imagine he'd drive you all the way out there and then walk back."

"I didn't see anybody on my way out, but it would've been easy enough for him to duck into the woods."

I sipped some coffee, then gave in and grabbed a donut for myself. Mia said, "Think it was Pierce?"

"I guess it's possible, but I really don't think it was. This guy sounded older — maybe forties — and not from around here. He had a Boston accent like Matt Damon did in that movie about the math genius. Not quite that harsh, but similar."

"Think he knows Pierce?"

"He claimed he didn't, and that he was working security for someone who lived around there. But that was a weak cover. If he was under the impression that I thought he knew Pierce, but he really didn't, wouldn't he want to leave me with my mistaken impression? Why would he offer up any information at all? It seemed obvious that he was trying to steer me away from the truth. So, yeah, I'd say he's connected to Pierce."

"Let's assume so. Then the question is: Why would he be working security for a 26-year-old dishwasher?"

"Man, I have no idea."

"Something weird there."

"Oh, I agree totally. We're missing a big piece of the puzzle. At least one piece."

Mia seemed to be enjoying our conversation — the speculation, the mystery, the unanswered questions — quite a bit.

So I said, "You realize that this sort of thing is completely out of the norm. Most of what I do, and what you would be doing, is pretty damn boring. You know that already."

"Yes, I do know that, and I notice that you said 'would.'"

"Yeah?"

"You should be saying 'will.'"

"You still want to do it, huh? Be my partner?"

"Can't be any more dangerous than working at the bar. You know how often I have to fend off creeps in the parking lot?"

"Where else am I supposed to wait for you?"

She smiled for a second.

I said, "Here's the other problem. This thing with Brian Pierce — whatever it is — it isn't actually a case now. Heidi pulled the plug. What that means is, ain't no money coming our way for it."

"So?"

"So if you really want to be my partner — and I'm glad you do — why not wait until the next case comes in? Then we'll jump right in."

"Nope."

"Nope?"

"Somebody mistreated my friend Roy, and they aren't getting away with it."

Frankly, I was touched. "That's, uh — "

"Sweet?"

"Really dumb. Working for nothing?"

"You're an ass. Let's go over it again. Repeat the entire conversation.

Word for word, if you can remember."

So I did, as best as I could recall. Mia listened quietly until I got to the part where the guy asked about the dryer in the driveway. I was starting to think of him as "The Guy."

"Wait a sec," she said. "What about the camera?"

"What about it?"

"Why would he mention the dryer rather than the camera?"

"I'm not following you."

"If you admitted to me that you'd been watching Pierce, I'd say, 'Oh, so you're the one who hid the super-secret spy camera beside his driveway.' But, instead, he asked about the dryer."

I thought about it. "Well, since I'd admitted that I was watching Pierce, it was obvious the camera was mine, whereas the dryer could've been dumped by anybody. He was probably just curious. Tying up loose ends."

"Maybe, or maybe he never found the camera."

"But I asked him about it. I asked if I was gonna get my camera back."

"Wasn't that when he was in the back of your van, pawing through all your equipment? He might've thought you were talking about one of the cameras you keep in the van."

That stopped me for a second.

She continued. "Did you say 'camera' or 'rock camera'?"

"I don't remember."

"How did he respond when you asked about getting it back?"

"He told me to shut up."

"So you've just been assuming he found the rock camera, but maybe he didn't. Maybe it was the dryer that made him suspicious. Did you reach the cedar tree before he zapped you? Did you get a chance to see if the camera was there?"

I had to think about it. "It's hard to remember. But now I'm starting to think I didn't."

"So the camera could still be sitting there, and if we're lucky, maybe it'll tell us a little more about this guy. Or about Pierce. Or the woman in the Jetta. Or all three."

"Damn, you're good."

"Thanks. We should go check it out."

"Absolutely."

"When?"

"Right now."

We took the van. We could've taken her car, but I'll admit it was a matter of pride. I guess I wanted to prove to myself — or maybe to Mia, or even to The Guy — that I wasn't afraid to show myself again, as plain as day. Also, on the more practical side, it made sense to keep Mia's car in our hip pocket, never seen before, in case we needed it later.

I didn't bother driving past Pierce's place and turning around. I simply pulled to the shoulder and stopped not far from the cedar tree. And I immediately liked what I saw.

"Is it there?" Mia asked.

She was temporarily crouched down in the back. No sense in letting The Guy know anyone was working with me.

"Hell, yeah, it is. Back in a sec."

"Be careful."

Once again, no cars were coming from either direction. Which was why, as I exited the van and made my way toward the rock camera, which was still resting in the same place I'd put it, I carried my Glock by my side, in plain sight.

It was a strange moment. I wanted to get away cleanly, without any trouble. No question about that. But there was also a small, irrational part of me that wanted The Guy to pop out from behind a tree so I could draw down on him and start to get some payback. Make him lie facedown in the dirt. Plant a foot on the back of his neck. Make him feel helpless and weak.

But nothing happened.

I grabbed the rock camera with my left hand and carried it back to the van, glancing behind me only once. I set the camera on the floorboard and tucked the Glock into the glove compartment, then closed the driver's door and pulled back onto the pavement.

When I stopped at the intersection with Circle Drive, Mia returned to the passenger seat and buckled in. She didn't say anything, but she was beaming. I stuck my fist out and she bumped it.

"Thanks, pardner," I said.

24

Later, I hovered above Mia and placed a comforting hand on her shoulder. I said, "Don't be nervous. It'll be a learning experience. We'll take it nice and slow."

I could tell that she was excited. Her face was flushed with anticipation. "I don't want to screw up."

"Don't worry. You won't. Just follow my instructions and you'll be great. Start by inserting the SD card into the card reader, then plug it into the USB slot."

She was seated in the chair in front of my laptop in my apartment. I was behind her, guiding her through the process.

I said, "First thing we'll do is import the video into iMovie. That'll take a minute or two, but it plays more smoothly directly from the hard drive, and it's good to have a back-up."

When the video had finished copying, I said, "Now go to the File menu and click 'New Project.' Okay, good. See there, at the bottom? That means we have a little more than eight minutes of video to review."

"That's all?"

"Remember, it's motion-activated. The camera isn't shooting all the time. So go ahead and hit Play and let's see what we've got."

The video began with me backing the van into Pierce's driveway. I hopped out, opened the rear doors, and unloaded the dryer. I was impressed with how quickly I got it done.

Mia said, "Shouldn't you have put the dryer in place first, then the camera, so you wouldn't have caught yourself on video?"

"Well, sure, if I was a seasoned professional and I knew what I was doing."

On the screen, I was getting back into the van, just about to drive away.

"Seriously," I said, because I didn't want her to think I was an idiot, "you have a good point. But I figured if anyone noticed me dumping the dryer, I didn't want them to see me positioning the camera afterward. So, yeah, it wasn't ideal, but I put the camera in place first."

"Makes sense."

After I drove away, the dryer was more or less in the center of the screen. To the left of the dryer, several feet out of the shot, was Thomas Springs Road. To the right, visible on the screen, was Brian Pierce's gate. After a period of inactivity — maybe twenty seconds — the camera turned itself off.

Nothing happened for the remainder of Saturday.

At 8:17 A.M. on Sunday morning, the camera activated as the nose of the Jetta entered the screen from the right, coming from Pierce's house, and stopped at the gate. If I had turned the rock a little bit more clockwise when I had hidden it, we would've seen more of the car. But that would've meant seeing less of any vehicle that might've pulled up on the other side of the gate to enter the property.

"This is very cool," Mia said.

"What, the camera?"

"The whole thing. I feel like a spy."

"That wears off, believe me. Watching normal people go about their daily lives is tremendously boring."

"Too bad we can't make out the license plate."

Ten seconds passed. Then twenty. I figured the brown-haired woman who had arrived in the car on Friday was perplexed by what she was seeing in front of her. It was taking her a moment to react. And then she stepped into the frame. She was standing near the front tire of her car, and it appeared that she was holding a cell phone to her left ear. Couldn't see her face very well at this point. She was wearing different clothes than she had been the previous time I had seen her, which meant she had packed an overnight bag, or she had some clothes at Pierce's house.

"Just let it keep playing?" Mia asked.

"Yeah. Let's see if she gives us a better view of her face."

The woman continued talking for quite some time, and now she was getting quite animated, gesturing toward the dryer on the other side of the gate.

"There's a goddamn dryer blocking the way," Mia said, using a high-pitched cartoon voice as she guessed what the brown-haired woman was saying. "Yes, a goddamn dryer. It's sitting right in the goddamn middle of the goddamn driveway."

I was becoming happier every minute that I had come up with this partnership idea.

After a little more conversation, the woman snapped her phone shut and leaned against the fender of her car, waiting, and giving us a good look at her face.

"Let's pause it right there," I said.

Mia complied, and I explained how to forward or reverse the video one frame at a time, so we could choose the best possible frame. Then I showed her how to save a still shot, and how to crop it as needed. Now we had a better photo of the woman's face than the one I'd gotten when she'd arrived on Friday.

"Okay, let it roll and let's see what happens."

The woman remained against the fender for about one minute, then she looked to her left, which was our right, and she behaved as if someone was coming from the house. She came off the fender and waited.

Sure enough, here came a man, not wasting any time, walking right past the woman, who followed him to the gate. The man was average height, sort of burly, with black hair and a full beard, closely trimmed. Nothing special about him. Middle-aged, maybe mid-forties. I was trying to decide whether the voice of The Guy matched up with this man. Maybe.

He unlocked the gate and swung it open enough that he could slip through. Then he walked over to the dryer. Gave it a test push, as if checking to see that it really was just a dryer. Not a Trojan Horse or a nuclear warhead. He opened the dryer door and looked inside. Nothing in there, of course. Then he shoved the dryer out of the driveway, so traffic could pass. At one point, he was more or less facing the camera head-on, so I asked Mia to save a still shot of his face.

After he moved the dryer, the woman, who had been watching from the other side of the gate, said something. He gave a shrug and a brief reply. Then the woman walked out of the frame, evidently to get into her car. The man went to the gate and swung it all the way open, and the Jetta passed through. The man closed the gate, chained it, and locked it. Then he walked out of the frame, back toward the house. Half a minute later, the camera turned itself off.

The next action took place nearly four hours later. At that point, the front end of a white Ford F-150 — Pierce's truck — appeared from the right. Then the man with the beard walked into the frame. He opened the gate, drove through, and left in the truck. Apparently, he was only turning around, because he came right back twenty seconds later. He pulled halfway through the open gate, then stopped, just past the dryer. Then he hopped out and managed to wrestle the dryer into the back of the truck.

"Must be a pretty strong guy," Mia said.

"Well, dryers aren't really that heavy," I said.

The man got back into the truck and pulled all the way through, stopped, locked the gate, then drove away with the dryer, heading toward Pierce's house. I said, "I can see as how you'd think this is super-exciting."

"Beats serving pitchers to drunks who want to bitch about their ex-wives."

The last action captured on video was from the previous evening. Of course it was. That's when I went to retrieve the camera and it didn't end well. I knew the video wouldn't show much, because, for obvious reasons, it doesn't have a flash. It works okay in low-light conditions, but there comes a point when it's just shooting darkness, more or less.

In this case, when the video began to play, you could tell that something was happening, and that someone was using a flashlight, but that was about it. The light was coming closer and closer to the camera, and then the light dropped to the ground, illuminating the grasses surrounding it.

"And that's when I got ambushed by a gutless coward."

Mia didn't say anything.

"He sucker-punched me," I said. "Or maybe I should say 'sucker-Tasered.'"

No reply.

"Not a fair fight," I said.

"Don't get mad," she finally said. "Get even."

25

We took a break for lunch, and then I told Mia about my fictitious Linda Peterson Facebook account and asked her to log in to it.

Mia was shaking her head as she tapped the keys. "You are one devious bastard. You friended Pierce?"

"But of course."

"And he was dumb enough to accept?"

"Hey, Linda's a hottie. It's hard to resist her feminine wiles. She also looks marvelous in a swimsuit. She's no Mia Madison, of course."

"I never accept requests from strangers."

"You might if Robert Tyler sent you one. He has the chiseled good looks of Matthew McConaughey, without that look of smug self-satisfaction on his face."

"That actually works? Women fall for it?"

"Well, sometimes. Admittedly, men are much less discriminating online."

"And everywhere else."

"Point taken."

Mia had clicked on Linda Peterson's friends list and was scrolling downward.

I said, "We'll go to Pierce's photos and compare the Jetta woman to some of his friends. I narrowed it down the other day. I'm pretty sure there are four candidates. Maybe you can help me pick a winner. Or maybe she isn't on there at all."

"Fine, but...he's not here."

And he wasn't. Brian Pierce no longer appeared on Linda Peterson's friends list.

Mia laughed. "Dude, I think you've been busted."

"Well, crap. Go up to the search bar and let's see if we can find him that way."

She did. A lot of Brian Pierces showed up in the results, but not the one we were looking for.

I said, "That means he not only unfriended me, he might've blocked me."

"Hold on," Mia said. She logged out, then logged in to her own account. She searched again for Brian Pierce — and there he was, confirming that he had blocked me, or rather Linda Peterson.

"Damn it," I said.

"Should I send him a friend request?"

"I don't think so. Not right now. He might figure out that you're connected to me."

"How?"

"Because you have all those photos of me in your albums. Typical obsessed female."

She elbowed me. "I think I have three photos of you."

"Whatever. Anyway, let's not. I can't think of anything to gain by risking it. I could try sending a request from Robert Tyler, but I think we should hold off on that, too, until we can figure out what's going on."

"Isn't this pretty good proof that the guy who Tasered you is working for Pierce? He caught you watching Pierce, so now Pierce is suspicious about everything, including new Facebook friends?"

"Maybe, but it could also be that Pierce accepted the friend request, then checked out Linda Peterson's page and decided he didn't know her, or that she'd mistaken him for another Brian Pierce. Either way, it seems like something is going on with Pierce."

"But what?"

"No idea. Luckily, when I sorted through Pierce's friends list the other day, I screen-captured the profiles of the four women who sort of look like the woman in the Jetta."

I directed Mia toward the folder containing the profiles, and she opened them, one at a time, and compared them to the photo of the woman in the Jetta.

"Definitely not her," she said immediately about the first one.

"How can you tell?"

"Cheekbones are totally different. And the eyebrows."

She moved on to the second one. "No. This woman has a much higher forehead."

She opened the third one. "For god's sake, Roy, are you kidding me? This woman looks nothing like the Jetta girl."

"Well, if you squint..."

"Not even a little bit. For starters, this woman looks Hispanic. The woman in the Jetta is about as Caucasian as you get. Very fair-skinned."

"Okay, okay."

That left one remaining photo. Mia opened it and didn't say anything for a few seconds. Then, "Yep. This is her."

"You sure?"

"Absolutely. See the shape of the eyes? And the nose? Plus, look at that mole on her chin. Same on both photos. Didn't you notice that? It's pretty big."

"Uh..."

"She has a different hairstyle now, but it's her."

"Erica Kerwick," I said. "Let's check her out."

Mia found the woman's Facebook profile, but her privacy settings were tight. She lived in Austin and was born on February 17, and that was about all we could see of her profile. We couldn't view her wall, her photos, or her friends list.

But here's the thing many people don't understand or simply forget about Facebook: The privacy settings you place on your own wall don't apply to your posts elsewhere on the site. So if you make a comment on someone else's wall, and that person has looser privacy settings than you do, your comment is visible to more people than you might like. If your privacy settings are "Friends Only," but you post a wild party photo on the wall of someone whose privacy settings are "Everyone," the photo can be seen by anyone with a Facebook account.

Which often makes it a lot easier to poke around and learn things about people like Erica Kerwick.

"Go to Google," I said. "Now click on that little gear thingy in the upper right. Okay, select 'advanced search.' Where it says 'this exact wording or phrase,' put 'Erica Kerwick.' Now, down lower, limit the search to Facebook dot com."

"I didn't know you could do this," Mia said, typing away.

"Yeah, and the good news is, I doubt there's another Erica Kerwick on Facebook, so we won't have to wade through a bunch of irrelevant junk. It's always easier when the person has an uncommon name."

Mia hit return and we got hundreds of results. Apparently, Erica Kerwick was quite the busy little Facebook user, and lucky for us, she had some friends whose privacy settings allowed us to see their Facebook content.

One comment from Erica Kerwick said: *Happy birthday, Jane. Wow, you are still so gorgeous! Let's catch up the next time you're back in town!*

Another comment, on a page started by a new restaurant: *The chiles rellenos were outstanding. Can I get the recipe for the salsa!? ;)*

On another friend's wall, in a thread about some B-list celebrity I had never heard of, Erica Kerwick had written: *That outfit was ridiculous. Doesn't she have a wardrobe person that's supposed to warn her against wearing anything that ugly?*

There were dozens of other comments like that. Tedious. Mundane. Boring. Trivial. Useless. That's how it goes.

And then, if you're damned lucky, out of the blue, with no real skill on your part, you hit paydirt. You see something so unexpected that it takes a moment to even comprehend what you've just learned. That's what happened now.

Erica Kerwick had left a comment under the status update of a young man who had recently graduated from high school. The graduation part was obvious, because the kid was wearing a cap and gown in his profile photo, and because he had said, 'Done with high school!' So you can understand how I pieced it together.

The comment from Erica Kerwick read: *I am so proud of you! We all love you and know you have a bright future ahead! xoxo Aunt Erica*

But it wasn't the outfit or the comment that caught our attention. It was the kid's name.

Curtis Hanrahan.

26

"Wow," said Mia.

"Yep."

"She's related to a kid named Hanrahan. No way that's a coincidence."

"Absolutely not." I could feel my pulse beginning to pick up speed. This was big news.

Mia said, "So, what, is she Patrick Hanrahan's sister? Kerwick is a married name?"

"I don't know. Could be Kathleen Hanrahan's sister."

"Or, if either of them — Patrick or Kathleen — has a brother, Erica Kerwick could be married to him."

I said, "If she was married to Patrick's brother, her last name would be Hanrahan. Assuming he doesn't have a half-brother."

"Or unless she kept her maiden name."

"Right."

"Does it really matter?" Mia said. "We know it has to be one of the above."

"True, but it's always nice to have all the facts when you can. Let's check the kid's wall."

"It's called a timeline now."

"Whatever."

The kid — Curtis Hanrahan — had created a "Family" section on his wall. A lot of people don't bother with this feature, but some do, and it can be useful.

Mia said, "The kid doesn't list any uncles with the last name of Hanrahan. Or any uncles at all, for that matter. And no other Kerwicks at all."

"Could mean nothing more than they aren't on Facebook. It appears neither Patrick or Kathleen has an account, or they've set them to be unavailable to the general public."

"You can do that?"

"I know you can fix it so you don't show up in results for Google and other search engines."

"But can you set it so you don't show up in Facebook search results?"

"I think so."

We explored the Help section of Facebook for about ten minutes, trying to answer this question, but it wasn't as easy to find the information as it should have been.

"Okay," I said, "let's just assume I'm right — "

"Big mistake — "

"Smartass. And go back to Curtis Hanrahan's profile. I just want to confirm that he's related to Patrick and Kathleen Hanrahan, and if we learn how Erica Kerwick is related to them, too, that'll be a bonus. We just need to make that connection, that's all. Verify that the kid having the last name of 'Hanrahan' isn't the most unlikely coincidence either of us has ever experienced."

Mia had bookmarked Curtis Hanrahan's page, so it took just one click to return to it. She said, "Seems like the easiest thing to do is just check all his relatives, one by one, and see what we can learn. Agreed?"

"Agreed."

There were about twenty family members listed, with many of them identified as cousins, and those cousins all looked to be close to Curtis Hanrahan's age. Youngish people, anyway, rather than a generation older. Seeing a list of relatives like this made you realize how many different surnames one family might have.

"I'll start with the middle-aged people," Mia said.

"Good idea."

She clicked on the first middle-aged person listed: Craig Marks, an uncle. He didn't have a Family section, so Mia went straight to Craig's photos, which is what I would have done. Craig had plenty of albums to sort through, but he was one of those people who, when he was uploading a collection of photos all at once, simply let the date serve as the name for the album. But first in the list of albums was Craig's past and present profile photos, which Mia skipped, clicking instead on Craig's album called "Wall Photos."

"See, they're still calling it a 'wall,'" I said.

She gave me a dismissive snort as the album opened into a page full of thumbnail photos. Lots of people at parties and eating in restaurants. At the lake. Dogs. Children. Somebody had bought an expensive-looking sports car. Nothing helpful. Mia scrolled downward. There were literally hundreds of thumbnails on the page. Craig liked his camera. Liked snapping photos of just about anything.

"Here we go," Mia said.

She was right. We'd just reached a photo of yet another gathering of some sort. A backyard, near a pool. Group shot. Everybody smiling.

There was Craig.

There was Erica Kerwick.

There was Kathleen Hanrahan.

The caption read: *Pat and Kathleen's place in South Padre.*

"Bingo," I said.

"Really? That's what you say in these situations? Bingo? I always wondered."

"Save that photo," I said.

She dragged it to the desktop, creating a copy.

We kept going and found Kathleen Hanrahan in several other photos, and we eventually found Patrick Hanrahan in a couple, all taken in or around a nice beachfront home. We didn't ascertain how everyone was related, but that probably wasn't too important. Right now, it was enough to know that the Hanrahans knew Erica Kerwick, and obviously Erica Kerwick knew Brian Pierce.

And I was back on the see-saw, convinced once again that I had in fact seen Tracy Turner at Pierce's house five days ago. Hell, at this point, it was virtually undeniable. But it felt great. Honestly, I was totally buzzing with vindication.

"What are you thinking?" Mia asked.

"There aren't many possibilities. First theory that pops into my head is that Erica Kerwick and Brian Pierce kidnapped Tracy Turner and they will eventually ask for ransom."

"But wait — how would that work? Later, when they released Tracy, wouldn't she identify Erica Kerwick as one of the kidnappers?"

"That's assuming they are going to release her."

"Oh, man I don't even want to think about that."

"Or they aren't letting Tracy see her aunt, so she can't identify her."

"But they are letting her see Pierce."

"Evidently."

"It just seems so cold-hearted. One of Hanrahan's own relatives kidnapped his daughter?"

"It happens. Desperate people do desperate things."

"What now?"

"I think we need to look through every album — every last photo — and see if Pierce is in any of them. If we can find one, maybe it'll give us some idea how Erica Kerwick knows him."

"In that case, we'll probably need to go through all the photos of all the relatives."

"No argument here."

"You'd better pull up a chair."

"Harder to look down your blouse."

"Grab a chair, you perv."

We spent the next two hours wading through all of the Facebook pages of the people listed in Curtis Hanrahan's Family section. Sometimes those pages led to yet more pages of additional people. It was back to being boring, mind-numbing work. But I'm glad we kept digging, because there was one more big break to come. Maybe the biggest break yet. Certainly the most unexpected.

We were sorting through more photos, this time in an album owned by a man named Skip Grogan.

"Skip," I said. "Who names their kid Skip?"

"Probably a nickname."

"Still."

Mia took a moment to stretch her arms. "I'm losing track. How is this guy related to the Hanrahans? Or Erica Kerwick?"

"Hell if I know. I can barely keep track of my own relatives. You want a Coke?"

"Love one."

I went to get refreshments while Mia continued with our chore. When I came back with two cans and a bag of tortilla chips, Mia was clicking through photos of some fancy black-tie affair. She said, "You know, there's a theme here: Seems like everybody in this family has money."

"Which family?" I asked. "The Grogans or the Hanrahans?"

"I hope that's a rhetorical question."

"Indeed."

I sat back down in the chair beside her, and if I'd been just a second later, I would've missed it. A photo was on the screen, but only for a split second before she clicked to the next one. I had seen something. Well, someone. Or I thought I had seen someone. Couldn't be. Impossible. I was tired. Seeing things. Had to check, though. Just as I'd had to check when I had seen — or thought I'd seen — Tracy Turner.

"Go back," I said.

"Huh?"

"Go back one photo."

And she did. I was staring at a bunch of happy people in tuxes and cocktail dresses seated at a long dinner table. Not a posed shot, a candid shot, as when a photographer floats through a ballroom and takes discreet photos documenting some ritzy event. The kind of photo that shows up in the society column of the newspaper.

Off to one side of the photo, and more in the background than the intended subjects of the shot, was a waitress. A blond waitress. My waitress. Jessica.

Mia could tell I was stunned. "What is it?"

"That's the girl I just went out with."

"Sorry, guy, but you're gonna have to narrow it down a little."

"The waitress from the other day. Jessica."

"Oh, that one. She's pretty. Really pretty. What in the world is she doing in this photo?"

"You tell me, because I don't have a clue."

"You think she knows the Hanrahans or Erica Kerwick?"

"I am completely and totally baffled. Let's try her Facebook page."

Jessica appeared in the search results, but her privacy settings didn't allow us to see much. Couldn't see her wall or her photos. But we could see her friends list, and none of the people we'd been investigating were on it.

"I got nothing," I said.

"Well, regardless, we have to go to the cops, right? Call that detective you talked to?"

I didn't answer right away.

"Roy?"

"Think about it from the cops' perspective. What exactly do we have? I'll tell you. We have evidence that Brian Pierce knows a woman who knows the Hanrahans."

"Not just one woman, two. Erica Kerwick and your new girlfriend. Pierce knows both of those women, and those women know Hanrahan."

"She's not my girlfriend, and we don't know whether Jessica knows the Hanrahans."

"But she was a waitress at some event they attended!" Mia was starting to raise her voice.

"Exactly," I said. "She was a waitress at some event they attended. So what? Despite how that looks to us, it could actually be a coincidence. She might not know the Hanrahans from Adam — and Eve."

"Do you believe that?"

"I don't know. I do know that we don't have evidence that Pierce knows the Hanrahans. In other words, we still don't have anything that will compel Ruelas to act. He won't be able to get a warrant."

"Are you sure?"

"He's still going to think I'm a nutjob and that I've got some sort of obsession with Pierce."

"But it's logical. The Hanrahans' daughter went missing, then you saw her with someone who has a connection to them."

"Yeah, but I don't have any evidence that I saw her. And, again, we don't know that Pierce knows the Hanrahans."

"He has to."

"It seems likely that he does, but that doesn't make it so. I bet a rich power couple like the Hanrahans know a lot of people, so that means there are a lot of people who know someone who knows the

Hanrahans."

"Weak, Roy."

"You think? Let me ask you something: Have you ever friended someone on Facebook, only to learn that you have a mutual friend in common that you never knew about?"

She rolled her eyes. She was resisting me, but I thought it was a good thing. This debate was forcing me to think things through more than I normally do.

"Come on, Mia."

"Yes. I have."

"Okay, then."

"That's a lame comparison and you know it. Bottom line — what if Pierce has the girl, Roy? Pierce and Erica Kerwick and the guy who attacked you. What if they kidnapped her?"

I sat silently.

She said, "If they have the girl, and you don't go to the cops with what you know, and then something happens to her..."

I let out a sigh of frustration.

Damn it.

27

Emily's temperature finally came down after two harrowing days, but the ordeal — the fear he felt about losing her — made him realize that he might have less time with her than he had thought. He had to move things along more quickly.

He was not a brute. He was not an abuser. There would be no force involved. He would need to gain her trust. Her affection. But it wasn't proving easy so far. She didn't seem to dislike him, and she didn't actively avoid him, but she had most certainly not warmed up to him — not by any stretch of the imagination. And she was not forgetting as quickly as he had hoped. It was a problem.

Just this morning, as she sat at the breakfast table, she refused to eat the eggs he had prepared for her. He thought it was the lingering effects of her illness. She hadn't regained her appetite yet.

Then she said, "I miss my mommy."

He didn't reply. Didn't react at all. Just kept buttering a piece of toast.

"I want to go home."

"You are home, Emily."

"That's not my name."

Jesus, not this again.

"Your name is Emily and my name is Jimmy."

She didn't reply. He resisted looking at her for the longest time, but when he couldn't help himself any longer, he glanced over and saw that she was tearing up, her lip quivering, her face contorting in prelude to an emotional outburst. A tantrum. These had been rare. Only a couple. Admittedly, he wasn't sure how to respond to these events, and he hadn't been consistent.

He went back to his toast, but before he was finished, the dam broke, and Emily began to wail.

"I want my mommy!"

Blubbering and hiccoughing so much she could barely get it out. Under different circumstances, it might be humorous.

He ignored her.

"I want to go home!"

"You are home, Emily." Persistent. Don't give in.

"I am not! I want to go home!"

"You are home. This is your home." He was showing a calm exterior, but it was beginning to eat at him. His patience was running thin.

Now Emily simply resorted to ear-piercing screams. But he knew it was simply a ploy to make him give in. He was stronger than that.

"Eat your breakfast," he said.

She gulped air, then began to scream again.

"Hush, Emily, and eat your breakfast. I went to a lot of trouble to make it for you."

In mid-scream, she shook her head. Being a brat. He could feel the heat rising in his face. She had no appreciation for him at all.

"Emily, I'm going to say it just once more. Eat. Your. Breakfast. If you don't, you won't get anything else until lunch."

She let loose with her loudest scream yet, the little bitch, and his anger flashed, white hot, making him raise his hand, wanting to strike her. He grabbed her plate instead and hurled it across the room, where it shattered against the wall.

28

Detective Ruelas was staring at me with a total poker face. No emotion whatsoever. It was just after five o'clock — the earliest he'd been able to meet with us. I had almost finished giving him the complete story — everything that had happened since I had called him three days earlier.

I'd told him about the woman arriving at Pierce's place in the Jetta. Told him about Emma Webster seeing a little girl in Pierce's truck earlier that year. Told him about setting up the rock camera and putting the dryer in Pierce's driveway. Described how I was ambushed and temporarily abducted when I went back for the camera. (He exhibited no empathy at all and possibly even looked skeptical.)

I mentioned that Mia had cleverly deduced that the camera might still be on the right-of-way. At this point, he'd glanced appreciatively at Mia, who was sitting beside me. He'd been glancing a lot, which I thought was a good thing. We'd predicted that having her along would give me credibility. I wouldn't look so nutty with someone backing me up.

Then I'd shown Ruelas the video — which I had edited down to the important parts — on my laptop. We were sitting in the same interview room as the last time I'd visited the substation, Ruelas on one side of the table, us on the other, which allowed us to watch his face as the video played.

No expression. Like his face was made of stone.

When the video stopped, I said, "We were able to identify the woman through Facebook. I friended Pierce a couple of days ago, and she was on his friends list."

"You friended Pierce?" The first words he'd spoken since we'd sat down.

"Yeah. Well, one of my alter egos did. Pierce has since unfriended me, but not before I was able to dig through his friends list and save some important information."

Maybe — just perhaps — I saw a tiny bit of grudging respect in his eyes. Like he was thinking, *Okay, that was pretty clever of you.*

He tried to cover it up by saying, "Where are we going with all this?" Impatient. Busy man with urgent stuff to do and important people to see.

"Just give me thirty more seconds."

I swung the laptop around where I could see it and opened a folder of jpegs on my desktop, talking at the same time. Time to drop the bombshell. "Just so you can see it yourself, here's a screen capture of the woman's face from the video. And here's a capture of her Facebook timeline. As you can see, her name is Erica Kerwick. Here's one of her own photos — a better shot of her face, so you can compare it to the frame from the video. Same woman. Agreed?"

"Sure. Any idiot can see that. Same mole on the chin."

I might've heard a tiny sound from Mia. Stifling a giggle.

I was glad that I was about to shove this guy's condescending attitude back in his face. "Here's a capture of a post she left on her nephew's wall. The nephew is named Curtis Hanrahan."

Boom! Detonation.

He looked at me and one of his eyebrows went up. In the scheme of things, it was an overpowering display of emotion. Then he looked at the screen again and verified that what I was saying was true. Before he could speak, I said, "And here is a photo of Erica Kerwick with Patrick and Kathleen Hanrahan."

He leaned forward for a better look. Studied the photo closely. Now I think I had him hooked.

I said, "We don't know exactly how they are related, but clearly they are. So Pierce knows Kerwick, and Kerwick knows the Hanrahans. There's a connection. And while I'm not one hundred percent sure that I saw Tracy Turner at Pierce's house, I'll say that I'm almost positive I did, and now there's a good reason to check it out."

Ruelas kept his eyes on the screen for a few more moments, then he leaned back and looked across the table at me. Had a trace of a smirk on his face. Hard for a man like him to deal with the idea that I had been right all along. He turned toward Mia. "How long have you worked with this guy?"

She dodged the question a little. "I've known him for a long time."

"Is he nuts?" I guess he just had to get his digs in.

Mia laughed and started to answer. Then she gathered her thoughts and said, "He's hardheaded, cocky, sometimes smug, occasionally arrogant, and even a bit egotistical, but no, he's not nuts. Not even close."

"Arrogant?" I said.

She didn't look at me, nor did he. They were still looking at each other. I think it would qualify as lingering eye contact. What the hell?

"You helped him with this research?" he asked her.

"Yep."

"You can vouch that he didn't Photoshop this all together or something?"

I wanted to answer that myself. With a long string of insults and profanities. I managed to restrain myself.

"Absolutely," Mia said. "But feel free to get on Facebook and double-check our work."

Smart.

He drummed his fingertips on the table. Again. And again. I knew what drove guys like him. He was the type who loved to make people wait for him to make Critical Decisions. Because he was an Important Man.

Finally, just as I was about to stand up and leave, he looked in my direction. "Okay. I'll check into it."

I waited for him to say more. He didn't. "You'll check into it?"

"Yes."

"May I ask what that will involve?"

He shook his head.

"Can you get a warrant?"

He looked at Mia. "You should add 'pushy' to your list."

She laughed. He grinned. I didn't know he was capable of it.

"I bet you have enough to get a warrant now," I said.

Ruelas said, "Also add 'repetitive.'"

And Mia laughed again. She was just playing along. Trying to make things go more smoothly.

I think.

Walking out of the substation, I said, "You know, it pisses me off a little."

"What does?"

"He wasn't grateful at all. Didn't say, 'Thanks for bringing this to my attention. Good work. Well done.' Nothing. What an ass."

She didn't reply. I unlocked the van and we climbed in.

"Don't you think?" I said.

"What?"

"That he's an ass?"

She shrugged. "He seemed okay. Just a cop. He has to deal with the public, and the public can be filled with idiots. I know that firsthand."

I started the van and backed out of the parking spot. "Still, there's no reason to act like an ass when you're dealing with people who *aren't* idiots. And to not even let us know how he's going to proceed..."

"You did the right thing, Roy. Now it's out of your hands and you don't have to worry about it. Think positive. Be optimistic."

I pulled out of the parking lot onto Ranch Road 620. We rode in silence for about a mile.

"You two seemed to be getting along well," I said, with an unmistakable implication in my tone.

"Oh, shit, Roy, did you really just say that?"

"All I meant was — "

"Who's being the ass now?"

I can't even tell you how fortunate I was that my phone alerted just then. Heidi emailing. Saying she'd be sending a new case by noon tomorrow.

29

After we got back to my place, Mia took off, and I ordered a pepperoni pizza. I was looking forward to a quiet, uneventful evening.

I hadn't realized until after our meeting with Ruelas how much the Tracy Turner thing had been stressing me out. It did feel good to know it was out of my hands now. I had no idea what that situation entailed, but the fact that someone related to the Hanrahans was involved made me much more confident that Tracy wasn't in danger. A stranger was much more likely to do harm.

But there was still one little detail lingering in my mind. One odd little circumstance that was difficult to dismiss as a coincidence, even though I'd earlier argued that it might be just that.

Jessica.

What was she doing in one of the Hanrahans' photos? What were the odds? Better question: Why was I worried about it? It was on Ruelas's plate now. Not my concern.

Of course, as Mia had pointed out on the drive home, I hadn't mentioned Jessica to Ruelas.

"Didn't see why I should," I'd said.

"Really?"

"Why would I drag her into it?"

"'It's always nice to have all the facts when you can.'"

I had a feeling she was tricking me. "That sounds familiar."

"You said it earlier today. I'm sure Ruelas would agree."

"Well, I never said I was a genius, but I'm flattered that you can quote me."

And that had been the end of it.

Okay, not completely. It was starting to eat at me. Both things — Jessica being in the photo, and my not telling Ruelas about it. But there was a solution. Call her up, make a date, and simply ask her about it. Discover that it's a coincidence, or that there is some harmless explanation, and be done with it.

I got voicemail.

"Jessica, my name is Vladimir and I'm a producer with the Playboy Channel. We received your audition tape and I'm pleased to say we were intrigued. That thing you did with the kumquat was unexpected but very creative and entertaining. Quite a show. So we would be very interested in speaking to you further. Please give me a call at your earliest convenience."

She called back five minutes later.

"You are one sick puppy."

"Who is this?"

She used a soft, sultry voice. "My stage name is Lola, and I can do interesting things with fruits and vegetables."

"Even, say, canned green beans?"

"You'd be surprised."

"I'm sure I would. Speaking of food, are you at work right now?"

"No, I worked the day shift. Why?"

The pizza I'd ordered went straight into the fridge for tomorrow night's dinner, and an hour later Jessica and I were seated at a Tex-Mex joint called Rosie's Tamale House, because it was Jessica's favorite place. It's located in a large metal building on Highway 71, south of Lakeway. That was convenient for Jessica, because it turned out that she lived in some condos not far away. Nice condos. Nicer than I would've expected.

"I worked at a barbecue joint when I was a teenager," I said as we waited for our food to arrive. "Which meant that I got more than my fill of barbecue. Considering where you work, I was surprised that you wanted to eat here."

"Oh, I don't eat the food at work. If I did that all the time, I'd be as big as a house. I have to save enchiladas for a special occasion."

I don't think she even realized that she'd just referred to eating dinner with me as a 'special occasion,' but I found that I was happy she felt that way. Bottom line: I liked her. Smart, funny, sweet, and beautiful. Great combination. Tonight she was wearing khaki shorts, sandals, and a red sleeveless blouse. Stunning. Great tan on her arms.

I said, "It's been years since I've been here, but things don't seem to have changed much."

The décor consisted of faux oak paneling, velvet paintings of Spanish conquistadors and horsemen, and an entire wall of yellowing Polaroid pictures — photos of regular customers throughout the years, going back three or four decades, including homegrown Texas celebrities like Willie Nelson and Tom Landry.

"The lights on the paddleboat are always a crowd pleaser," she said, nodding toward a painting on the wall nearest us.

"Not often you see artwork that requires an electrical cord," I said.

"I like it. It's kitschy."

"Whether it was originally intended that way or not."

She smiled. "It was good to hear from you again."

"It was good to be heard."

"But you have more questions for me, don't you? About Brian Pierce."

I offered a weak grin. "Wow. Busted. How did you know?"

"Intuition."

"But I was planning to call you anyway."

She dipped a chip in salsa and didn't reply.

"You don't look convinced," I said.

"We'll see. Go ahead and ask your questions."

"You sure?"

"Yep."

Right then our waiter brought our food, warning us that the plates were hot, and then he scooted away.

"My question isn't so much about Pierce," I said. "It's about a photo. I saw you in a photo, waitressing at some black-tie event attended by Patrick and Kathleen Hanrahan." I waited a beat, to see what sort of response I got. Not much of one. Her expression didn't change. She was busy with her food. "Do you know them?"

"Well, sure. Very weird what's happening to them right now. Where did you see this photo?"

"Facebook."

"On whose page?"

"One of Patrick and Kathleen's relatives."

"Wait. You're losing me. Why are you digging around on Facebook for pictures of the Hanrahans?"

I wanted to get more answers from her, but it appeared I'd have to give her some answers of my own first. So I said, "Can I tell you some things confidentially?"

"Hey, I haven't said a word to anybody about this thing with Brian so far. Why would I start now?"

"I appreciate that, but this is bigger than that. This has nothing to do with Brian's insurance claim."

"Okaaay," she said, starting to look at me with suspicion. "What exactly *does* this have to do with?"

I lowered my voice. "The abduction of Tracy Turner."

She stopped with her fork in mid-air. "Roy?"

"Yeah?"

"Are you a cop or something?"

"No. No, I'm not. I'm a videographer, like I told you. Scout's honor."

"Then why — "

I held up my hand to stop her. Then I told her all of it, straight up. Yes, it was a big risk. But my gut was telling me that I could trust her — completely. There was just no way this woman was involved with a kidnapping or an abduction. And she'd been so open with me so far, I felt that it was only fair to return the favor. She ate slowly while I talked, occasionally frowning or looking surprised at key moments — like when I described seeing Tracy Turner at Brian Pierce's place, and when I described being waylaid by The Guy, and when I identified the Jetta woman as a relative of the Hanrahans. I even told her about meeting with Ruelas and that I had seen no reason to mention seeing her in a photo. By the time I was done with all this, I'd been talking for a solid fifteen minutes.

I expected her to say something like, "Why didn't you tell me all of this from the beginning?" But then again, she was a smart gal, and she must've understood why I hadn't volunteered all of that information without a compelling reason. Instead, she asked a much less predictable question.

"I get the feeling you don't know who owns La Tolteca, do you?"

"No idea," I said.

"Patrick Hanrahan."

30

Son of a bitch! How had I missed that?

I had picked up my fork, but I put it back down. "You are friggin' kidding me."

"Nope."

"For how long?"

"Since it opened. He opened it."

"I feel pretty damn stupid for not knowing that."

"Well, it's not like his name is on the door. He owns a lot of stuff, and restaurants are just a small part of it. Nowadays he owns maybe a dozen restaurants across the country. That's where I first met him."

"Where?"

"When I was working at a high-end seafood place called Chowders about, what, six or seven years ago. That was Patrick's, too, and he was a lot more hands-on back then, because he wasn't quite so high in the stratosphere yet. I mean, I think he was doing pretty well, but he hadn't reached that level of wealth where he owned places that he never even visited. Anyway, I worked there, and so did Kathleen. And so did Brian Pierce."

My mouth literally fell open. I couldn't believe I hadn't discovered the connection between Pierce and the Hanrahans until now. Sloppy of me. Unprofessional. Just plain embarrassing. I felt like I needed to call Ruelas and tell him. Then I thought: He must know by now. After all, he was a cop, not a dumbass videographer.

I said, "Hanrahan hired his own wife to work there?"

"No, this was before they got married. She was a waitress, too. Your food is getting cold. You should eat."

I picked up my fork again. "Kathleen was a waitress?"

I was having a hard time picturing the woman I'd seen on CNN as a waitress, but I'm glad I didn't say that out loud, because it would've sounded insulting, and that wasn't how I meant it. Just the opposite; Kathleen Hanrahan seemed the type who would think that sort of job was beneath her. Serving food to common people?

"That's where she and Patrick met, and a little more than that," Jessica said. "She was sleeping with the boss. She was pretty wild back then. Party girl. Big drinker, and into drugs, I think. And she was married at the time."

"To the Turner guy. Tracy's dad."

"Right."

"Was the affair before or after Tracy was born?"

"After, I think. Yeah, she was already working there when she had Tracy. She took a few months off for maternity, came back to work, and that's when this thing with Patrick started up. The affair was a dirty little secret but everybody knew about it. Patrick would act as manager two or three nights a week, and Kathleen would always hang around after closing until all the other employees had left, so that it was just her and Patrick there. I think they use to have sex in his office, or that's what people said. It was just, I don't know, a pretty gross situation. So much so that when she got pregnant, everybody was saying Patrick was the dad."

I was having a tough time squaring this description of Kathleen Hanrahan with the woman I'd been seeing on TV. Goes to show that you can't judge people by their appearances.

"But they never acknowledged what was going on between them?" I said.

"Not until she filed for divorce, and then they acted like they had just started dating, and then, surprise, like six months after that, they ran off to Cozumel or someplace and got married."

I couldn't remember ever getting so much useful information from one person in such a short period. This was fantastic.

I said, "So you and Pierce have worked for Patrick Hanrahan all this time?"

"Well, I have. Good pay and good benefits, because I've been with the company for so long. New employees don't get the same hourly rate that I get, in addition to tips, so I'm hanging with it until I get my doctorate, which is another story. Anyway, after Chowders closed down, most of the staff disappeared, but Patrick asked a couple of us to work at La Tolteca. Brian — I don't know where he went, but he showed up at La Tolteca early last year, I think. I had forgotten about him, to be honest, because I hadn't known him that well back at Chowders. His first day at La Tolteca, he said hello as if he knew me, but it wasn't until later in the shift that I even remembered who he was. Not really the memorable type. Back then, at Chowders, he hung around more with the busboys, who were all teenagers, rather than with the wait staff, who were mostly in their twenties."

"What did he do at Chowders?"

"Same as now. Dishwasher."

"He must've been pretty young."

"I guess so. Eighteen, nineteen. Which is another reason I didn't recognize him right away. He wasn't a teenager anymore. Looked more like an adult. Also, I should mention — when you were grilling me about Brian the other day? Asking if he was creepy? He really isn't. He's just a quiet guy. Sort of a loner, but not a serial killer type of loner." She laughed. "Well, not as far as I know."

I was trying to think of other questions to ask. I wanted to make sure I got it all. "So what's your take on this situation with Tracy Turner?"

"I really have no idea. I feel bad for Patrick, and for the girl, of course."

"No gut feeling?"

"Well, what you're saying — that you saw her at Brian's place — that just doesn't make any sense at all. And this other woman..."

"Erica Kerwick."

"Right. She's related to Patrick and she was at Brian's place? Are you positive about that?"

"Or she's related to Kathleen."

"I don't know what to tell you. I don't know anything about her. Don't think I've ever heard the name."

"Did Brian have some sort of friendship with Patrick? Then or now?"

She laughed a little. "Uh, no. Brian was always way too low on the totem pole. I mean, Patrick would hire Brian to do odd jobs outside of work, like paint his house. Stuff like that."

"How well do you know Patrick?"

"Fairly well, I guess, but only as a boss and an employee. It wasn't like we were ever friends, either. If you simply said the name 'Jessica,' he wouldn't think of me. He'd need a last name. That sort of relationship."

"What about your relationship with Kathleen?"

"I steered clear of her. Not the kind of person I'd want to be friends with, then or now."

"Does Patrick come into La Tolteca?"

"Not much anymore."

"When was the last time you saw him or Kathleen anywhere?"

She thought for a minute. "Last fall, I think. See, Patrick is involved with various charities, and they sometimes have banquets or galas or whatever, and some of us earn extra money by waitressing at those events. Very good money."

"So that explains the photo I saw on Facebook."

"Right."

"Any idea which event that was?"

"I couldn't tell you without seeing the picture, but the one last fall was a thing for autism. You know what happens when Kathleen sees me at one of those gigs?"

"What?"

"Absolutely nothing. She acts like she never met me before. It's kind of funny and pathetic at the same time. I think she likes to pretend she was always a rich man's wife and she doesn't want any reminder of what she used to be. And I notice she still puts away a lot of wine. She seems half-sloshed most of the time."

I couldn't think of any other questions. So I said, "You mind if I excuse myself for a minute?"

"Sure."

I headed off toward the bathroom area, but stopped just outside, where I could see her across the restaurant. Took out my cell phone and called her number. I could see her at the table, reaching for her purse, retrieving her cell phone, then smiling and shaking her head when she saw who was calling.

"Roy?"

"Hey, you remember when I said I was going to call you anyway, even when I didn't have any questions?"

"Yeah?"

"Well, I don't have any more questions, so I'm calling now. Will you go out with me again? Say, right now? Maybe we can go have tea and a margarita?"

"You are a goofball."

"That means yes, doesn't it? I'm pretty sure it does."

"Better idea. Let's go get some ice cream."

"Ooh, that *is* a better idea."

"And take it back to my place."

Things I learned in the next few hours:

She had been born in Dallas, but her dad had gotten a job at Dell in the early days, so they had moved down to Austin while she was in high school. Her dad had retired with a boatload of money — not just from his salary, but from the stock he owned in the company. He was what people call a "Dellionaire." So Jessica had family money.

She also had one brother, no sisters. The brother was a web designer in New York City. She went up there a couple of times a year to see him.

She had a master's degree in art history and was on her way to earning a Ph.D.

She loved AC/DC, ZZ Top, and Johnny Cash.

She'd spent a year in Europe right before college.

She played competitive soccer on a women's team every weekend.

I'll keep the rest to myself.

31

It was a great night. Wasn't going to be such a great day, although it got off to a fairly normal start, back home at my apartment, talking on the phone.

I felt like I'd spent a good portion of the past week giving long-winded explanations to people. I'd explained things to Harvey Blaylock, to Mia, to Heidi, to Jessica, to Travis County deputies, to Ruelas, to Emma Webster, to The Guy, to Jessica again, and now I was explaining things to Mia once more.

Telling her everything that Jessica had told me the night before. Well, not everything. Just the pertinent stuff. I figured she deserved to know all of it, and we had time to kill until Heidi sent that new case she'd promised. (She'd replied to an email this morning by saying, "Soon! Just putting everything together. Look for it before lunch.")

"You need to tell Ruelas," Mia said, referring to the fact that Brian Pierce worked at a restaurant owned by Patrick Hanrahan. That was the connection.

"He'll know that already and I'll look like an idiot."

"That's never stopped you before. But wait — why will you look like an idiot?"

"Because I didn't figure out the link sooner. For God's sake, Pierce *works* for Hanrahan."

"Well, first, you're a videographer — a damn good one — and not a private investigator. There's no reason you should have figured that out. That's not your job."

"But I — "

"And second, who cares if he thinks you're an idiot?"

She waited. I didn't have a good response. I mean, really, why did I care what Ruelas thought?

"Call him," Mia said. "Then, once and for all, this thing is out of your hands. You can move on with a clear conscience."

"Uh, why wouldn't I have a clear conscience now?"

"You know what I mean. Poor choice of words. What I mean is, you'll know you did everything you could."

I sighed deeply.

"I have to say, this partnership is quickly going to become tiresome if you're going to make me do the right thing all the time."

"What's the plan when you hear from Helga?"

"It's Heidi. I'll sort through it quickly and see how we need to proceed. I'm thinking we can work it together and that will let me show you the ropes. Literally, I carry ropes. You need to see them. It's quite a collection. Blue ones, red ones — "

"I'm hanging up now."

And she did.

It was tempting to procrastinate and call Ruelas later, after I'd had a chance to grab a shower and get squared away for the day. But, no, I did the right thing. Called his cell. It rang four times and I had high hopes that I'd go into voicemail. Perfect. Just leave a detailed message and probably never have to talk to the jerk again in my life.

Then he picked up and ruined my plan. Wherever he was, it was noisy, like a coffee shop or a restaurant.

"It's Roy Ballard," I said.

"I was just about to call you." There was something in his voice I didn't like.

"Yeah? What's up?"

"That guy we've been talking about?" He wasn't using names, so I gathered that he was in a public place. Being cautious. "We visited him bright and early this morning. Had all the proper paperwork, too,

GONE THE NEXT   153

if you know what I mean."

"You had a warrant."

"Right. But, hell, the way he reacted, we could have showed up without one. He seemed genuinely confused, and when we told him why we were there — what we were investigating — he just about insisted we come in and look around. You know why? There wasn't a damn thing there. Not a trace. Not a toy, not any kids' clothes, not a stray goddamn hair. It looked exactly like you'd expect a house to look when a twenty-six-year-old single guy lives there alone."

I could feel my face flushing. *They'd moved her.* That was the only explanation. Moved her and cleaned house. Taking no chances after The Guy discovered I'd been watching.

"You got anything to say?" Ruelas asked. The background noise had faded, like he'd stepped outside or down a hallway where it was quieter. "You just made me look like a first-class asshole."

"I don't know..."

"Damn right, you don't know. Wasted my time. You need to see a shrink, you want my opinion."

"Did you interview him?"

"Of course I goddamn interviewed him! There was nothing there!"

"I'm sorry about that. How about Erica Kerwick? You could get a warrant for her place."

"Holy Christ. If you think I'm going off on another wild goose chase based on what you think you saw, you're crazier than I thought."

"Did you at least talk to her?"

He hung up without answering.

I sat there for a very long time, unmoving, holding the phone, until it buzzed with the incoming email from Heidi.

"You had nothing to apologize for," Mia said. "That's his job, to check into stuff like that."

We were in the van, heading north on Loop 1, one of three major north/south highways in Austin. She was at the wheel. I figured, hey, if this was a partnership, she could do half the driving.

"Now I say it's time to forget about it all," Mia continued. "That was the whole point of talking to Ruelas, wasn't it? To stop thinking about it and get back to work?"

"I thought it was to do the right thing, in case Brian Pierce had the girl."

"Don't be a snot. Of course it was that, too. My point is, you've done all you can be expected to do."

We went another mile without saying a word. I liked her driving style; very fluid, and she wasn't afraid to do some lane changing to get around the slowpokes.

Mia said, "So are you going to tell me about this new case or not?"

"There was a girl there," I said. "At Pierce's place. Maybe it wasn't Tracy Turner, but there was a little girl in Pierce's doorway."

She didn't say anything until she realized I was staring at her, prompting her to speak.

She said, "I don't want to pick a fight, but..."

"But what?"

"You've wavered on that point yourself."

She was right. Not only had there been times when I didn't feel confident I had seen Tracy Turner, there had been times when I wasn't even sure I had seen any little girl at all.

"Emma Webster said she saw a little girl with Pierce," I said. "I believe her. I also believe that I saw one. You *know* that Ruelas must have asked Pierce if there had ever been a little girl there, and we know there has been, and if it wasn't Tracy Turner, why wouldn't Pierce say, 'Oh, that was my friend's daughter,' or whatever? And if Pierce had said something like that, Ruelas would have told me, and he wouldn't have been pissed, because he would have realized that I actually had seen a little girl."

"I don't have an answer for you, Roy. Maybe Pierce didn't say anything because he thought it would only make Ruelas more suspicious, even if it really was some friend's daughter. So he lied. Now tell me about the new case."

It felt wrong to let it go, but Mia was right. It was time. I opened my laptop and clicked on the folder Heidi had sent. I had already sorted through the documents, but I hadn't briefed Mia yet.

"Guy's name is Timothy Burke. Thirty years old. He's a roofer for a local homebuilder. Claims he slipped off a ladder and fell. Injured his back, which can be difficult to diagnose, meaning it's hard to prove he didn't injure it. That's something you should know: Almost all of the cases we'll investigate involve injuries that are hard to diagnose."

"Makes sense. If they were easy to diagnose, your clients wouldn't need you to verify or discredit the injuries, would they?"

I turned toward her again. "*Our* clients, Mia. Our clients."

She smiled broadly but kept her eyes on the road. "Thank you."

What I needed today was a slam dunk — something that would give me a sense of accomplishment and closure, all rolled into one.

Timothy Burke was kind enough to deliver.

Not twenty minutes after we parked down the street from his small three-bedroom home in northeast Austin, he came out, climbed into his truck, and hit the road. Mia followed at a discreet distance.

"It's weird, but my heart is actually racing," she said.

"Feel like you're doing something a little sneaky?"

"Exactly. Worried that he'll catch me following him."

"Remember that he's the one who should be worried."

"Have you ever gotten caught?"

"By a subject?"

"Yeah."

"A couple of them have looked at me kind of funny — like they were getting suspicious — but most of them are too dumb to piece it together."

Timothy Burke followed Parmer Lane over to Interstate 35 and went north on the access road. Before he reached Howard Lane, he pulled into a McDonald's and went through the drive-through. Made me hungry. Then he drove to the Home Depot right next door.

"Oh, this could be good," I said.

"What?"

"I bet he's collecting workers' comp and doing some small jobs on the side. Double-dipping."

Timothy Burke had already parked and was walking inside. Mia parked two rows over.

"Just use your amazing skills," I said, "and I'll be hanging around."

There was a moment after we walked inside that I thought we'd lost him, and that would've been a major bummer, but we found him in the lumber aisle. It simply could not get any better than that. The lumber aisle.

Mia grabbed one of those low, flat carts and slowly moved in his direction. Burke had a cart of his own, and he stopped it beside the cedar pickets and began to load up. Pretty good indication he was building a fence.

I used the video camera on my phone, which would be plenty good enough, because I was no more than fifteen yards away, poking my head around the corner just enough to see him.

Mia stopped her cart near Burke — who was still methodically loading pickets onto his cart, so focused on his task that he hadn't even noticed Mia yet. She looked back at me, as if to say, 'Isn't that enough?'

I shook my head. Those pickets didn't weigh more than about two or three pounds apiece. I needed something better. Something heavier.

So Mia approached Burke and said something. I couldn't make out the words, but just like a week ago with Wally Crouch, it didn't take a neuroscientist to figure out the general gist of the conversation — especially when Mia gestured across the aisle, toward the bags of cement.

Can you help me load a couple of these?

Oh, sure. No problem.

And that's what he did. Eighty pounds each. Loaded them up, then watched with no subtlety whatsoever as Mia slowly retreated up the aisle in her well-fitting jeans. She was smart enough to proceed toward the back of the store, away from me, so as not to draw Burke's attention my way. I recorded another few moments — long enough for Burke to stop ogling and go back to loading his cart, showing no ill effects from hoisting the cement.

A few minutes later, Mia and I met outside at the van, where we exchanged a high-five. We had been inside the store for eight minutes.

"How can guys be so clueless?" Mia said.

"Just our nature, I guess." To be more accurate, I figured most women would just never understand why a man would respond to a woman who looked like Mia, especially when she was asking him to help with some task that would allow him to show how big and powerful he was.

"How much did we earn just now for doing that?"

I told her.

"Jesus. Really?"

"Yep."

"We should've partnered up a long time ago."

32

So I got the slam dunk I wanted, and I was back home by noon feeling pretty good about it. Emailed the video to Heidi, who replied by saying, "Wow, you are fast! Thank you. By the way, it occurs to me that your hottie does all the work and you just run the camera. Guess I'd better not point that out to her."

Nothing else on the to-do list, so I ate lunch and took a nap. After that, I had time on my hands, which isn't always a good thing. Especially for a guy like me.

There are times when I torture myself with my own thoughts. Ruminate. Weigh the odds of this or that. Contemplate all the possible actions I could have taken, and what the likely result of each would have been. Or what the result might be if I acted now. That can lead to some bad places. Bad decisions.

Or maybe that's lame and a shrink could give a better analysis for why I decided to do what I did that night. I guess, bottom line, there could be a grab bag of reasons.

Guilt.

Shame.

Maybe a need to do something, simply because there was a time when I couldn't do anything.

Because, let me tell you, until you've had your daughter snatched right out from under you at a public park — there one minute, gone the next — you have no idea what helplessness feels like.

On that horrible day, and into the night, the police interviewed me for about nine hours. The same questions, over and over. Poking, prodding, dissecting, until I realized they were looking for contradictions in my story.

"Wait a sec. I thought you said Susan Tate had brown hair."

"No, I said blond!"

"That's right, blond. You have no idea what you might've done with her phone number?"

I was starting to clench my teeth. "I told you, I never got it. I couldn't find her!"

"I need you to stay calm, Mr. Ballard."

"I am calm, but we're wasting time. I need to be out looking for Hannah. Where is my wife right now?"

"Believe me, we have people looking — a huge team of people. Best thing you can do is talk to me. You might have something useful and — "

"I've told you everything a dozen times!"

"And the thirteenth time might be the one that does the trick. Maybe you'll remember a certain car in the parking lot, or a jogger who slipped your mind until now. You could have the key to this whole situation. And we really need that, because nobody else at the park saw anything. We can't even find anyone who remembers seeing you and Hannah there. Or this Susan Tate."

That's when I knew things were bad. Did they think I'd gone to the dog park alone, for the purpose of claiming that Hannah had been with me and someone had grabbed her? And that I'd invented Susan Tate?

I said, "We were sitting off by ourselves. Susan Tate was the only person I talked to."

"And that's why I'd really like to find her."

"So she can confirm my story?"

"Well, there's more to it than that. Honestly, we need to rule her out."

For a second or two, in my agitated and exhausted state, I let that get my hopes up. Of course! She was one of the abductors. She'd conspired with someone else to make it happen. That's why they couldn't find her now. She didn't want to be found.

But it made no sense.

I'd gone back to look for her of my own free will. Abductors couldn't have predicted or arranged that. So the real reason they needed to find her was simply to verify that I wasn't making her up. Right now, she was a phantom, which was raising red flags in the cops' minds. And word began to get out to the media. When a police spokesperson says something like, "We're still working to confirm various events at the dog park," reporters run with it and often speculate as to what it means.

Even more frustrating, the police wouldn't release Susan Tate's name and announce they were looking for her. Maybe they had their reasons, but I don't know what they were. Maybe they were simply *that* skeptical that she was a real person. Maybe — regardless of whether she existed or not — the fact that she couldn't be found gave the cops leverage against me, and they wanted that, until they were absolutely positive that I hadn't harmed my own daughter. See what I mean by ruminating?

It wasn't until the following day that Susan Tate surfaced, and it quickly became obvious why it had been difficult to locate her. Yes, I'd seen her jogging several times, but she actually lived about three miles away. The cops had only been looking in my neighborhood for someone by her name.

Second, because she was currently separated from her husband, she had been using her maiden name, but in all legal documents, she was identified by her married surname, Weiser. No Susan Tate in the tax records, in the voting records, or even in the phone book.

And in the worst stroke of bad luck, right after she'd been at the dog park, she'd flown to Miami for a convention and had heard nothing about Hannah's disappearance until the next morning. Fortunately, she'd called the police immediately and confirmed my account of events.

Didn't matter. The damage had been done. In many people's mind, I was a viable suspect. Rumors were swirling. I was back home by then, and my own wife was treating me with a degree of hostility that I had never experienced. Some of my friends called and dropped by, but there was a reserved nature to their behavior — as if they were wondering if I could be trusted. Did they know the real me?

Not that I cared at that point. I just wanted to find my daughter. But where do you start? How do you find a puff of smoke that has disappeared in the wind?

Helpless.

Now, nine years later, I had to wonder if either Patrick or Kathleen Hanrahan — or maybe even both of them — were feeling that way.

I knew that the circumstances didn't look particularly good for either of them. It started when Kathleen grew tired of being interviewed and refused to speak to the police anymore. Then Patrick couldn't pass a lie detector test, which raised enough suspicion that he'd hired an attorney and joined his wife in refusing further interviews. Then it came out that Kathleen had recently seen a divorce attorney and had been considering a split for years. Even I had thought that looked bad for Patrick, making me wonder how he might've reacted when he learned what Kathleen had been contemplating.

It was worth reminding myself now that none of those facts meant either of the Hanrahans were guilty of anything or that they were involved in the disappearance of their daughter. Especially when you threw in the things I had learned about Brian Pierce and Erica Kerwick.

So, yeah, there was a chance — maybe a slim one, but I don't know — that they were feeling as helpless as I had. That's why I couldn't just let the whole thing go.

33

It's easy to spend three or four grand, or even a lot more, on a pair of night-vision goggles. Or you can do what I did a couple of years ago and get a six-hundred-dollar Generation 1 pair that would satisfy just about anyone short of a Navy Seal or that psycho in *Silence of the Lambs*.

Truth is, since I'd bought them, I hadn't had much opportunity to use them. But they'd come in handy tonight.

An hour after sundown, I drove the van west again, to Thomas Springs Road. Drove past Brian Pierce's gate, which was closed, as usual. Nothing out of the ordinary going on, as far as I could tell.

When I reached the intersection at Circle Drive, I pulled in to the Circle Country Club. It was a Tuesday night, but there were a fair number of cars and trucks scattered around the paved lot. I found a parking spot as far away from the front door as possible, and I sat in the van for a few minutes, until I was sure nobody else was in any of the nearby vehicles. Then I climbed out, locked up, and casually walked out of the lot to Thomas Springs Road and headed back toward Pierce's place.

At most, it was half a mile. I kept to the shoulder, with the NVGs and my holstered Glock dangling in one of those plastic sacks they give you at a convenience store. I looked like a guy walking back home with a six-pack. Not unusual. But it didn't matter, because nobody drove past the entire time.

I passed the little church on the other side of the road. No deputies hanging around. As soon as I reached the near corner of Pierce's tract, some fifty yards before his gate, I veered off the shoulder, toward the barbed-wire fence running along the front property line.

Anybody who's spent time in rural areas knows there are three ways to cross this kind of fence. Climb over, and probably end up with a tear in the crotch of your jeans. Slip between two strands, and get a tear on the back of your shirt. Or the third option, the one I chose: Drop to the ground and shimmy under the lowest strand. Works fine as long as you don't have a big gut. I reached back for the plastic sack and hurried into the cover of the cedar and oak trees.

Now I couldn't see much of anything. Very little light under the canopy. The crescent moon wouldn't be up for several hours. I slipped the NVGs onto my head and turned them on. Ah. Much better. I tucked the plastic sack into my pocket. I kept the Glock in my right hand.

Over the next ten or fifteen minutes, I worked my way extremely slowly and carefully through the woods toward Pierce's house. There were so many dried leaves and twigs on the ground, it was impossible to walk silently, but I came pretty close. It was comforting that I couldn't see anything moving anywhere in the green-tinted woods around me. The Guy wasn't lurking behind a tree, as far as I could tell.

Eventually, the trees thinned a bit and I began to see the glow coming from Pierce's windows, about thirty or forty yards away. I took a few more steps, right to the edge of the clearing that surrounded the house, and I stopped. Removed the NVGs. Stood totally still for ten solid minutes.

Nothing.

No dog lunging at me. No sounds except for some crickets and a screech owl. No movement in any of the windows. Pierce's white Ford F150 was parked out front, but I didn't see the Jetta or any other vehicles.

Fortunately, none of the exterior lights were on — not even a porch light. That was good, because it meant I could walk right up to the house. And it was bad, because it meant I could walk right up to the house. Yeah, I'll admit I was nervous. Not only was I trespassing, I was armed, and that was not a good combination for a guy on probation. Not that I was expecting or wanting a confrontation. Just the opposite. I was here to sneak up and install a tap on Brian Pierce's phone. Illegal as hell, and nothing I learned would be admissible, but if I was able to discover Tracy Turner's whereabouts, I didn't care if I did it illegally or not.

I waited another ten minutes. Still nothing, although I did hear two cars pass on Thomas Springs. Time to get closer.

The front of the house faced south. I approached up a slight slope from the west side, where two windows were lit and one was dark. Could be somebody in that window watching me, or aiming a shotgun, but it was a chance I had to take. I didn't see the exterior telephone box mounted anywhere on this side of the house, but I wanted to get closer anyway, because if there were people inside, it would be good to know where they were.

Ten more minutes. That's how long I took to cover the distance. When I was within five yards of the house, I was far enough up the gentle slope that I could begin to see into one of the windows. Saw a dresser, so I knew it was a bedroom. A few steps closer and I saw the bed. Nobody in it. Nobody anywhere in the room. The door into the room was closed. But now I could hear something. Murmuring. A conversation from somewhere inside the house.

I went to my left, toward the rear of the house. Past the darkened window. Now I could see that curtains were drawn across it, with no light showing around the edges. Relief. It was probably a bedroom, too. If there were people in there, perhaps lying awake, they wouldn't see my form passing across the window.

I reached the corner at the rear of the house and peeked around it. There was enough stray light from the windows in back that I could see a large patio with four wrought-iron chairs encircling a limestone fire pit. A good place to kick back with friends and enjoy a crisp winter evening, telling stories around a crackling fire. But right now, it looked bleak and desolate and sort of sad in the darkness.

My Nikes were quiet on the concrete as I edged past the first rear window, which also had curtains drawn. After twenty more feet I could see through the three small ascending windows built into the back door. I was looking up a hallway which led past the two bedrooms on the right. There were also two open doorways on the left — more bedrooms, or more likely a bedroom and a bathroom. Couldn't see into them from here. No light coming from those rooms either. It appeared that the hallway fed into the living room at the front of the house. I could see the back of a couch and, beyond it, a bookshelf against a wall, but I wasn't willing to get any closer to the back door for a better view. Nothing moved, but the murmuring was louder. Sounded like two men talking, maybe sitting in the living room, just out of sight from my vantage point.

I continued in a clockwise fashion around the other rear corner of the house, and now proceeded slowly along the east-facing exterior wall, past windows with more drawn curtains.

Slowly. Carefully. Toward the front of the house.

And now I was approaching a lighted window that likely looked into the living room. I stopped beside the window, my back to the wall. The conversation I'd been hearing was at its loudest yet, although I still couldn't make out any specific words.

Was it The Guy? Talking to Brian Pierce?

Only one way to find out. Go ahead and peek. I knew that with the lights on inside, they wouldn't be able to see me outside. The glare on the inside of the pane would prevent it. Still, I'd feel obvious and vulnerable.

But I did it.

I leaned ever so slowly past the edge of the window, and the room slowly came into view. First I saw that same bookcase against the front wall. Leaned a little farther and saw a loveseat against the far wall of the room.

Then I saw the TV viewing area — two easy chairs facing a flat-screen mounted on the wall. The TV was tuned to a talk show of some sort. Not like a Letterman or Leno type of talk show, but more of a PBS one-on-one type of show — host and guest, around a table, with no band, no sidekick, no audience, no elaborate set. That was the conversation I'd been hearing.

The Guy was nowhere to be seen. Neither was Erica Kerwick or Tracy Turner.

But Brian Pierce was there, stretched out on the floor between the chairs.

Well, I think it was him. It was hard to tell, because a big piece of his face was missing, and what was left was covered with blood.

34

Mia didn't know what to say at first. That much was obvious. It was the next morning. I hadn't slept at all, wondering if I'd made the right decision. Still didn't know.

"So he was shot?" Mia finally said.

We were at my apartment, one of us on either end of the couch.

"Guess so. It was hard to tell."

"You didn't go inside?"

"Hell, no."

"What if he was still alive?"

"He wasn't. Not a chance. I can guarantee that."

She took a deep breath. I don't blame her. I had just made her an accomplice to a crime. Failure to report a violent death was probably a felony.

She said, "I'm just...I don't..." At a loss for words.

"Would you rather I hadn't told you?"

She thought about that for a moment. "No." She shook her head. "No. I'm glad you did. We're partners. Even though it was pretty shitty of you to go over there without me."

"Would you have gone with me?"

"No."

"Would you have tried to talk me out of it?"

"Of course I would have. That was the whole point of turning it over to the cops. That's what they do. They're the pros. And now you might have contaminated the crime scene."

I had already thought about that, obviously. Not just last night, sitting in my apartment, pondering it for hours, but there at Pierce's window, when I'd had to make an immediate decision. It wasn't an easy choice. Report it, or get the hell out of there and don't look back? It had occurred to me pretty quickly that if I reported it, I would be the number one suspect. So, after several long minutes frozen at that window, I'd chosen option number two.

I'd left, and not nearly as slowly and quietly as I'd arrived. Back through the trees, not bothering with the NVGs this time. Hoisted myself over the fence, because it was faster than crawling under, and snagged my jeans on a barb. Hustled along the shoulder of Thomas Springs Road, lying flat in the tall grass when one solitary vehicle passed by. And finally made it back to the Circle Country Club parking lot, where I tried to appear casual as I walked to the van, and when I was pulling out, I noticed a guy leaning against a truck, smoking a cigarette, watching me leave. Crap. A witness. I'd told Mia all of this.

"This is really bad, Roy," she said.

"I know."

"Did you touch anything? Any windows?"

"No."

"You might've left footprints."

"The ground seemed pretty dry, but yeah, it's a possibility. That's why I ditched my shoes."

I'd thrown them in a dumpster behind a strip center, but she didn't ask.

"Who would've shot him. And why?"

"No way of knowing. Maybe Erica Kerwick. Or The Guy. Or he could've shot himself, for all we know."

"Did you see a gun on the floor?"

"No, but it could've been under him or just hidden from view behind one of the chairs."

"Are you going to report it?"

"I can't, Mia. Think how it would look. Ruelas would say, 'What were you doing over there? You thought Pierce was a child abductor. Considering your history, maybe you thought you'd dish out a little justice on your own?'"

"You could call it in anonymously."

"I'm not sure I could — not in a way that they couldn't eventually trace back to me. I think it's best if I do exactly what I would have done if I'd never gone over there."

"Which means do nothing."

"I'm afraid so."

She was shaking her head. "Roy, Roy, Roy."

"I know."

"You never should have gone over there."

"Hindsight."

"Hindsight, hell. You should've known that *before* you went. Your judgment really sucks."

I sat there quietly for a beat or two, wondering how she'd respond to what I was about to say. "I'm in this thing, Mia. I think I've made that obvious by now. Tracy Turner was at Brian Pierce's house, and Erica Kerwick knew it. She was part of it, whatever *it* was. Now Pierce is dead, Tracy is still missing, and neither of the Hanrahans will talk to the police. Meanwhile, Ruelas and his fellow Keystone Kops can't seem to uncover clue number one. Or maybe he just doesn't care."

"Roy..."

"I'm not giving up, Mia. I've made up my mind. Call me smug, cocky, or arrogant if you want, but I'm gonna figure it out. I'm close already, I know it. So everything else has to go on the back burner until I'm done, it's that simple. I realize that's not what you want to hear from a brand-new partner, but there it is. I don't expect you to help me. I'm not asking you to help me. In fact, it's probably better if you don't get involved."

"Then why did you call me and tell me what you did last night?"

"I don't even know. Seemed like I should tell somebody. You yourself just said my judgment sucks."

She got up off the couch and walked over to the sliding glass door that opened onto my patio. I knew she was thinking things through — maybe even wondering if she should kill this partnership right now.

Then I heard her giggle. Didn't expect that. Apparently she'd just remembered something amusing.

"What?"

She said, "I almost forgot, because you kind of distracted me with all this, you know?"

"What?" I said again.

She turned around, grinning, like we were about to share a joke. "Ruelas asked me out."

I think I literally flinched, just a little. "He — really?"

"Called me up and asked if I wanted to meet for drinks."

"When was this?" She was backlit from the sun shining in through the glass door, so I held my hand up to block the light and get a better look at her expression.

"Late yesterday afternoon."

I waited for her to say more, but she didn't.

"What did you say?"

"Really? You can't guess?"

"You said no."

"Of course I said no, you dork. Not my type at all."

"What is your type?"

"Well, I'm not totally sure, but he isn't it."

"Good-looking guy. Makes a good living."

Why was I listing that jerk's attributes? Like I was daring her to go out with him?

She said, "My point in telling you is that I agree that he's not very focused on this case. What kind of detective tries to hook up with a witness when he's working a big case? I guess I'm a witness. Right?"

"Yeah."

"But you're even more of a witness."

"I am. I wonder when he'll ask me out."

"Anyway, it just seems like he's crossing a line. Kind of sleazy."

"There might even be a policy against it."

"I didn't think about that."

She came back to the couch and sat down. Took another long breath. Finally said, "Do you always get into fixes like this? Should I expect this on a regular basis?"

"Just trying to keep life interesting."

"Yeah, great. So what's our next step?"

"Are you saying you're in this with me?"

"Well, damn, Roy, I don't have much choice. What kind of partner would I be if I bailed every time things got messy? So what's our next step?"

"Take a wild guess."

Mia remained on the couch while I called Jessica on my cell phone. Considering how things had progressed the last time I'd seen Jessica, I thought about going into the other room to make the call, but that seemed sort of juvenile.

She answered by saying, "Hey, there."

I said, "How's it going?"

"Working right now, but it's slow. I've been thinking about you."

"Same here."

"You've been thinking about you?"

"Exactly. I find myself very interesting."

Maybe I had a weird tone in my voice, but Mia was giving me a strange look, along with a raised eyebrow. I turned the other way.

Jessica said, "I'm glad you called."

"You thought I wouldn't?"

"I knew you would."

"We should get together soon."

"I'd like that. When?"

"This weekend?"

"Sounds good. I'm off on Saturday and don't have to work until two on Sunday."

"Excellent. In the meantime..."

"Yeah?"

"I need to ask a favor."

"What's up?"

"You might not even be able to help, but I figured it wouldn't hurt to ask."

"This must be some favor. Spit it out, dude."

"Do you happen to have a phone number for Patrick Hanrahan?"

I started with a text:
I saw Tracy at Pierce's house one week ago today.
Then we waited a few minutes.

"Think he'll respond?" Mia asked.

"I wouldn't. At least not yet."

And he didn't, not after ten full minutes. So I sent a second one:

I saw Erica at Pierce's house five days ago.

More waiting.

"So what's the deal with this Jessica?" Mia asked. "You getting serious?" Needling me, and making no effort to conceal it.

"Well, she's definitely interesting. I really like her a lot. But here's the thing. The other night, we started to get a little bit intimate, and I don't want to share all the details, but it turns out she's a dude."

Mia simply shook her head slowly. She had known a line of bullshit was coming. "Always deflecting," she said.

"Me?"

"Absolutely. When you don't want to share, you turn it into a joke."

"You weren't sort of joking when you asked? Giving me a subtle jab?"

I looked down at my phone. Still no reply. So I sent a third one:

Three days ago, I was attacked at Pierce's place.

Then a fourth one:

A man abducted me, interrogated me, then let me go.

I figured Hanrahan was getting curious by now. Or maybe he wasn't, depending on whether he already knew any of this stuff.

"Okay, yeah, I apologize," Mia said. "I was teasing you a little."

"She's very nice," I said. "I like her."

"Wow. This is real progress."

"Teasing again?"

"You're right, I am. It's hard not to."

"Oh, you can tease me all you want. I have no problem with it."

"Because it gives you justification to deflect."

"What are you, a therapist now?"

"Just a concerned friend."

"Did I say something at some point that makes you dislike Jessica?"

"No, of course not. I've never even met her."

"She actually reminds me of you, you know."

"Oh, really? That's interesting. In what ways?"

"Well, like you, she has a burning passion for her collection of Cabbage Patch dolls. She is also a devotee of Romanian folk dance.

Oops. I'm deflecting again, aren't I?"

"At least it's always amusing, Roy."

"Thank you. But I do appreciate your concern for my welfare, so I will do my best to give you an honest answer. Bottom line, I like Jessica because she is intelligent, interesting, and drop-dead gorgeous. She also has a great sense of humor."

Mia was grinning. It was a cat-that-ate-the-canary type of grin. "Those are the ways she reminds you of me?"

"Ha. I didn't necessarily say that."

"Well, if she — "

My phone chimed. An incoming text from Hanrahan's number.

"He's asking, 'Who is this?'"

"You have to be straight-up with him, right?"

"Yep."

I wrote: *My name is Roy Ballard. We need to talk.*

He replied: *Are you a cop?*

No, I'm a fraud investigator. I saw these things while investigating Pierce.

He didn't respond for several minutes. Long enough for him to Google my name and learn some things — not just about my own experiences with abduction, but about my involvement as a witness in a handful of lawsuits. Wouldn't take Hanrahan long to see that there really was a guy named Roy Ballard who investigated insurance fraud. After that, he'd have to decide whether or not to believe I was actually that Roy Ballard. It would be tempting for him to suspect that I was an enterprising reporter from some tabloid journal or television show.

Then he finally replied: *Come to my office in one hour.*

35

The highrise at 301 Congress was one of the most prestigious business addresses in Austin. Nice-looking place, too, with an angled-glass crown that made it stand out on the downtown skyline. Back in 1985, when they were excavating for the foundation, they'd uncovered fossils from a mastodon and a saber-toothed tiger. Those fossils were displayed in the lobby, but we were more concerned with the seventeenth floor.

Up we went, just the two of us in the elevator.

"Got a plan of any kind?" Mia asked.

"No, but I'm open to suggestions."

Her silence indicated that she didn't have any.

When the elevator doors opened, we were immediately confronted by a very wide and imposing reception desk — the kind with a counter so high you can hardly see the person behind it. In this case, that person was a perky brown-haired young woman in a blue business suit and a white blouse, with a red scarf knotted around her neck. She was also wearing one of those hands-free telephone headsets, and it was obvious she was in the middle of a call, but that didn't prevent her from giving us a big smile as we stepped from the elevator and approached the desk.

While we waited, I took the opportunity to quickly scan the surroundings. Above the woman, mounted on the wall, was a logo formed out of three letters: PAH. Hanrahan's initials, no doubt. Named the company after himself.

The place gave off a vibe of understated wealth. Everything classy and well designed. To the right of the reception desk was a small waiting area with leather chairs and a couch, and beyond that, a door with no knob, meaning it was an exit only. So, to get into the offices, you had to go left, through a double glass door.

But first you had to pass a smaller desk, at which was seated a security guard roughly the size and weight of an industrial refrigerator. It was odd the way the desk was sort of stuck to one side, almost like it was a temporary arrangement. A permanent guard station would've been designed to blend in better. The behemoth caught me looking and gave me a slow nod of greeting. I nodded back then looked away.

When the young woman ended her call, she looked up at me and said, "Good morning. May I help you?"

I said, "We're checking in for the eleven o'clock flight to Los Angeles."

Mia sighed.

The young woman, still smiling, said, "My outfit, right? I look like a flight attendant. The scarf is probably too much."

"Not at all," Mia said. "I like it. Is it silk?"

"It is."

"Very nice."

The young woman looked pleased.

I said, "It appears we also have to pass through security after check-in," meaning the meathead at the small desk.

She gave a polite laugh and said, "And you're here for..."

"We have an appointment with Patrick Hanrahan."

"Your names?"

"Roy Ballard and Mia Madison."

I noticed that she didn't need to check an appointment book, and she didn't have us sign the register on the countertop. Instead, she punched a button on her phone console and, a few seconds later, said, "Roy Ballard and Mia Madison are here for Mr. Hanrahan."

The whole operation was very smooth and professional. I was prepared to usher Mia over to the waiting area, but before we even made a move in that direction, a woman emerged from the glass doors to greet us.

Not just any woman. It was Erica Kerwick.

I'm pretty sure Mia and I both managed not to react with surprise, but I guess it didn't really matter. I had already told Hanrahan that I had seen her at Pierce's, so she likely knew that I knew.

She was neither friendly nor brusque. She simply stepped past the guard station and said, "Come with me, please."

And we did, past the guard, who simply watched us pass with no emotions on his face whatsoever. Through the double doors and into a long, carpeted hallway. Erica Kerwick led the way quietly, and when we reached the end of the hallway, where it made a 90-degree turn to the right, she instead turned to the left and rapped softly on a closed door. Big slab of walnut or mahogany or who knows what.

I didn't hear a response, but Erica Kerwick opened the door and stepped into the office. We followed. It was a damn nice space — oil paintings, expensive furniture, floor to ceiling windows with an amazing view of the river winding through the city below — but I didn't have much time to appreciate it, because here came Patrick Hanrahan from around a huge desk. Great-looking guy. Black hair with some silver in it. He was dressed casually in a blue golf shirt and some dark slacks. When he reached us, he stuck out a hand. "Patrick Hanrahan."

We shook.

"Roy Ballard, and this is Mia Madison."

They shook too, and I heard the door close behind us. Erica Kerwick had left without so much as an offer of coffee. I didn't know whether I should read something into that or not.

Hanrahan said, "Shall we sit?" and extended an arm in the direction of a cluster of furniture near the windows.

"Great view," Mia said.

"I like it," Hanrahan said. "In fact, you can actually see my house from here, out in Westlake Hills. It's just a dot, but you can see it. I didn't even know that when we leased this space. See that hill with the transmission tower on it?"

"Yeah."

"I'm on the hill just to the right of that. A white house."

We pretended to see it, but there was too much haze in the air.

"Anyway," Hanrahan said, gesturing again toward the furniture. Mia chose a plush upholstered chair facing the window, so I sat to her right and Hanrahan sat opposite her.

"I imagine you get a lot of sun in the afternoon," Mia said.

We were making small talk, and there was really no way around it. I'd been in enough similar situations to know that people who have just met don't jump into serious conversations without a little meaningless babble first.

"I lower the blinds when it gets really bad," Hanrahan said. "Winter is okay — the sun is lower and at more of an angle — but now, in the summer, yeah, it can be a little too much."

Enough.

I said, "I'm very sorry about Tracy."

"Thank you."

"And I'm sorry you're having to deal with the media."

He gave me a sort of pained grin that was also part grimace. "That means a lot, because, uh, I know you are familiar with this sort of thing yourself."

"Yeah."

"I did some Googling..."

"Don't blame you."

"And it sounds like you went through hell."

"Pretty much."

"But I have to admit I'm not clear why you're here."

I nodded. "Let me summarize it. I was investigating Brian Pierce for insurance fraud, based on his workers' comp claim after the accident at your restaurant. Just routine stuff. This was the day after Tracy went missing. I was walking along his fence line, using binoculars, and I saw a little girl in the doorway at Pierce's house. I'm all but certain it was Tracy."

I gave him a moment to respond, but he didn't, and his expression didn't change. Maybe he was just numb. I could understand that. Or maybe he was one of those men who, when under extreme stress, intentionally remained cold and analytical, rather than letting their emotions get away from them. Another possibility — maybe the cops had already questioned him about Pierce and my alleged sighting of Tracy, in which case this wasn't news to him. But whatever the reason, his face didn't give anything away.

So I continued. "Unfortunately, I didn't get video."

"How far away were you?"

"Maybe a hundred and twenty yards." I realized I was trying to make the distance sound insignificant.

Hanrahan was waiting for me to go on.

"Two days after that, I watched a woman in a white Jetta visit Pierce's house. I set up some video surveillance equipment, got some good footage of that woman, and we were able to get on Facebook and determine that her name was Erica Kerwick."

Hanrahan still said nothing.

I said, "Same woman who just brought us into your office. I believe she's related to you somehow?"

Hanrahan said, "Where did you hear that?"

No reason not to tell him. "There's a kid named Curtis Hanrahan on Facebook — "

He was nodding. "One of my nephews."

"And she called herself 'Aunt Erica' in a comment on Curtis's page."

"She's my cousin."

"How long has she worked for you?"

"About seventeen or eighteen years."

I changed gears abruptly, on purpose. "Can you tell me if that *was* your stepdaughter at Brian Pierce's house?"

"Please don't do that."

"Do what?"

"Call her my stepdaughter. As far as I'm concerned, she's my daughter."

"I apologize. Can you tell me if that was your daughter at Pierce's house?"

This time, he didn't say anything right away — just cocked his head and appeared to be contemplating whether he *should* give an answer. Finally he said, "I wouldn't know whether it was or not. I probably shouldn't even be talking to you. My attorney would go ballistic. You know as well as anybody how words can get twisted around, get taken out of context. I've had it happen in my professional life, and I can't afford for it to happen here. I'll just say this: Nobody on this planet cares more about Tracy than I do. I would go to any lengths to ensure her safety and well-being."

"What was Erica doing at Pierce's place?"

"I don't know specifically, but she and Pierce are employees of the same corporation. Use your imagination." Big, fake, patronizing grin.

Intuition told me he was being deceptive.

"So it was work related? That's what she told the police?"

"She didn't speak to the police."

"They didn't contact her?"

"Oh, they contacted her, but she didn't speak to them. I asked her not to. I'm sure you understand why, with your experiences."

"I can, yeah. Do you know where Tracy is now?"

He gave me the type of frown that suggested my question was in bad taste. Then he said, "My daughter is missing. I don't know where she is, and if I did, she wouldn't be missing. I was hoping you might have some useful information for me, but it seems like all you have is questions."

"I'm sorry. If you have questions for me, by all means, go ahead."

He looked out the window for a minute, out at the skyline and the river, or at nothing at all. Then he said, "How sure are you that it was Tracy at Pierce's house? Honestly. Please don't exaggerate."

"Let me put it this way: I would bet a whole lot of money on it."

"Would you bet your life?"

"Pardon?"

"Would you literally bet your life?"

Now it was my turn to pause and consider. I said, "No, I wouldn't."

"How clear is the video of the woman in the Jetta?"

"Plenty."

"You are positive it's Erica?"

"Yes."

He looked at Mia. "You agree?"

"Absolutely. It's her."

"Both of you would bet your life on it?"

"Yes," I said.

"I would," Mia said.

I didn't have the slightest clue whether Hanrahan was shocked or surprised by these revelations.

He said, "Let's stop beating around the bush. Are you implying that Erica and Brian Pierce have kidnapped my daughter?"

I almost laughed. "We don't know what to think, but doesn't that look like a possibility to you?"

"Absolutely not. No way. Erica would never do that. You yourself just said you wouldn't bet your life it was Tracy."

"Only because there is almost nothing I *would* bet my life on."

He was squirming in his chair, about to stand up. "This is a waste of time."

"We're trying to help you, Mr. Hanrahan. We're just trying to find out what happened."

"Why?"

"Why what? Why do we care?"

"Exactly. You aren't cops."

"No, but if we can help find your daughter, why wouldn't we?"

"I have to be honest, Mr. Ballard. Some of the things I saw online made me wonder about your credibility."

"Hey, I understand."

"You say you saw Tracy at Brian Pierce's house, but you were all alone. Nobody else saw her."

I remained calm. "I have no reason to make it up."

"But people make stuff like that up all the time. That's one of the drawbacks of offering a reward. The cops told me about all kinds of nutcases who have called in about Tracy. No offense. I didn't mean for that to sound like you're a nutcase."

"Been called worse."

"What is this you said about being attacked on the side of the road?"

I told him, very briefly, what had happened, including the part where The Guy tried to claim he was working for someone else in the area.

He said, "You think this man was protecting Pierce?"

"Seems obvious."

"You don't appear injured."

"Just my pride."

"Nobody else can verify your story."

This time I did laugh. "Well, the man who attacked me can verify it. And he will, one of these days." It was obvious from his body language that Hanrahan was about to call an end to this meeting. So I said, "Have you received a demand for ransom?"

"You think I'm going to give that kind of information to a complete stranger? Here's something for both of you to think about. You obviously have this notion that you might be able to help find Tracy, to bring her home safely. I appreciate that. I truly do. But you should also consider the possibility that you might be endangering her. That's why you should leave the investigation to the professionals. Let them do their job."

He stood up. The meeting was over.

In the elevator, Mia said, "That was a very odd encounter, don't you think?"

But I was busy with my phone.

She said, "I couldn't tell what to believe and what not to believe. The man was like a robot."

No time to talk. I was opening the folder that contained sent texts. Now I held my phone up for her to see. "Tell me what this text says."

She looked at me, puzzled, then looked at my phone and read, "'Three days ago, I was attacked at Pierce's place.'"

I clicked to the next text. "And this one."

"' A man abducted me, interrogated me, then let me go.'"

I snapped my phone shut. "Five minutes ago, Hanrahan asked me about being attacked on the side of the road."

It took Mia about a nanosecond to process the relevance of that remark, and then she smiled broadly. "How would he know it happened on the side of the road?"

36

She wouldn't stop.

Asking for her mommy.

Asking for her daddy.

Saying she wanted to go home.

Crying for no discernible reason.

It weighed on him. Kept him up at night. Why couldn't she simply forget those things? Everything would be perfect if she would just forget.

It finally reached a point where he knew he couldn't wait for her to change, but would instead have to take action. Make her change. Make her forget.

He had also known that, eventually, he'd have to leave the house with her, once she had proven that she could behave. He had been playing it by ear, gauging her emotional state, and trying to decide how much he could trust her in public. Now he realized he could kill two birds with one stone, so to speak.

"Do you like McDonald's?" he asked her late one morning.

She nodded, but didn't make eye contact.

"How about if we go have lunch there today?"

"Okay."

"And I have a surprise for you. Your mother is going to meet us."

Her head immediately popped up, her eyes more lively than he had seen them in days, but he could tell that she was suspicious.

"Would you like that? To see your mother?"

"Yes."

"Okay, then. Let's get you cleaned up and we'll go."

On the drive over, he said, *"I'm counting on you to behave yourself, okay?"*

"Okay."

"No temper tantrums. No screaming or crying."

"Okay."

"I think sometimes you forget how much I do for you, and how I take care of you."

Emily didn't reply.

"Now I'm taking you to see your mother, so I want you to be grateful. No more of that bratty stuff, okay?"

"Okay."

"Don't speak to anyone except me or your mother. Is that understood?"

She nodded.

Later, when he pulled into the parking lot, Emily craned her head left and right, looking for the family car, no doubt. Of course, it was nowhere to be seen.

"She's not here yet. We're a few minutes early, so we'll go inside and order."

His heart was beating wildly as he took her by the hand and they began to walk into the restaurant. He had to remind himself that there were thousands of little girls all over the city who looked like Emily. And time had passed since she had gone missing. In today's world, it was already old news. Nobody would be paying attention.

They went inside and Emily stuck close to his side, just as he had hoped she would. They looked just like any other dad and his daughter, stopping off for a burger. He ordered cheeseburgers with no onions, fries, and two Cokes. Then they sat at a booth in a corner and began to eat.

Emily kept watching the door.

Waiting for mommy.

Anxious. Excited.

"She'll be here in a little bit. Go ahead and eat."

She did, reluctantly. One small nibble at a time.

This was going to be as cruel as anything he'd ever done, but there was no avoiding it.

Finally, when Emily had eaten most of her meal and it was plain she wanted no more, he said, "Tell you what. Let's go wait outside. I'm sure she'll be here any minute."

On the way out, they took a few last slurps from their Cokes, then tossed their trash into the garbage can.

"Let's wait in the car."

And once he got her all buckled in, he acted as if his cell phone had vibrated. He pulled it from his pocket and pretended to take a call. "Oh, hi...Yeah, we're here...We already finished eating...I see... Really?...I understand...No, I'll tell her...Okay, bye."

When he hung up, she looked at him expectantly, but he didn't say anything right away. Not yet. Too many people coming and going from the parking lot.

He waited until he'd started the car and pulled out. Then he said, "That was your mother calling. She can't make it."

And Emily was already beginning to cry. Just like that.

"She doesn't know when she'll be able to see you again. Maybe never. She said it might be best if you forgot about her and your father."

Now Emily was taking a tremendous gulp of air, followed by an ear-splitting scream that drilled to the very center of his brain.

He gritted his teeth and rode it out.

"It's just you and me, Emily. Just you and me."

37

This time, Mia didn't cajole me into calling Ruelas and telling him what we had learned. Maybe it was because she was starting to think we could do a better job ourselves, or maybe she understood that the cops couldn't do much with that information as long as Hanrahan refused to talk, or maybe she was just hooked on the rush that came from learning what we had just learned.

Patrick Hanrahan was involved. He had to be.

She drove as we talked.

"What're you thinking?"

I said, "He knows that Tracy was at Pierce's place. They are all working together — Hanrahan, Pierce, Erica Kerwick, and The Guy. Nothing else makes sense."

"But what are they working on? Why is he hiding his own daughter?"

I didn't have a solid answer. All I could do was speculate. "If Kathleen Hanrahan was planning to divorce him, chances are good she'd get custody, despite her problems with alcohol."

"Yeah, but would that upset him enough to stage an abduction? Why not just ask for joint custody? With all his money, he could hire an army of attorneys."

"I don't know. Maybe Kathleen's problems are worse than we know, and Patrick couldn't stand the idea of Tracy living with her even part of the time. In fact, let me check something..."

I opened my laptop, connected my USB modem, and logged on to the Texas Department of Public Safety's criminal records database. Didn't take long to search.

"Kathleen has been busted twice for DWI in the past three years," I said.

Mia said, "I wonder if Tracy was in the car either of those times."

"Even if she wasn't, Patrick probably figured it was only a matter of time."

We rode quietly for a minute.

I said, "Well, regardless of whatever reason Patrick might've had for grabbing Tracy, if he did do it, he'd need a place to stash her."

"Yeah..."

"Jessica said Brian Pierce does all kinds of odd jobs for Patrick. So what if Patrick paid Pierce to keep Tracy at his place? Not by himself, of course. Erica Kerwick stays over there, too. It works out perfectly, because Pierce is already on leave from work because of his injury." Then something else occurred to me. "You know what? You need to turn around."

"What? Why?" She moved into the left-hand lane to make a U.

"There are only so many players in this thing. Pierce is dead. That leaves three. We need to be keeping track of them as much as possible. Hanrahan would have to be crazy to go anywhere near Tracy right now. But Erica Kerwick..."

"We need to keep an eye on her."

"Exactly."

Like most highrises in Austin, Hanrahan's building had a parking garage with reserved spots on the lower levels for tenants. We spotted Erica Kerwick's Jetta on the second floor, not far from the elevators. There were no spots for guests on that level, but, fortunately, there was only one exit out of the garage.

"Just find a metered spot on the street and wait for her," I said. "She goes anywhere — anywhere at all — you follow her. And if Hanrahan goes anywhere, send me a text."

"What does he drive?"

That stopped me. "I don't know. You'll need to use binoculars and check each driver that comes out."

"What are you going to do?"

"Get a cab back to my place. I'll need your car keys."

"Where you going?"

"We got what we could out of Hanrahan. Now I want to see if his wife will talk."

Less than an hour and a half later, I was in Mia's Mustang, cruising west on Bee Cave Road. Keeping it under the speed limit, because Westlake cops are fond of running radar, and they'd love to pull over a car like this one.

I turned right on Westlake Drive, followed it through the intersection at Redbud Trail and along the twisting road into the heart of one of the most affluent areas in Austin. Lots of business hotshots lived up here in these steep, heavily wooded hills, including Michael Dell. He had something like 33 acres, complete with a thirty-thousand-square-foot mansion and a helicopter pad.

The Hanrahans lived off a street called Toro Canyon. Easy enough to get their home address off the tax records, which showed that they owned half a dozen properties in Travis County. That's what wealthy people did. They owned a lot of stuff.

It didn't surprise me when I reached their place and saw that their entire estate — four acres — was surrounded by a wrought iron fence. Eight feet tall and spikes at the top.

No news crews hanging around, but that didn't surprise me either. The two-lane road was narrow, with no shoulders and no place to park. The cops in a little municipality like this would run those guys off in a heartbeat if they created a traffic hazard by lingering or loitering.

I drove past, just to give myself time to think. Couldn't simply walk up to the front door. Wasn't about to trespass. Didn't know Kathleen's phone number, and I really doubted Patrick would give it to me. I wondered if he was even staying here now, after the revelation that Kathleen planned to divorce him.

I turned around at a street called Fast Fox Trail and moseyed back to the Hanrahans' place. I pulled into the driveway and stopped at the gate. To my left was a keypad, which would magically open the gate if I knew the right numbers to punch in. Or I could punch a button and summon someone inside the house, which I couldn't even see from where I was idling.

Nothing to lose. I punched the button.

I wondered if the Hanrahans had servants of any kind. Maid. Gardener. Pool boy. Butler. Au pair. Was there somebody back there who would be shirking his or her responsibility by failing to answer the buzzer?

So far, nothing, so I gave it another punch.

Now I noticed a small, discreet video camera tucked into the English ivy growing to the left side of the gate. It was just me, one guy, in a Mustang, not a news van, and maybe that's why Kathleen Hanrahan decided to see what the hell I wanted.

"Yes?" she said through the small speaker mounted beneath the keypad. The sound was surprisingly clear — enough so that even with just that one word, I recognized her voice from the times I'd seen her on the news.

I didn't waste any time. "Mrs. Hanrahan, my name is Roy Ballard. I just came from a meeting with your husband and I'd like to speak to you, too, if you have a minute. I am not a police officer or a reporter of any kind."

"What...who is this?"

"Roy Ballard, ma'am. I have some information I'd like to share about your daughter Tracy."

There was a long enough delay that I wondered if she was there, or if she was going to answer.

Finally, she said, "Are you one of the news people?"

I was tempted to believe that she couldn't hear me well, but I could hear a telltale sign in her voice. Slight confusion. A hint of a slur. She'd been drinking, or taking pills, or something. Which could make my job a whole lot harder or a whole lot easier.

"No, I'm a videographer," I said. "I investigate insurance fraud."

Gave her a few seconds to reply. Not a peep. I really didn't want to spill my guts out here on the intercom, but I didn't have any choice.

So I said, "Mrs. Hanrahan, I saw your daughter last week, the day after she went missing. I saw her at the home of a man I was investigating

— a man who worked at one of your husband's restaurants. I really think we should sit down for a few minutes and talk about it. This isn't a joke or a trick or some sort of scam. Hear me out, and if you want me to leave, I'll leave immediately."

Still nothing.

"Mrs. Hanrahan, you have my word."

The gate began to swing open.

Not quite noon and she was drunk, no question about it. Not tipsy. Not buzzed. Inebriated. I could tell from the moment she opened the door, swaying, glassy-eyed. There was also a small purple splotch on the front of her white blouse, which told me that her drink of choice was wine. This was not the well-put-together woman I'd imagined her to be.

She looked past me, out to the parking area in front of the house, as if to make sure there hadn't been additional people hiding in the Mustang.

Then she looked at me again. "What was your name?"

"Roy Ballard."

I stuck out a hand and she shook it. It was obvious from the circles under her eyes and a general sag to her face that the past eight days had weighed on her.

"Thanks for stopping by," she said, as if she'd invited me. "Come on in."

The Hanrahan home, which was gorgeous from the outside, was every bit as stunning inside. Very modern. The ceiling of the entryway was so high above me, I felt like I was in an auditorium. Everything was black and white, including the checkered floor.

Kathleen led me into the living area, which had a lot more color, including a red L-shaped sectional sofa so sprawling that three matching blond-wood coffee tables served the longer side. The far wall consisted of blackened steel surrounding an immense fireplace. The artwork on the other walls — contemporary oil paintings — looked damned expensive even to a bumpkin like me. The two floor lamps looked like something a team of designers had spent months creating.

There was no TV on the wall, no piles of mail on any of the tables, no dirty dishes or socks on the floor. Did anybody really live here? Or maybe the maid had cleaned that morning. Maybe she cleaned every morning. Maybe she never stopped cleaning. Maybe it was like painting the Golden Gate Bridge — a nonstop process. Weird the way the wealthy lived. The only hints of personalization in the room were a full glass of red wine and an iPad on one of the coffee tables. Evidently Kathleen had been sitting in here on the couch when I rang the buzzer, and this is where she now sat again, on the edge of the couch cushion, at full attention. I sat a few feet away.

"You saw Tracy?" she asked. She appeared genuinely and pathetically desperate.

"I am virtually positive it was her." I recalled what her husband had asked me. "I would bet just about anything on it."

"Where? When was this?"

And, for what seemed like the hundredth time, I told my story about seeing Tracy. Kathleen was my most rapt audience yet, and she appeared particularly stunned when I mentioned Pierce's name, as if she hadn't expected it. I saw anger flash in her eyes when I brought up Erica Kerwick. She *wanted* to believe everything I was telling her — that much was obvious. Before I was even done, her face was a mask of drunken confusion and pained disbelief, and tears were streaming down her cheeks. I stopped without giving the details of my conversation with her husband.

"Brian Pierce and Erica have Tracy? Patrick has to be in on it. That lousy, lousy bastard. We need to tell the police." Her voice was urgent.

"I have already. They know all of this."

"What are they doing about it?" She wiped at her nose with the back of her hand.

"I know they searched Brian Pierce's house and came up with nothing. Tracy wasn't there."

"Why wasn't that on the news?"

"Well, I don't think cops routinely announce when they are going to search someone's home. That could cast suspicion on a lot of innocent people. Do you need a Kleenex?"

She nodded and pointed toward a hallway to the right of the fireplace. "There's a bathroom..." she said.

"Be right back."

I wandered down the hallway and found it easily enough. It was a guest bathroom, but it was enormous. There was a box of tissues resting on the granite countertop. I grabbed it and returned to my place on the couch, noticing that the previously full wine glass was now about half full.

Kathleen grabbed a tissue and dabbed at her nose.

I said, "I understand you worked with Pierce."

She nodded. "A long time ago. He still works for Patrick."

"When was the last time you saw him?"

"Patrick?"

"Brian Pierce."

"I don't know. Last year? Maybe when I was in the restaurant at some point."

"Doesn't he do odd jobs for your husband?"

"Sometimes, but it's been awhile."

"Has he ever babysat your daughter?" I was thinking about what Emma Webster had told me — how she had seen Pierce with a little girl in his truck.

She shook her head. "We have a nanny. We've had a couple."

Her breath smelled so strongly of alcohol, it was difficult not to recoil.

"What about Patrick's cousin?" I said. "What can you tell me about her?"

Now Kathleen really looked confused. "His cousin?"

"Erica Kerwick."

"She's not his cousin. Where did you get that?"

Because that's what your husband told me.

Instead I said, "She referred to herself as 'Aunt Erica' on a Facebook post by your nephew Curtis."

It took her a minute to decipher what I was saying. Bringing up her nephew seemed to have puzzled her. Then she said, "What she meant was — you know how you might refer to an old family friend as an aunt or uncle? Like that. She's not his aunt, but she's known him since he was just a kid, so he calls her Aunt Erica. So does Tracy."

Why would Hanrahan lie to me about that? Protecting Erica? Protecting himself? Whatever the reason, it was more evidence that he was hiding something, and that he was involved with the disappearance of his own daughter.

I said, "Is she a family friend or just an employee?"

Kathleen let out a sharp, cynical laugh — almost like a quick bark

— but then, in an instant, her face crumpled with emotion. After a few moments, she regained her composure enough to say, "Patrick has been fucking her for years."

38

I didn't push her. I just sat quietly and let her sob for a minute. It didn't seem right to put my hand on her shoulder or make any other comforting gesture, so I didn't.

Meanwhile, of course, my mind was racing. I was wondering how much money it would take to get a guy like Pierce — living on a dishwasher's paycheck, with property taxes to pay on 20 acres every year — to go along with an abduction scheme. Whatever the amount, Hanrahan could likely afford it a hundred times over. Or a thousand.

And since Patrick and Pierce didn't have a friendship — just an employer/employee relationship — the cops would have no reason to check Pierce out. Not any more than they'd have reason to check out all of Hanrahan's employees, and he likely had hundreds, or even thousands.

The 'why?' was still puzzling me. Was the threat of divorce enough of a motivator? Sometimes, in the middle of divorce proceedings, or after custody had been granted, the losing parent would grab the kids and hide them, or just take off, never with much of a plan in place. Just an angry or fearful reaction, which made it even harder for that parent to have access to the kids afterwards. But rich, successful, intelligent men like Patrick Hanrahan didn't do it that way. They didn't run, they did the opposite. They hired lawyers and went on the attack. They used the full weight of their financial resources to tear their spouses to shreds. We had to be missing an important piece of the puzzle.

Kathleen had just said something.

"Pardon?"

"He denies it now, but it's true. I caught him, and he admitted it, and he said he ended it, but he didn't. It makes me so mad. He doesn't have the guts to admit what he's still doing."

Now I was confused enough that I had to wonder whether she was even right about the affair. Maybe it was just the paranoid delusions of an alcohol-soaked brain.

"You caught him? How did you find out?"

She sniffled and gave me a grim smile. "It sounds so cliché, but I hired a detective. I had suspected the cheating for several years, and I finally couldn't stand it anymore, so I hired a man to tell me if it was true."

"When was this?"

"Three or four years ago."

"And what did you learn?"

"That I was right. He was cheating. I threatened to leave, but he said he'd end it, and he begged me to stay. So I did. But he didn't end it. He lies about it, only now he knows he has to be more careful."

It was ironic to hear this woman complaining about her cheating husband, when, according to Jessica, Kathleen had cheated on her first husband with Patrick. What a hypocrite.

"That's what you meant when you said he denies it. He denies that it's happening now."

"Yeah."

"But he admitted it four years ago."

"He had to. I had photos."

"What sort of photos?"

Another short, barking laugh. "Patrick and Erica having sex in Erica's house. The detective took pictures through a window."

This just kept getting better and better. And maybe this was the piece we were looking for. Sure, Kathleen was a drunk, complete with multiple DWI arrests, and Patrick could use that against her in a divorce. But would Patrick be willing to have those photos entered as evidence in court? Kathleen's lawyer would stress that Patrick was a cheater who couldn't be trusted, and was that the type of man who should raise a child?

But I had to wonder why Kathleen hadn't demanded that Patrick fire Erica Kerwick. So, trying to be tactful, I said, "I'm a little surprised she still works for Patrick. Doesn't that bother you?"

Kathleen looked like she didn't want to respond to that, but she eventually did. "Everyone else in Patrick's family is close to her. She wasn't just going to go away. She'd still be around."

Okay, I had an idea what that meant. It wouldn't be possible for Patrick to fire Erica without the rest of the family wondering why. Which meant the affair would eventually come out. I'm guessing none of them — Patrick, Kathleen, or Erica — wanted that. So Kathleen had chosen to leave things as they were. She didn't want anyone to know about the affair. Over the years, that had been more important to her than making sure her husband had no contact with his lover. Pitiful.

"Do you see Erica often?" I asked.

"As little as possible. I should call my attorney."

"About what?"

"They can find out what the police have done about this. Patrick should be in jail. All of them should be. You're a witness. You saw Tracy with Brian Pierce and Erica."

I didn't correct her by saying that I had not seen Tracy with Erica — only with Brian. I didn't see the point in it. The woman was far enough in the bag that she would forget in a few minutes.

"Look," I said. "The cops didn't believe me, especially after they searched Pierce's place. They think I'm a nutcase. So the best thing you can do, if you agree that it appears Patrick and Erica were involved, is start talking to the police again. Tell them about the affair Patrick had with Erica. Do it through your lawyers if you're more comfortable that way. But share that information with the cops. You should do it as soon as I leave."

She was starting to bawl again. I didn't know if that was because she thought I was reprimanding her, or if she was just overwhelmed by everything she'd been through, or if it was simply because she was drunk.

My phone vibrated in my pocket. An incoming text.

"When does Patrick usually get home?" I asked.

"You kidding me? He's staying at a hotel. He'll never sleep under this roof again."

I checked my phone. Mia had sent a text:

Erica just left. I'm following.

Which was good, and now that I knew Patrick wasn't staying here, I was less worried about him suddenly showing up and finding me interrogating his wife. When I looked up from my phone, Kathleen was finishing the last of the wine in her glass.

I said, "I understand you'd been thinking about a divorce for quite some time. Did something happen between you and Patrick recently? Something that set him off or freaked him out?"

She shook her head.

"Nothing?" I said.

She shook her head again but didn't make eye contact.

"No arguments or anything? Maybe you gave him an ultimatum or something like that?"

Another small head shake. She was holding something back, and I was tempted to push her on it, but I also didn't want her to stop talking to me. My best guess at that point, considering what I learned, was that she had threatened to make the photos public, maybe put them on the Internet. Patrick, in a rare rash moment, responded by showing what he could do in return — take Tracy. Maybe it was just a display of power, but it got out of hand when Kathleen called the cops. Who knows? Maybe none of this was accurate.

I hated to ask what I was about to ask, but there was no avoiding it.

"Tell me about the day Tracy went missing."

Her face scrunched up again. I could see the pain there as clearly as the freckles across her cheeks.

I said, "I know it's not easy, but what you tell me might help me find her."

She nodded. "She was in her room, and then she wasn't. Just like that. I went in to check on her because I realized it had been awfully quiet, and she wasn't there."

I had noticed that the Hanrahan house was wired to the gills with a kick-ass security system.

"No alarm went off?"

"The system wasn't set. We only set it at night."

"No video from the front gate?"

She shook her head. "It wasn't on."

"So she simply...disappeared?"

"It was my fault. I was taking a nap."

Or passed out? I thought.

"Where was Patrick?"

"Working."

Which meant nothing. Patrick — or someone else — could have slipped in and grabbed Tracy with no problem.

There was only one more thing I wanted to ask about. "Kathleen, has Patrick ever hired a bodyguard or security service for any reason?"

"Not that I know of. We've never had a reason to."

"Okay. Well, if he needed somebody to act as a bodyguard — someone he could trust without question — does that bring anybody to mind?"

She didn't hesitate. "His brother."

"Oh, yeah? What's his name?"

"Sean."

"Tell me about Sean."

"He used to be a cop until he got fired. I don't know what he's doing now."

"You don't keep in touch?"

"Patrick talks to him on the phone a lot, but we only see him a couple of times a year."

"Why's that?"

"He lives in Brockton."

"Where is Brockton?"

"Massachusetts."

Son of a bitch.

"I don't suppose you have any video of Sean, do you?"

She was drunk, but not so drunk that she wasn't curious. "Where are you going with this?"

"I'm not sure yet, but if you have any video, that would be very helpful."

She grabbed her iPad and switched it on. Opened Facebook. Then she queued up a video and held the tablet up for me to see.

"This is Sean's toast at our wedding. He was the best man."

What I saw was the man in the video from my rock camera. Sean Hanrahan, in a tux, holding up a glass of champagne. Another brick had just fallen into place.

Patrick Hanrahan.

Erica Kerwick.

Brian Pierce.

And now Sean Hanrahan.

Those were the four players. Was there a fifth? The Guy? Or was Sean Hanrahan The Guy? Was he the son of a bitch who Tasered me?

Kathleen hit the play button, and the moment Sean Hanrahan began to speak — saying, "Today we're here to celebrate Kathleen and Patrick" — I knew the answer was yes.

39

Lynette Taylor tried her best not to spoil her five-year-old daughter, Ashley, but Randy said she was too much of a pushover. Randy was Lynette's husband — a sweet man and a great dad, and he somehow had the ability to resist all of Ashley's tricks. He was immune to the begging, the pleading, the whining. Even when Ashley kicked it into crying mode, which she seemed to do more and more these days, Randy didn't give in. But Lynette did, all too often, and it was becoming a problem.

Ashley was turning into a brat.

Hard to admit it, but it was true. Not all the time — she was still sweet most of the time — but boy did she have her moments. Hissy fits in public. Major kicking-and-screaming meltdowns. Bad enough that Lynette had actually spoken to her pediatrician about it.

"As long as you keep giving in," he said, "and as long as you keep rewarding her bad behavior, then she's going to keep right on doing it. Wouldn't you?"

He said Lynette needed to be firm. Don't be manipulated. Set boundaries and expectations, and stick with them. In short, be the parent.

Sometimes easier said than done.

Say, for instance, you've had a bad day at work, and now you can feel a migraine coming on. And on your way home from preschool, Ashley starts asking for a milkshake, because you've stopped for a milkshake in the past. A kid her age doesn't understand why it's okay to stop for a milkshake on one day but not on another day. Sure, you can explain it, but come on — she's five years old. The rational, logical part of her brain isn't quite developed yet. You can say something like, "Honey, it's okay to have a treat like a milkshake every now and then, as long as you don't do it too often," but you might as well be speaking Latin.

The kid wants a damn milkshake.

So what Lynette had been doing lately — and, again, she knew this wasn't smart — was giving in before it got ugly. She rationalized it. If Ashley started screaming and Lynette gave in, that meant Ashley would scream more in the future. So on those days when Lynette just flat-out knew she didn't have the ability to withstand Ashley's emotional assault, Lynette would say okay before it even got that far.

"Can I have a milkshake?"

"Okay, but that means you can't have another one for awhile."

Yeah, Lynette would try to sound tough — like she was in control — but bottom line, Ashley got her milkshake.

Today was one of those days.

Ashley asked, and Lynette was so not in the mood for a fight, so she caved immediately. Felt bad about it, but she just couldn't handle any drama right now. Not today, after she'd felt a strange lump in her breast that morning in the shower. Probably nothing. Almost certainly nothing. Going to the doctor tomorrow to get it checked, but in the meantime, it was weighing on her mind, and the last thing she wanted was a battle with Ashley. Hell, Lynette deserved to have a calm, peaceful afternoon.

So she stopped at McDonald's, and they weren't sitting in the booth for two minutes when Lynette saw something that grabbed her attention. Rather, she saw someone.

A little girl, not much older than Ashley. Sitting with a youngish man at a booth in the corner of the restaurant. Lynette looked, then looked again. She couldn't help herself. Because the little girl in the booth looked a lot like a girl who had recently gone missing. Her photo had been all over the TV and in the newspaper. The entire nation knew about her.

Just my imagination, Lynette thought. *Couldn't be her. No way would a child abductor waltz right in to a McDonald's and have lunch. How stupid would that be?*

But what if it really was the missing girl? How bad would Lynette feel if she didn't call, and then she later learned she could have saved that girl's life? Obviously, that would make her feel a million times worse than calling the police and learning she'd been wrong.

Either way, she had to make a decision, because the man and the little girl had gotten up from their booth and were heading toward the door. They took one last slurp from their Cokes before they tossed their trash away. Then they went outside.

Lynette watched through the glass as they crossed the parking lot. What would Randy think if she came home babbling about seeing an abducted girl? It sounded so crazy. So unlikely. Like something out of one of those cheesy crime shows.

Yeah, it did. But she knew what Randy would say. He'd say, "Did you write down his license plate number?"

40

I didn't learn until later that Kathleen Hanrahan didn't take my advice. She didn't call the cops, and she didn't call her lawyers, because her lawyers were actually her husband's lawyers. She considered them the enemy now.

What she did instead was continue drinking wine, until a poorly conceived plan of action blossomed in her mind.

I was in the Mustang, now going east on Bee Cave Road, back toward town. My thoughts were spinning off in a dozen directions. I'd learned a lot, but I had no idea what to do next. So I called Mia. Got her voicemail.

I said, "Check this out. According to Kathleen Hanrahan, her husband has been having an affair with Erica Kerwick for years. She's not Patrick's cousin, she's his goddamn mistress. I told Kathleen to tell all this stuff to the cops, but I don't know if she will. Oh, and I know who The Guy is now: Sean Hanrahan, Patrick's brother. Used to be a cop. You nailed it when you said it was a Boston accent. I heard him on a video. He's lived in Massachusetts for about twenty years. Anyway,

I'm heading back to my apartment right now, because I don't know what else to do at the moment. I'm sure I'll think of some way to make myself useful. So you stay on Erica's ass and let me know what's happening when you get a chance." I paused for a second, then said, "They have her, Mia. No question about it. We just need to figure out where she is now. As far as I'm concerned, proving they did it — I don't care about that. Let's just find Tracy."

There was a certain sense of momentum that I didn't want to lose. We were making progress. Slowly digging up facts. Putting pieces of the puzzle in place. Granted, there were still big sections missing, but I knew a hell of a lot more now than when I had gotten up this morning.

One thing I didn't know, as I'd mentioned to Mia, was what to do next. So I made it up as I went along.

Back in my apartment, I sat down at my computer and started researching Sean Hanrahan. Problem was, there were a lot of hits. Nearly fifty thousand. Too many Sean Hanrahans in the country. But the one I was looking for kept a low profile. Didn't find him on Facebook. Didn't find him on LinkedIn or any other professional networks. No big surprise. Contrary to dire warnings about privacy issues, your average middle-aged American doesn't have much of a record on the Internet, especially if he or she hasn't actively *participated* on the Internet.

So I narrowed down the results by searching for a combination of "sean hanrahan" plus "police officer." That immediately dropped the number of hits to 87. First hit was a newspaper article written by a guy named Sean Hanrahan about a burglary arrest in Tucson. Nope. Unrelated. That article was repeated on about a dozen other sites. In fact, the more I dug, the more I saw that most of the hits were useless.

But there was one that caught my eye. Sean Hanrahan, a cop in Brockton, Massachusetts, had received an award for pulling a woman out of a burning car after an accident. This was four years ago. The accompanying photo told me it was the right Sean Hanrahan, but I had already assumed as much. I read further. Hanrahan had been with the Brockton Police Department for fifteen years and had received several other awards in that time. He was quoted as saying, "I was just doing my job. This is what they train me to do, and what they expect me to do."

Then I found a more recent article. One in which Sean Hanrahan wasn't quite so heroic. Last fall, he'd been suspended for improper conduct during an arrest. He had Tasered a guy in handcuffs.

Bastard was fond of his Taser.

The suspension led to a hearing, which led to his eventual dismissal. The victim — who had two prior convictions for aggravated assault — was suing the department, and so was Sean Hanrahan, for wrongful termination. He claimed that the Tasering was justified because the guy in cuffs had headbutted him, making him groggy, and he was afraid the guy was about to run away. The victim said, "That's a crock. If I'd headbutted him, the dude would still be sleeping it off." There was no dash-cam video of the incident.

My phone vibrated.

A text from Mia: *She went out for lunch. Brought food back to office.*

I replied: *Stay on her. Get my voicemail?*

She said: *Yes. Vry interesting. What r u doing?*

Me: *Researching Sean H. Has a history of Taser abuse.*

Mia: *Keep me posted.*

I went back to my research, but my phone interrupted me again, this time with an incoming call. I knew it wasn't Mia, because the personalized ringtone I'd selected for her long ago was "Brick House" by the Commodores, whereas this was just a generic tone. I checked the caller I.D. No name came up. But I recognized the number.

Ruelas.

I was torn. Maybe he had something good to tell me. Or very possibly not. Answer or no? I chose no. He surprised me by not leaving a voicemail. Now I was curious as hell.

I kept looking but didn't find anything else useful about Sean Hanrahan, so I tried to learn more about Erica Kerwick. The last time I'd checked her Facebook page, her privacy settings were tight. Now I couldn't find her page at all. She'd deactivated it or changed the settings. Didn't want anyone snooping around.

My phone rang again. Ruelas for a second time. No voicemail. Damn.

I did find Erica Kerwick on LinkedIn. Her employment history said she'd worked for PAH, Inc. for eighteen years, just as Patrick Hanrahan had said. Prior to that, she'd worked briefly at a travel agency in Austin. She'd attended Austin High School, followed by the University of Texas. Didn't list the dates she'd graduated from either.

I felt like I was fumbling around. What was I searching for? Was I likely to find it online? I sat back and thought for a moment.

Someone had entered the Hanrahan home while Kathleen was sleeping and taken Tracy. I was guessing that Brian Pierce was the only person on that list who probably didn't do it. No, they'd send someone Tracy knew and trusted.

Patrick Hanrahan wouldn't do it himself, because once Tracy went missing, his actions beforehand would be scrutinized endlessly. He'd need an airtight alibi.

That left Sean Hanrahan or Erica Kerwick. My money was on Erica, because she was like a regular part of the family, even if Kathleen hated her guts. Erica took part in Hanrahan family events, at least occasionally. She saw Tracy on a fairly frequent basis and had almost certainly developed a bond with her. If Aunt Erica suddenly arrived at the Hanrahan house and told Tracy it was time to go, Tracy would go.

Okay, then what?

Erica takes Tracy directly to Brian Pierce's house? Probably. Was Sean Hanrahan already there? No way of knowing, but I assumed so. How would Tracy react to this sudden change, with neither parent around? Again, no way of knowing. Some kids would freak out, while other kids were happy just about anywhere, with just about anyone. But it didn't really matter whether Tracy was upset or not, did it? She had to go along, one way or the other.

What came next? They kept her at Pierce's house, but they moved her later. And somebody killed Pierce, for some unknown reason. Maybe Pierce was starting to have a hard time with the situation, and was about to blow it for all of them. Maybe he was ready to take Tracy back to her mom, and Patrick Hanrahan wouldn't hear of it. And his brother — the tough cop with a history of violence — took care of the situation.

Maybe.

None of that mattered, really. The only thing that mattered was figuring out where Tracy was now.

Damn phone rang for a third time, but this time I heard "Brick House." Mia. I took the call.

"What's up?"

"You talk to Ruelas?" Anxiety in her voice.

"No. He called you?"

"Just now. They found Pierce."

41

The lead detective had been on the job long enough to be realistic, if not quite cynical. Big case with lots of publicity meant hundreds of leads, and sometimes thousands. Most of them were bullshit, of course. They had to be.

But every last one had to be checked out.

So you talk to each person claiming to have seen the missing person — in this case, a little girl — and hear what they have to say. Some of them, it takes about half a minute to rule them out. When someone claims the girl was snatched by a secret cabal of neo-Nazis headed by George Clooney, all you can do is say thanks, we'll look into it. Sometimes you find yourself actually wanting *the caller to be an obvious head case, because then he or she wouldn't waste any more of your time.*

Conversely, the rational, reasonable, credible callers ate up resources and man-hours. When someone says, "I'm not positive it was her, but it sure looked like her," well, hell, you couldn't just let that go. Too many cases were solved as the result of calls like that.

So one of your team members takes each call and starts asking questions, looking for cracks in what this person is telling you. Which city are you calling from? What day did this happen? What time? If the missing person was supposedly seen in Buffalo on Wednesday at three o'clock, but you had her on video in Tucson at about the same time, you could hang up. How tall was she? Four feet? How sure are you about that? Nope. This missing girl is about a foot shorter than that. On and on, like that. How long was her hair? Weight? Color of her eyes? Scars? Type and color of clothes? How far away were you? Did you speak to her? Who was she with? Overhear any conversation? Did you hear any names?

Little by little, you whittle away. Find a fatal flaw that means this is another dead end, and you say, "We certainly appreciate your call. We'll let you know if we learn anything." And that was it. On to the next one.

But some of the credible calls can't be dismissed that easily, so they make it past the initial screening. You have to expend even more time and resources on them.

Like this McDonald's lady.

Says she saw a little girl earlier today. Description was spot on. Right age, height, weight, hair color, et cetera. Says the girl was with a white male, approximately 25 to 30 years old. Average height and weight. Brown hair. Clean shaven. Nothing particularly memorable about the guy. Nothing that raised any red flags, except that the little girl looked familiar. She looked like the missing girl. So the lady had written down the man's license plate number, just in case. And later, when she got home, she pulled up the missing girl's photo on the Internet.

And oh, Lord, she immediately knew she'd been right.

Are you positive? "Yes, it was her. I have no doubt about it at all."

How many times had he heard that? Simple enough in a situation like this to run the plate number and get a name. Then run the name and see who you're dealing with.

So the detective did that, and what he learned made him wonder — without getting unduly excited about it — if maybe he'd found a needle in the haystack. Because this guy, despite his appearances, wasn't as ordinary as he looked.

His name was Daniel Wayne Bertram. Twenty-seven years old. Record was almost spotless. Almost. But that one entry sure raised a red flag.

Three years earlier, Bertram had been arrested for public lewdness. A sex crime. Worth calling up the file and digging deeper. And the detective saw that the crime had taken place at a public swimming pool. The report said Bertram had sat just so, purposefully, with his legs splayed open, and he had tugged his suit over in a way that would allow a woman nearby to get a look at his genitalia. Had done it several times, until the complainant "knew it wasn't an accident." What she had done then — oh, man, why couldn't every complainant be as clever as this one? — was videotape the son of a bitch.

And the woman had been especially pissed off about it, because she wasn't alone. Her four-year-old daughter had been with her.

42

"Was he still dead?" I said.

"That's not funny, Roy."

"It's a little funny." But, at the same time, I found myself looking over at my front door to make sure I'd remembered to lock the deadbolt.

She said, "I'd say you were right, that Ruelas is thinking of you as a suspect."

"Who found the body?"

"He didn't say."

"Did you ask?"

"Yeah. All he said was he wanted to talk to you. He asked where you were."

"What did you tell him?"

"That I didn't know."

My doorbell rang. I can't tell you how quickly my heart sank when I heard that. I was hoping I'd have a little more time.

"Roy?"

I got up quietly and walked softly into the bedroom.

"Roy?"

"Yeah?" I whispered.

"Was that your doorbell?"

"Yep."

"What are you going to do?"

"Hold on a sec." One window in the bedroom faced the parking area in front of my apartment. I peeked around the edges of the blinds and saw a patrol car parked along the red-curbed no-parking zone. "Cops are here," I said. I sat on the edge of the bed. "Does Ruelas know I'm driving your car?"

"No."

"If you talk to him again, definitely don't tell him that."

I was glad I had parked Mia's Mustang in the far reaches of the lot so it wouldn't get dinged. Less noticeable over there. Meanwhile, the cop at my door had probably been told to look for the van.

"I'm not an idiot. What are you going to do, Roy?"

"Not much I can do, for the moment."

The doorbell rang again.

"Could they have gotten a warrant?"

"Search warrant or arrest warrant?"

"Either one."

"With what probable cause? I'm betting Ruelas just wants to grill me."

"Maybe you should talk to him."

"Not in person. No way. Not right now. Not gonna let that buffoon waste my time. We're too close to figuring this out."

"Honestly, Roy, I don't feel close."

I heard a car door close. I peeked out the window and watched as the patrol car pulled away.

I said, "Cops just left. For the moment, anyway."

"Did you hear what I said?"

"That you don't feel close to solving this? I don't understand why you'd say that."

"We have no idea where Tracy is. They could've taken her anywhere."

"Okay, let's talk about that. At this point, we have to conclude that Tracy is with Sean Hanrahan, right?"

"Most likely."

"Almost certainly."

"I guess."

"So think about this. If you were him, would you attempt to travel a great distance — even by car — in the company of the most sought-after missing person in the nation? A huge portion of the population has seen photos of Tracy."

I gave her a few seconds to mull it over.

"No," she said. "I'd hole up somewhere. That's what they were doing at Pierce's."

"Exactly, but something went wrong and Pierce ended up dead. So where did they go?"

I wanted to get her spirits back up. Answering questions — even in the form of informed conjecture — would make her realize we *were* close.

"I wouldn't go to a hotel or motel," she said. "Too easy to get spotted. Plus, you can't check in anywhere nowadays with just cash, so he'd be leaving a paper trail that might be used as evidence later, or to track him down if they start looking for him. Hey, what about — "
She stopped.

"What?"

"I was thinking about the photos we saw on Facebook. The ones taken at the Hanrahans' place on South Padre Island. If they own a vacation place down there, that might be a good place to hide. But we already agreed that Sean Hanrahan wouldn't want to drive a long distance, and that's, what, six hours?"

"If you don't speed, yeah, about that. It's tempting to consider, but I think you're right. Too far."

"Still. If he drove after sundown, so nobody could see inside the car..."

"All it would take is one simple traffic stop and he's screwed. I just don't think they'd risk it."

"But we're guessing."

"Bottom line, yeah, we're guessing. That's all we *can* do, short of driving down there."

The line went quiet as we both considered other possibilities.

Mia said, "What if there's a fifth person involved? Someone we don't know about?"

"I guess it's possible, but I don't know who it would be. And right now, we don't have any reason to think there's a fifth."

"Well, I'm running out of ideas."

"Can you stay on Erica Kerwick?"

"Yeah."

"If anyone's going to lead us to Sean Hanrahan, it's her, not Patrick."

"Agreed."

"I'd come spell you, but I think it's best if I keep my distance now, considering."

"Are you going to go anywhere?"

"You mean to avoid the cops, or to look for Sean Hanrahan?"

"Either."

"Don't know yet. Wouldn't know where to go. The cops can't just break into my apartment without a warrant. In fact, I could answer the door and tell them I'm not interested in talking. But I think I'd rather not let them know where I am."

"What should I do if Ruelas calls again?"

"Voicemail. No, wait. Don't worry, he won't call you again."

"Why? What are you going to do?"

Call him back. That's what I was going to do.

But first, I dug around on YouTube until I found a video that featured airport announcements. Really. Who would upload that sort of crap? I didn't really care, to be honest. I simply queued it up, with the sound turned low, then I dialed Ruelas and he answered on the first ring.

"Thanks for getting in touch. Have you spoken to Mia?" The pseudo-cordial patter of a bureaucrat on autopilot. Not an asshole this time.

"We use smoke signals."

"I'm assuming she's told you that Brian Pierce was found dead."

"She did."

"Listen — where are you right now?"

"At the gym, working my pecs. I am so jacked. I'm huge, bro."

"Really, where are you?"

"Why?"

"I think we should talk about this. Maybe you can help me figure some things out."

"Yeah, that's you. Always looking for help from guys like me.

Because you're so humble and you understand your limitations."

It didn't faze him in the least. "Can we meet?"

"We can talk now."

"If we could just sit down for a few minutes and — "

"We can talk now. That's the only way it's going to happen. Take it or leave it. I don't have much time."

I'll admit I was taking an inordinate amount of pleasure in giving him a hard time. And I just knew the faint airport sounds were driving him crazy.

He sighed — which meant he was shedding the nice-guy persona — and said, "I understand you had a little chat with Kathleen Hanrahan."

"I did. Did she call you?"

"She's the one who found Pierce's body. Sounds like you got her all hyped up about Pierce, then sent her over to his house. That how it happened?"

"Nope. What else you want to know?"

"She rammed her damn SUV through Pierce's gate and went stomping all over the crime scene. Drunk as hell. Lucky she didn't kill anybody along the way. Nearly incoherent, but she did manage to tell us that you told her Tracy was at Pierce's house."

"I didn't say that. I said I was almost positive I saw Tracy there on Wednesday of last week. I didn't say anything about Tracy being there now. In fact, I told her you searched the place and didn't find anything. Has she told you Patrick Hanrahan had an affair with Erica Kerwick, and that she thinks the affair is still going on?"

The silence told me I'd taken him by surprise, and it made me realize just how reluctant Kathleen was to have the affair become public knowledge. Too ashamed or embarrassed, or simply too much pride. But I had no problem divulging these details to Ruelas. Maybe the information would help him find Tracy. I didn't care who found her, as long as she was found.

When Ruelas recovered, he ignored what I'd just told him and said, "Have you ever been to Brian Pierce's house?"

"Well, he did host a Tupperware party once."

"Yes or no?"

"You know I have. I told you I saw Tracy Turner there."

"No, I mean actually on the property. Or inside the house."

"No comment. But I can tell you that I didn't kill Pierce. That's what you're wondering."

"How do you know someone killed him? He could have died naturally."

"Because you just called it a 'crime scene.' Are we really going to play these games? I understand that I'm an obvious suspect, but strike me from the list or you'll be wasting your time."

"You know I can't do that. Not until I get some answers."

I was getting frustrated. All of those old buried feelings — cops not believing what I was telling them — were coming back. "Jesus, I know you're not that dumb. You're an asshole, for sure, but you're not an idiot. I didn't kill Pierce. I know you know that. So move on. Find Sean Hanrahan. Surely you've figured that part out by now. You know about Patrick's brother and why he was fired. You figured out he's the guy in the video I showed you. Find Sean Hanrahan and you'll find the girl. Not only that, you'll be a step closer to knowing who killed Pierce."

Ruelas didn't respond for a very long time. I waited. I wasn't going to give him any additional details that could cause me problems, but maybe I could learn something from things he might say. Finally, he said, "We've been looking for Sean. No luck so far. He won't answer his phone or return our calls. You got any ideas?"

Once again, his tone had changed. Sounded like he was acknowledging what I was telling him and now he was just wanting to be practical and stop chasing dead ends. He didn't seem bothered at all by the outright insult, but in his line of work, he had probably become immune to all sorts of abuse.

I said, "It's a long shot, but the Hanrahans have a place in South Padre."

"Already had it checked out. No luck."

"Then I'm out of ideas. That's the truth."

Another silence followed. Then he said, "By the way, you're not fooling anyone with that airport bullshit."

I reached for the mouse and closed my browser, killing the video. I said. "Fair enough. And if you ask Mia out again, I'm gonna kick your ass."

I heard a chuckle as he hung up.

43

I spent more time in front of the computer, rooting around for information about the Hanrahan brothers. I wasn't looking for anything in particular, because I didn't know what to look for. But sometimes that approach works. You stumble on something that you couldn't possibly have known, and it proves useful.

Not this time, though.

I dug through dozens of old newspaper and magazine articles about Patrick Hanrahan and his slow but steady rise to success. He wasn't some flashy Internet genius who burst onto the scene and quickly made a zillion bucks. No, he did it the old-fashioned way, starting businesses and nurturing them with hard work and long hours. His first venture, nearly twenty years ago, was a pizza franchise. A well-known Texas brand that had been in business for two decades. That did well, so he opened two more. Started making some pretty good money.

Then he tried something much different than pizzas. He opened a Toyota dealership. This, as far as I could tell, was his only career misstep. He had no experience in that industry, and it did not go well. Not a total disaster, but he did lose some money, so he sold it after a few years.

Went back to restaurants. This time, he came up with an idea of his own. A place called Texas Taco. Fast food, more or less, but healthy. Lean beef and fresh vegetables. It was a big hit immediately, and before long he had three more. Pretty soon, another regional chain bought him out. Rumor was that he got about ten million in the deal. This was fourteen years ago.

After that, he opened a high-end seafood restaurant in downtown Austin. Patrick's Pier, it was called. I'd heard of it but hadn't ever been there, not being a fan of seafood. And, until now, I couldn't have told you who the Patrick in the name was.

Then he opened Chowders — where Kathleen, Jessica, and Brian Pierce had all worked. Also seafood, and not cheap, but not quite as high-end as Patrick's. According to the articles I found, Hanrahan realized the two places were competing with each other, so he closed Chowders.

Then he opened La Tolteca, which was another big hit for him. There was only one in the Austin area, but there were about a dozen more scattered around the southwest. Made a rich man even richer.

This was all very inspiring, but none of it was helpful.

I jumped onto Facebook and went back to Curtis Hanrahan's page. From there, I snooped from one Hanrahan page to another. I didn't know how most of these people were related to Patrick, Sean, and Kathleen, but they were all family, I knew that much, so maybe I'd see something that would help. Maybe a mention of some other vacation home. Or some innocuous comment about Sean's recent whereabouts. But I found nothing.

I received a text from Mia a little after six in the evening, telling me that Erica Kerwick had just left the office. Did I want Mia to follow her? I said yes, let's see where she goes. I was really hoping Erica would take us directly to Sean Hanrahan and Tracy Turner, but no such luck. She went straight home to a cottage in Tarrytown. Nice area. Homes more expensive than you'd expect an executive secretary to afford. Maybe Hanrahan had helped her buy it. Did that matter?

Three hours later, I had grabbed a bite to eat and was just sitting down at the computer again when Mia called. "She hasn't budged. Lights in the living room just went out. I think she's in for the night."

It was nine-fifteen.

"Is the van sticking out like a sore thumb?"

"No, there are lots of cars parked along the curbs."

"Do you mind hanging around one more hour?"

"Sure thing. What about tomorrow morning?"

What I wanted was for Mia to be staked out and waiting at sunrise, or even earlier, or maybe even spend the night watching Erica Kerwick's house. But Mia hadn't signed up for this bullshit. She wasn't even making any money on this fiasco. So I said, "Sleep late. I'll call you when I figure out what to do next."

"You sure?"

"Yeah. I don't want to burn you out and make you miss bartending."

"Yeah, right. Don't worry about it. Believe it or not, I'm enjoying myself. You learning anything over there?"

"Oh, you bet. For instance, did you know there's a young lady named Elizabeth Hanrahan who has an unnatural fondness for unicorns? She even writes poetry about them. Really bad poetry."

"And you're qualified to judge poetry?"

"Point taken. Have you seen anyone else hanging around? Cops?"

"No. Why?"

I told her about my conversation with Ruelas, and how I thought they might send someone to keep tabs on Erica Kerwick. Apparently, they hadn't done that, or they were so good at it, Mia hadn't seen them. Doubtful.

She said, "You think you're off the hook with Ruelas?"

"I think so, yeah. Guy's an asshole, and I told him that, but he's smart enough to know I didn't kill Pierce."

"Good. I was worried. A pretty boy like you would be eaten alive in prison."

"It's my high cheekbones," I said. "Irresistible."

"Tell me about it."

At that moment, I would not have believed I was six hours away from blowing this case wide open.

Once, while waiting in my dentist's office, I read an article about "dream incubation," which was first researched by some smart professor at Harvard. Supposedly, you can use your dreams to solve problems. Sort of similar to lucid dreaming, the topic for the movie

Inception, but a little different.

You start by focusing your mind on a particular issue right before you go to sleep. Maybe even write the problem down on a piece of paper, and then, when you lie down, visualize the problem as a concrete image. Focus on it intensely. Then, when you wake up — *presto!* — you have a new perspective. Fresh ideas. A smarter way of approaching the problem. That was the gist of it, but it sounded like a truckload of horseshit to me.

But maybe it works, because when I finally went to bed, I couldn't think of anything other than finding Tracy Turner — I was obsessed, bordering on frantic — and when I woke up just after one in the morning, I realized I'd overlooked something.

Not South Padre.

But the same train of thought.

When I'd accessed the tax records to get the Hanrahans' address earlier today — actually, it was yesterday now — I'd noticed they owned half a dozen properties in Travis County. I hadn't looked at the records closely, or at all, really. I didn't even think about the implications, because it wasn't unusual for wealthy people to own all kinds of real estate.

But now I was wondering: What were these properties? Business real estate owned by PAH, Hanrahan's corporation? Nope. Those wouldn't have shown up under the name Hanrahan. Those would be kept separate. No, instead, those listings in the records would be for homes, condos, townhomes, raw acreage, maybe a ranch in the rural part of the county. That sort of thing.

I sat up in bed. Wide awake now.

Went to my computer and clicked the bookmark for the county tax records. Typed in his name. Seven listings in total for Patrick and Kathleen Hanrahan. One, of course, was the home in Westlake Hills. The other six?

One was a small condo in a high-dollar high-rise downtown. Date of the deed was just three years ago. I was willing to wager that Hanrahan had purchased it simply to have a nice little getaway in the heart of the city.

Another listing was for an empty lot, and I realized it was simply a tract adjoining the tract on which their home was built. They'd bought two tracts and combined them into one homesite.

But the remaining four listings? Homes in various neighborhoods throughout the city. The oldest date of deed was twenty-two years ago. The newest was six years ago. If you plotted the value of these four homes on a chart, along with the home in Westlake Hills, you'd notice a steady rise in size and value.

I got a chill down my spine as I realized what this meant.

These were the homes Hanrahan had owned and lived in as his wealth slowly grew. He hadn't ever sold them. He had almost certainly held onto them as an investment, recognizing — correctly — that real estate in the Austin area would pay off very well. No doubt he hired a property-management company to lease those homes out for him.

The big question running through my mind right then, as I sat in front of my computer in my underwear in the middle of the night...

What if one of those homes was empty?

44

I printed the addresses of all four homes, along with a map to the one house that was in an area I didn't know well — Great Hills, in the northwestern part of town. But the remaining three were out west, in either Rollingwood or West Lake Hills. It wouldn't take long to check them all out.

I debated calling Mia and letting her know where I was going, but why wake her up? I was jazzed that I'd had this idea, but now that I was good and awake, I knew that the odds were slim. Sure, look into it, but don't expect too much. That's what the rational part of my brain was saying. But the rest was pumped by the possibilities. Buzzing. Adrenaline was flowing as I got dressed, grabbed the keys to the Mustang, and headed for the door.

And froze.

I heard a noise. Right outside my apartment. Not much of a noise, but enough. Hard to describe. A buzz, or a hiss. Then it stopped. And started again.

I stepped softly to my door and listened. Whatever it was, it was literally right outside, just a few feet away. My door is one of four in a breezeway between two buildings in the complex. Very private, without much foot traffic. I looked through the peephole and saw movement, but nothing that I could identify. My porch light was off. There was some ambient light — maybe from a neighbor's porch light — but it wasn't enough to let me see what was happening.

Ruelas.

That's what I was thinking. Maybe I hadn't really convinced him that I shouldn't be a suspect in Brian Pierce's murder. Anyone who watches real-life cop shows knows that arrest warrants are often served in the middle of the night. Catch the suspect off guard, in bed, confused. Was that happening here? If so, I had no place to go. There would be no getaway.

More hissing.

I looked through the peephole again, but it didn't help much. Still saw movement, but there could have been one person out there or an entire SWAT team. No voices. No lights. No muted crackle of radio communication.

The hissing stopped.

So strange. No idea what was happening out there, but I was damn sure going to find out. In one quick movement, I reached out with both hands, unlocked the deadbolt, and yanked the door open.

A dark figure was standing in front of me — surprised, I think — with his right arm raised and an object pointing at my face. Could've been a gun, a knife, but I didn't wait to find out. I launched myself at the figure, wrapping both arms around his torso and tackling him to the ground. I could tell it was a male, but, fortunately, this was not a large man. Didn't mean he wasn't strong, or driven by adrenaline.

He fought back. Hard.

We were on the concrete, wrestling, and neither of us had an advantage yet. Too dark to get a look at the guy. I had his left arm clasped around the wrist, so he couldn't get up and run away, but his right arm was still free. When I'd taken him down, I'd been aware of a clattering sound — something metal hitting the walkway. A strange tinny sound, with a rattle to it. Whatever it was, I was pretty sure it meant that I'd knocked loose whatever he'd been holding in his hand. In any case, I didn't feel the steely blade of a knife plunging into my back. What I felt instead was him flailing at the side of my head, trying to hit me, but not doing a very good job.

"Stop!" I said.

Yeah, like that would work. He kept whacking away, grunting with the effort, but his punching skills were poor. Of course, since one of his arms was free, that meant one of mine was, too. My left. Luckily, I've always been a bit ambidextrous. Not a lot of room to draw back and throw an effective punch, so I used my open palm to give him a quick, firm smack on the underside of his jaw. His teeth slammed together with an audible crack. You might be surprised how quickly this can take the fight out of someone.

Then I raised my arm high, fist straight up, and brought my elbow down directly on the bridge of his nose. I could feel the cartilage give, and he squealed in pain. While he was dazed, I quickly grabbed his right arm and held it tight, then straddled his chest. I had him pinned. Right then, the porch light went on at the apartment directly across the breezeway from mine, which allowed me to get a good look at him.

And I recognized the son of a bitch.

"Oh, you've got to be kidding me."

He'd grown a goatee and put on a few pounds, but there was no mistaking his identity.

Ernie Crenshaw. Ernie fucking Crenshaw. My old boss. The one who'd pressed charges when I'd broken his nose. I hadn't seen him since.

"Ernie, you idiot." I was short of breath. Amazing how thirty seconds of close combat can wear you out.

I looked to my left to see what he'd been holding in his hand. A can of spray paint. I twisted around to see my apartment door. He'd painted the word "ASS" in bright orange letters. He'd been in the process of writing "HOLE" beneath that, but he'd only gotten as far as the H and the O.

I heard the neighbor's door open. She was peeking out from behind a security chain.

"Rita?"

"Are you okay, Roy?"

"Yeah. Have you called the cops?"

"Not yet."

"Please don't, okay? Everything's fine. I'm sorry for the disturbance."

"You sure?"

"We were just goofing around and it got a little rough. Sorry to wake you."

She lingered in the doorway for a few more seconds, then closed the door.

Ernie still had not said a word.

"You flattened my tires on Sunday, didn't you? And on Thursday of last week."

He turned his head and spat out a fairly generous amount of blood. But his breathing seemed to be okay.

"It's always been you, right? All those times my tires got flattened. The broken antennas and smashed windshields. I thought I had a lot of enemies, but it was just you."

He said, "You broke my goddamn nose. Again."

"Jesus, Ernie, it's been three years. Isn't it time to move on?"

My thighs were starting to burn from sitting on top of him. I let go of his wrists. He wouldn't have the guts to try anything.

"I could call the cops," I said. "Tell them what you did tonight. But I'd say we're even now. You need to leave my van alone. And leave me alone. Otherwise, I'm coming at you hard, without the cops."

He didn't say anything.

"You understand, Ernie?"

After a few seconds. He nodded.

"I have to go somewhere," I said. "And while I'm gone, you'd better figure out a way to clean that paint off my door."

I started with the address in Great Hills.

Cruised past slowly and immediately saw signs of inhabitants. The lawn had been mowed recently. I could tell that much from the sweep of my headlights. Even more obvious, there was a car in the driveway.

And the clincher? There was light coming from a couple of different windows. Not a lot of light, with people still awake inside, but the faint light from a small lamp or even a computer's screen saver. There was always some amount of light in a home, even when everyone was sleeping.

Sean Hanrahan and Tracy Turner were not in there. If they'd decided to hide in one of the homes, that meant the home wasn't leased, which in turn meant that the electricity would not be turned on. The juice got turned off and back on between residents. That was standard.

A new renter had to arrange for the electricity to be turned on and put down a deposit. And if Patrick was hiding Tracy at one of these houses, he wouldn't be dumb enough to turn the electricity on. Big red flag.

I wasn't discouraged. Still had three houses to go.

At the second one, on Hatley Drive in Rollingwood, it was the same thing. Car in the driveway, light in the house. They weren't here either.

So I moved on to the third home, a few blocks away on Pickwick Lane. On first pass, it seemed to have possibilities. No cars. No lights. The lawn was a bit scruffy. It appeared to be empty. I drove past in both directions, slowly, looking for the slightest hint of light from any window that I could see. Nothing.

So I parked down the street, along the curb in front of an empty lot. Walked back toward the home. Turned onto the sidewalk near the mailbox and walked straight up the steps to the front door, as if I belonged there. *Yeah, it's the middle of the night, but don't mind me. I'm supposed to be here.*

Like most front doors nowadays — especially doors in nicer homes — this one had leaded glass inset in the top half. So I could see inside the house. No light anywhere. I knew it was a long shot that any of the neighbors were watching me right now — hell, it was a longshot that any neighbors could even *see* me right now — but I pretended to ring the doorbell anyway. I couldn't actually see the doorbell, so I just poked my finger out in the dark. Then I waited. Nothing happened, of course.

I retreated down the steps and walked over to the garage on the east side of the house. No windows in the garage door. I was hoping that a motion-activated security light might snap on, answering the question for me, but no such luck.

I stood quietly in front of the garage door for a few seconds, just listening. There could be a car or two inside the garage, which would explain why there were no cars in the driveway. Or the garage might be completely empty.

The only windows I hadn't been able to see so far were in the rear of the house. Had to go through a gate in a six-foot picket fence to get into the backyard. There was no lock on the hasp. I lifted the latch and slowly swung the gate open. Nice and quiet. Left it open and stepped into the backyard.

Stood there for a minute and let my eyes adjust. There was a wooden deck, but there was no outdoor furniture of any kind on it. Growing along the rear property line was a wall of bamboo, which provided plenty of privacy.

I moved forward, but after just five or six steps, I stopped cold. I saw a very faint glow in a window beside the back door. Light. Not much, but enough. The electricity was on. The house was occupied.

I retreated as slowly as I'd come in. Closed and latched the gate behind me. Proceeded down the driveway and back to the Mustang. Fired it up and eased away from the curb and down the street, feeling conspicuous as hell because of the growl of the big engine.

Now I was down to one. One house. If they weren't there, well, I didn't know what I'd do next. I had no ideas left. I still had the will to keep looking — tomorrow, the next day, the day after that — but I didn't know *where* to look. Not unlike nine years ago. Driving the streets aimlessly. Wracked with frustration because I didn't know what to do with myself.

One house.

I couldn't get my hopes up. Wouldn't allow it. Didn't want the disappointment. Instead, I just drove. Back onto Bee Cave Road, then west. Took a right on Buckeye Trail and began the steep climb to the top of the hill. Then I followed the twists and turns past homes tucked in among the cedar and oak trees. Similar to Hanrahan's current neighborhood on Toro Canyon, except maybe a tad less expensive.

I watched the addresses as I got closer and closer. This home would be on the right-hand side. I came around one more curve and saw the right numbers painted on a mailbox. The fourth house on my list.

The porch light was on. SUV in the driveway.

Damn.

I drove past.

It had been a great idea. Creative. But it hadn't panned out. I continued on Buckeye Trail, down the hill on the other side, to Westlake Drive. Took a left, then a right on Redbud Trail. Crossed the low-water bridge and turned right on Lake Austin Boulevard. Back into Austin.

I was waiting at a red light, so close to heading back to my apartment, when I finally realized my mistake.

45

Daniel Wayne Bertram was not an easy man to track down.

First call went to his probation officer, who had last seen Bertram at a regular monthly meeting three weeks earlier. She gave the detective all of Bertram's info, including an address, which turned out to be a rental. Convenient. Texas law allows a landlord to inspect a property just about any time he or she wants. The detective called the landlord to see if he'd cooperate, maybe take a peek inside, but the landlord said, "Yeah, he was in there until a few months ago, but he skipped out. Owed me about four grand in back rent."

"Any idea where he went?"

"Not a clue."

"Any references listed on his application?"

"Nope. I keep it pretty simple. If they pass the credit check and can cough up a deposit, hey, that's good enough for me. This is the first time I seriously got screwed."

"You got a phone number for him?"

"Yeah, but it was dead the last time I tried it."

"Let me have it anyway."

It was the same number that the probation officer had provided, *which the detective had already checked himself.*

So the detective called the work number that the probation officer had given him. Manager said Bertram had quit two weeks ago.

This was bad, but it might also be very good.

Why was Bertram suddenly breaking all the rules of his probation? You change your address or quit a job, you're supposed to report that immediately.

The detective figured it wasn't a coincidence.

So he dug deeper. Bertram had no siblings, and his parents were long dead in a car wreck. He didn't own any real estate in the county, or in any of the surrounding counties.

He had an uncle, though. Sid Bertram. Sid was nearly eighty years old and lived in a house he and his wife had bought forty-seven years earlier up in Barton Hills. A widower now.

The detective started to dial a number, then decided it was worth a drive. And once he got there, he was smart enough to knock on a couple of neighbors' doors first, just in case. Neighbor on the left didn't answer, but the neighbor on the right did. He was holding an acoustic guitar when he opened the door. Shirtless. Young guy with scruffy hair. Austin was crawling with wannabe musicians.

"Yeah?"

Despite what they say in books and movies, people can't peg a cop from looks alone, especially when you're wearing jeans, tennis shoes, and a golf shirt. So the detective quickly identified himself and showed his shield.

"You know Sid next door?"

"Sure. What's up? He okay?"

"I haven't talked to him yet. You seen anyone else around there lately?"

"Actually, yeah. Young guy. Sid told me he had a grandson, so I figure that's who it is. Wait, I mean a nephew, not a grandson."

"Have you talked to him?"

"The nephew? No, I've just seen him come and go a couple of times."

"With Sid?"

The man shook his head. "No, I haven't seen Sid in a couple of weeks."

"You normally see him more than that?"

"Almost every day — walking his dog, or out working in his yard. He's pretty active for a guy his age. Come to think of it, I haven't seen Jack in awhile either."

"Who's Jack?"

"The dog. He's a barker, always chasing squirrels. But now I'm realizing how quiet it's been around here lately. You're freaking me out a little. You think Sid's okay?"

"You mind if I come inside for a minute?"

46

Doorbell buttons are lighted.

I sat unmoving in the Mustang as the stoplight went from red to green to yellow and back to red again. There wasn't another vehicle in sight. Warm night, with the windows down, but I had goosebumps on my arms.

Doorbell buttons are lighted.

That way, when visitors are standing on your porch in the dark, they can see to ring the bell. In all but the most inexpensive homes, and maybe in some very old homes, doorbell buttons are lighted. But the doorbell button at the third home had not been lighted. I'd stood right there on the porch and not noticed it. I'd even poked my finger out into the dark, mimicking ringing the bell. But I hadn't been able to see the bell.

I could think of two possible explanations. The light had burned out or was otherwise malfunctioning. Or the electricity at the house wasn't turned on after all.

But what about the glow from the window I'd seen near the back door of the house?

So what? Didn't mean there was electricity. If I were Sean

Hanrahan, hiding out in an empty house with my six-year-old niece, I'd want light of some kind. A six year old might be freaked out in the dark. Hell, even without a six year old, I'd want some light. Some kind of battery-operated lantern. Maybe even a battery-operated TV. And a radio.

The stoplight cycled through again.

And I'd set up in a room to the rear of the house, where the picket fence and towering wall of bamboo would prevent neighbors from seeing faint light in a window.

My hands were starting to sweat. This was it. It had to be.

The light turned green and I made a U-turn.

I parked farther away this time. Two blocks. In front of a house, along the curb. If the owner were an insomniac and peeked out the window, he might wonder why this kickass Mustang was sitting out front, but that wasn't a concern at the moment.

Maybe I wasn't very creative, but only two plans had run through my head on the drive over, and I wasn't positive I was choosing the right one.

Plan A involved simply staking out the house and watching it. But for how long? Days? Weeks? Months? Sounded crazy, but it was possible it could stretch on that long. They could have laid in a stockpile of food. Even if Mia and I traded off shifts, it wasn't a realistic plan. Besides, I didn't have the patience for it. Tracy Turner was in that house. There was no other conclusion. So I was finally going to bring this ordeal to an end. No more delays.

Which meant Plan B.

Still sitting in the Mustang, I opened my phone and made a call. Three-thirty in the morning. Ruelas answered on the second ring, sounding groggy.

"Yeah?" he said. Didn't realize it was me. He hadn't ever bothered assigning a name to my number. Probably figured it wasn't worth the effort. Realistically, how many times would he talk to me?

"It's Roy Ballard."

I heard an exasperated groan. Then there was a long pause. Then he said, "What the fuck is wrong with you?"

"I inhaled paint fumes as a child."

"See, the problem is, you think you're clever, but you aren't. Your friends should be honest with you about that, if you have any."

I said, "I know where Tracy Turner is. I'm two blocks from the house where she is being kept."

"You're an idiot."

"I'm going inside in about ten minutes. You should join me. It'll be fun."

"Bullshit."

"That's fine. I'll go in alone." I used that tone of voice people use when they are about to hang up. It worked.

"Fuck it, I'll play along. Where is she?"

"We looked into South Padre, but we didn't follow that path far enough. We didn't think about other properties Hanrahan owns. The tax rolls show four houses in his name in Travis County."

I waited. The silence told me he hadn't known about the homes, or it simply hadn't occurred to him. All that manpower at the sheriff's office, yet none of them had checked into something that now seemed so obvious.

I said, "Tracy and Sean are in a house in Rollingwood, on Pickwick Lane."

"You've seen them?"

"No."

"Then how do you know?"

"There was light in a back window, but the doorbell wasn't lighted."

"Meaning no juice to the house."

I was a little bummed that he'd connected the dots so quickly. "Right."

"Or a faulty doorbell," he said.

"What are the odds of that?"

"Sounds like a wild-ass hunch to me."

"Fine. I'll go in by myself and take all the glory. Tell the media what a wimp you are. Tell 'em I gave you a chance to join me, but you weren't interested."

Another long pause, accompanied by the creak of some wooden furniture. He was sitting up in bed.

"What's the address?"

I gave it to him.

He said, "You hang tight and I'll — "

"Forget it. Ten minutes, whether you're here or not."

"You understand that you — "

"I don't want to hear it."

"You'll be committing a felony. I'll arrest you myself."

"You've got nine minutes."

I hung up.

I didn't know where Ruelas lived, but chances were slim that he could get dressed and drive to the address in nine minutes. Didn't matter. I would wait as long as it took — for him, or for whomever arrived first. I would wait just long enough for them to arrive and step from the vehicle.

A patrol car arrived in seven minutes. Rollingwood isn't a big place. A cop could reach just about any part of it in less than five minutes. So Ruelas had called, explained himself in about a minute, and they'd dispatched a car.

The unit came slowly up the street, no cherries, no siren, and by then I was on the sidewalk leading to the front door of the house.

My heart was pounding. Mouth dry. Palms sweaty. I was so ready for this all to come to an end.

The patrol car eased to a stop in front of the house. Not stealthy. Obvious as hell. But that didn't matter. Not for what I had planned. I could see the cop inside the car — just one guy, softly illuminated from the lights on the dashboard. He was maybe fifteen yards away from me. A few seconds passed. It was dark enough that I didn't know if he could see me. I could feel my phone vibrating in my pocket. Had to be Ruelas calling. I didn't look. I needed to wait and see what this cop would do. But he wasn't going to go inside the house with me. Neither would Ruelas, if he were here. No cop would — unless he wanted to be fired.

Now the patrolman turned on his exterior searchlight and quickly swept the yard with it. Landed on me and held steady. I held one hand up to block the light. Held the other hand out to my side, fingers splayed, to show that I didn't have a weapon.

Despite blocking the light, I couldn't see anything. I heard his car door open.

"Rollingwood police officer. Please face away from me and place your hands on your head."

No, he wouldn't go inside the house with me. But he'd certainly go in *after* me.

I turned away slowly, my hands remaining in plain sight, and then I began to trot along the sidewalk toward the house. The cop shouted something at me. I picked up speed, mounted the steps, and busted the front door open with one enormous kick.

47

It all happened so fast.

That's the classic remark from people who've been involved in a car wreck — or in any sudden, unexpected event that creates fear or panic. A street mugging. A fistfight. Getting caught in a flash flood. Being attacked by a dog.

Studies show that adrenaline enhances your memory, and that seems true to some degree. If you're in an airplane that makes an emergency landing, you're not likely to ever forget that, are you? But the smaller details? Those are what people can't remember. The color of the car that sideswiped them. The height of the man with a shotgun who held up a convenience store. Ask three people for a description of the robber and you'll get three different responses. The big picture is clear, but the details are fuzzy.

I remember this: When I went through the darkened doorway, I shouted, "Police!" as loudly as I could. Why not? Getting charged with impersonating a police officer was the least of my worries.

I could see very little. Just seconds ago, the cop had been aiming his spotlight at me, and now I was in the dark, and my eyes weren't adjusting. But I couldn't hesitate. The cop would be right behind me.

So I plowed forward almost blind. Fumbled my way through that room and went through an open doorway. No idea what type of room I was in now, because I still couldn't see a damn thing. Dining room?

And then there was some light. Not steady light, but dancing, swaying light, coming from behind. The cop — with a flashlight. He yelled, telling me to freeze. He was close. Very close.

I ran straight for a closed door. If I hadn't lost my bearings, that door would lead to a room that was in the rear of the house. The room I'd seen from the backyard. The room that had had light sneaking around the curtains.

I didn't even bother with the knob. I just hit that door full force with my shoulder, running at nearly top speed. It was a typical interior door. Not solid wood. Hollow core. Lightweight.

In the timespan of about a thousandth of a second, the veneer facing began to crunch under the impact, and then the door gave, swinging open violently and slamming into the wall at the end of its arc.

What happened next?

I can tell you, but I can't be certain of the details. Then again, do they matter?

I was standing in that doorway, facing a darkened room, and then a brilliant light hit me full in the face. Not from the cop, of course, because he was behind me. Someone was in this room with a powerful spotlight.

In hindsight, I understand that the person behind the light shined it on me just long enough to ascertain that I wasn't a cop — or at least I wasn't a uniformed cop — despite what I'd yelled when I came through the front door. And he wouldn't have guessed there was an actual cop following in my wake. It would have been crazy to shoot a cop, knowing that other cops would follow. But a civilian who appeared to be alone?

I remember the briefest pause, standing there in that doorway, out of breath, not knowing what to do next, and wishing I could see whether I had been right.

And then there was a sound. Extremely loud. Like a tremendous lightning bolt that strikes too close to home. I couldn't have told you it was the blast of a .357. But I guess I should have expected it.

The impact was enormous. I suddenly had no air, and I realized I was no longer standing.

I heard a high-pitched scream. My memory is hazy on a few things, but I remember feeling some comfort in recognizing that it was the scream of a little girl.

48

The detective remained by a window, keeping an eye on the house next door, waiting for a patrol unit to arrive.

The shirtless guy had put his guitar down. He didn't know what to do with himself. He knew something big was happening, but he didn't know what. "You want something to drink?" he asked.

"No, thanks."

"Can you tell me what's going on?"

"You ever see a little girl with Sid's nephew?"

"A little girl? No. Does he have a daughter?"

"Is Sid hard of hearing?"

"No."

"What does the nephew drive?"

"A little green sedan."

"What make?"

"Don't know. Sorry. Can you tell me what's going on?"

"You know, I think I will take something to drink after all. Maybe a glass of ice water? If you don't mind."

"Oh, sure. Be right back."

While the tap was still running in the kitchen, two patrol units *pulled to the curb in front of Sid's house. The detective called out "Thanks for your help," then stepped outside, closing the door behind him. He had a quick conversation with the two uniformed officers, telling them what was what. One of them moved along the side of the house and positioned himself against a chain-link fence, where he could keep an eye on the backyard. Make sure nobody snuck out the rear. The other officer followed behind as the detective approached the front door and knocked firmly.*

Weird how you feel at moments like this. You want it to be something, and you want it to be nothing. You want to catch the perverted scumbag who would abduct a little girl, but you want old Sid to be okay, too. Sometimes you can't have it both ways.

He knocked again, so hard that his knuckles hurt. Called out loudly, "Mr. Bertram? Mr. Bertram, sir, are you in there? It's the police."

Gave it thirty seconds, then knocked again. Pounded, really. "Mr. Bertram, we are concerned for your welfare." He opened the screen door and tried the doorknob. Locked.

He motioned to the uniformed cop, standing ten feet behind him, and the cop came closer. In a low voice, the detective said, "Check the garage. There's a window on the side. See if you can get a peek through the blinds."

While the uniform was gone, he pounded again. "Mr. Bertram, please come to the door. It's the police. Are you okay?"

The uniform came back and said, "All I can see is the fender of something green."

The detective nodded. The nephew's vehicle. The uniform retreated to his spot ten feet behind.

The detective pounded again. "Mr. Bertram, we are going to enter your home." He was practically shouting. This was all being recorded via the mike transmitting to the uniform's dash cam. Good. Documenting the authentic concern they all had for the welfare of an elderly gentleman. Establishing that they had the right to enter. "This is the police. We are going to break a window and enter — "

He heard the sound of the deadbolt unlocking. Then the door opened just a crack, with a security chain stretched across the gap. Young man looking out. Looking frazzled. Puzzled. Might've just woke up.

"What's going on?" he asked.

The detective identified himself. "Are you Daniel Wayne Bertram?"

"Yeah?"

"Sid Bertram is your uncle?"

"Yeah."

"Is he home right now?"

"He's sleeping. So was I."

The detective grinned. "Sid managed to sleep through all my banging?"

"I guess so, yeah."

"Would you check, please? I need to speak to him."

Bertram frowned. "I don't understand."

"Just need to speak to your uncle. Won't take but a minute."

"But I...really, about what?" Pale. Nervous.

"Mr. Bertram, I'm going to ask you to remove that chain and open the door."

"Why? What's — "

"Mr. Bertram, please — open the door so we can talk."

"But — "

"I just need to ask you and your uncle a few questions, then you can get back to your nap."

Bertram absolutely did not want to comply. That was obvious. But what choice did he have? He said nothing. A muscle twitched under his right eye.

"Mr. Bertram, I need to check on your uncle's welfare. I have a responsibility to do so, and I can legally enter this home to see if he's okay."

Bertram did nothing. He was no longer making eye contact. The detective realized that his entire body was tense. Heart thumping hard. He could feel the comforting weight of the revolver holstered on his hip, under his jacket.

"Mr. Bertram, I am about to kick this door open. You need to open this door. Right now."

Daniel Wayne Bertram was beginning to cry. His face was bunching with emotion. He nodded, then slowly closed the door.

The detective was ready. If it took more then three seconds for Bertram to unhook the chain and open the door again, he'd kick it in. Or go through a window.

But the door opened again. Bertram didn't even attempt to step out on the porch and close the door behind him. His body language said that the pretense was over. He was beaten. Tears ran down his cheeks. He was sniffling.

"Step outside, Mr. Bertram."

He did as instructed. The uniformed cop stepped up and guided Bertram off the porch, out into the yard, just to keep him out of the way for the next few minutes.

The detective entered the house. Called out. Nobody answered. Had his revolver in his hand now, because you just never knew. Maybe Bertram had a partner.

He poked his head into the kitchen. Nobody. Just the hum of a large freezer. With a lock on it. He was pretty sure he knew what he would find in there. But that would have to wait.

He turned from the kitchen and went down a hall. Slowly. Listening. Three doors, all closed. One left, one right, one at the end. Bedrooms, most likely. No rhyme or reason, he chose the one on the left. Opened the door.

And there she was.

Not tied up. Not gagged. Just sitting quietly, as she'd no doubt been warned to do. Holding a stuffed bunny rabbit. No expression on her face whatsoever.

The missing girl.
Hannah Ballard.

49

It's so trite, I can hardly stand it. The whole waking-up-in-the-hospital routine. But if you get shot, and you lose a lot of blood, and the doctors and nurses manage to keep you alive, that's where you're going to wake up. The hospital.

I didn't fade in and out, I simply woke up, more clear-headed than I would have expected, fully cognizant that I was in a hospital room. The TV mounted high on the wall was tuned to some old black-and-white movie.

There was a woman sleeping in a chair in a corner of the room. At first I thought it was Jessica, and then I realized it was Mia. I also realized that I was glad it was Mia, rather than Jessica.

On my left, there was a window looking out over a parking lot. It was daytime, with the sun low in the sky, but I couldn't tell if it was early morning or late afternoon. The left side of my chest was throbbing like a son of a bitch. When I attempted to sit up a little bit, it got worse. So I decided I was fine where I was.

There was some large medical device looming to my right. I couldn't turn my head enough to get a good look at the screen on the front of it. I had an IV in my right arm, but that was about it. No tube down my throat or mask over my face.

More than anything else, I was curious. What day of the week was it? How long had I been here? What had happened in that house? Why did —

"Hey."

I looked at Mia. She was smiling and coming up out of the chair, joining me beside the bed. She looked very tired, but still beautiful as hell.

"Hey, back," I said. "What day is it?"

It didn't hurt to speak as much as I thought it would. Let me rephrase that: Speaking didn't make me hurt any more than I already was.

She said, "Friday morning. Eight o'clock. About thirty hours since you got shot. How long have you been awake?" she asked.

"Just a few minutes. Your snoring woke me."

For half a second, she bought it. Then she grinned. "You must be feeling okay."

"Not too bad, but enough with the small talk. Was it Tracy Turner?"

A look came over her face. Pride, I think. Or just pure, off-the-charts satisfaction. She nodded. "Yeah. It was her. She was in there."

"She's okay?"

She nodded again.

Yes.

I closed my eyes and just took a moment to savor that information. For the second time in my life, I felt a sense of relief so profound as to be indescribable. You see, Tracy Turner — and my daughter Hannah — were two of the lucky ones. Children who had survived abduction.

I felt Mia's hand close over mine, so I opened my eyes.

"I was worried about you," she said.

"Mere bullets cannot stop me. Not for good, anyway."

"This one came pretty close."

"Yeah?"

Her eyes were welling up, but she didn't say anything.

"Where did it hit me?"

"Low on your chest. Through the ribs on your left side. It could have hit your liver or your kidney, but all it got was your spleen. They removed it."

"That's okay. I keep an extra in the freezer."

"Do you even know how lucky you are?"

"Enough that I feel like a cliché. See, if that bullet had been just an inch higher..."

Her face clouded. "This isn't funny."

"Uh...you seem a little angry."

She gave me a look that said, *Of course I'm angry, you incredible dumbass.*

I said, "What, uh — "

"You shouldn't have gone in there without me. Did that never occur to you?"

Oh. Right.

"I called the cops," I said feebly. "I waited for them to show up."

"Yeah, but I'm your partner, remember? Remember the talk we had after you went to Pierce's place?"

"You probably shouldn't say that too loud."

"I deserved to know what was going on, Roy. What if the tables had been turned? What if I'd seen Tracy Turner with Erica Kerwick and I'd decided to handle it all by myself?"

"Point taken."

"And maybe, with two of us going in, you wouldn't have gotten shot. Even better, I would've talked you out of it. It was a pretty dumb plan, you know?"

I was tempted to mention that the plan had worked, but now there were tears running down her cheeks. I realized that I hadn't handled things as well as I should have, regardless of whether I'd found Tracy Turner or not. Mia deserved better.

"You're right," I said. "I apologize."

She didn't say anything.

"Seriously," I said. "Won't happen again. Promise."

She finally met my eye and I saw a bit of forgiveness in there. This time, I took her hand.

"Tell me the rest," I said. "It was Sean Hanrahan?"

She nodded slowly. "He shot you."

No big surprise. "Where is he now?"

"He's dead, Roy. That Rollingwood cop who came in behind you — his name is Pryor — he shot him. Then he stopped your bleeding until an ambulance arrived. You owe him big time."

"How is Tracy?"

"She appears to be fine. No evidence of any abuse or mistreatment at all, although it was probably pretty traumatic seeing her Uncle Sean get killed."

"Yeah, I'm sure it was, but I am absolutely not going to feel any remorse for that."

"I know, and nobody is saying you should."

"What are Patrick Hanrahan and Erica Kerwick saying?"

She shook her head. "Nothing. Still won't talk. Everyone knows they were involved, but nothing's happening. Same as before."

"So they haven't been arrested?"

"Not yet. Apparently Ruelas got search warrants for Hanrahan's house and office, and Erica Kerwick's house, too. Don't know if they're finding anything. If it makes you feel any better, Patrick and Erica are getting crucified in the media."

It didn't make me feel any better, but I didn't say that. I tried to concentrate on the fact that Tracy was safe. And there was a pretty good chance she could describe what had happened to her in the eight days she'd been missing.

"What is Tracy saying? She could be the key to all this."

"I agree, but if she's giving them anything useful, Ruelas isn't sharing it with me. He's kind of pissed off. Won't return my calls."

"What the hell does he have to be pissed about?"

"I imagine he's just generally upset that you were right, and you found Tracy. From what I understand, that's a guy thing. Jealousy. Macho posturing and all that."

"You're going to tease me while I'm flat on my back?"

"Can you think of a better time? Besides, I don't want you to get a big head."

"About what?"

"Well, when I leave, and you start channel surfing, you're likely to hear people calling you a hero."

"Oh, yeah?"

"Yeah."

"Because of the way I faced down the North Korean army single-handed?"

She rolled her eyes. Her hand felt good in mine. Natural. Nothing self-conscious about it. I found myself hoping she felt the same way. For just a moment, we fell silent, just grinning at each other, and I thought we might kiss. Of course, I couldn't lean upward, toward her, so I was waiting for her to bend down. I *know* she felt it. I think. Or maybe I got my signals crossed. Or maybe it was whatever pain medicine they had me on.

But the moment passed. She released my hand.

I noticed a large bouquet of flowers resting on the windowsill.

"Who are those from?"

"Heidi. She stopped by a couple of hours ago."

"That was nice."

"She's a sweet gal."

"I'm glad you think so. She's our biggest client."

I was starting to get sleepy.

"I'm glad you're okay, Roy."

"Me, too." My eyes closed.

"I'll come back later this afternoon, okay?"

Not long after Mia left, after I'd slept for about an hour, I was visited by an investigator from the Rollingwood Police Department. His name was Barber, and he wasn't there long. That's because, as soon as he identified himself, I said, "Man, I'm not saying a word about anything. You want to charge me with something, go right ahead."

"I just need to hear your account of that night. For the record."

I said, "Nope." He opened his mouth again, but I said, "Seriously, dude. Don't bother."

It was a lost cause for him. I'm sure his department didn't like the way I'd forced their hand — getting an officer involved in a fatal shooting — but what were they going to do? Hassle a man that had been branded a hero?

"Well, I tried," he said. Then he gave me a wink, shook my hand, and took off.

I was released on Monday, stitched and heavily bandaged, but feeling halfway decent. Mia picked me up in her Mustang and took me to my apartment, where I was pleased to see that none of Ernie Crenshaw's spray paint remained on my front door. I'd never seen it cleaner.

There were various notes, business cards, and letters stuck between the door and the frame. These were from well-wishers — friends and neighbors — as well as eager reporters wanting to get the first interview. I was glad that none of them were hanging around the premises.

Mia followed me inside, then went back out to her car and wheeled in an ice chest filled with enough food to get me through the next several days. Fruits. Veggies. A lasagna. A casserole. Some baked chicken.

"So, I'm like a shut-in now?" I said.

"You shouldn't be going anywhere. Just rest and relax. Recuperate."

"That's all I've been doing for three days."

"Other than flirting with the nurses."

"Can you blame me? Did you see that redheaded one?"

"I did," she said. "He was cute."

"Well played."

I started to put the food away — using just my right hand, because it hurt to move my left side at all — but she stopped me and began to unload it herself. I watched.

"Thank you," I said. "This was really thoughtful."

"Hold your thanks until you try some of it. I've never claimed to be a good cook. Gross. What is in this Tupperware container?"

"Uh..."

"It's gray, and I don't think it's supposed to be."

I was thinking back on the hand-holding at the hospital. Maybe it was just a gesture of concern. Of friendship. Nothing else meant by it.

"You should come by tonight and eat some of this with me," I said.

She kept unloading the ice chest, rearranging the contents of my fridge in the process. Making sure nothing else looked deadly. "How about tomorrow night?"

"What, you have plans tonight?"

"I do, yeah."

She didn't say any more. Didn't make eye contact.

"What, a date?" I said.

"Yes, actually."

"Please. For the love of all things holy. Tell me you're not going out with Ruelas."

She stopped unloading and looked at me. "Are you truly that much of an idiot?"

"Of course I am. Haven't I made that clear?"

"No, not Ruelas. Just a guy I met at the gym a few weeks ago. I can call it off if you want."

"No, tomorrow night is great," I said.

An hour later I was alone again, settled on the couch, zoning out in front of the TV.

There was still nothing new on the case, according to media reports. Part of the problem was that Kathleen Hanrahan was not allowing police to speak to Tracy. I wasn't sure what the law prescribed in such a situation. Could the cops demand access to interview a six-year-old witness? Could Kathleen tell them to take a hike?

Here, as with the investigator who'd visited my hospital room, the cops had to walk on eggshells or suffer the wrath of the public. Maybe the cops were being patient because they had already gotten all they could from Tracy — but it was unclear whether they had even had a chance to ask her questions. Legally, they wouldn't have been able to interview her without a parent being present.

There was also the fact that witnesses that young were notoriously unreliable. If an interviewer said, "Tracy, name some of the people you saw while you were staying with Uncle Sean in that house," and Tracy said, "Daddy and Aunt Erica," you couldn't always be sure that was accurate. Maybe she only wished she'd seen them. Or maybe she dreamed it. Or she thought that's what the interviewer wanted to hear.

I took a short nap, then finally decided to tackle the chore of listening to the voicemail on my cell phone. Eighty-seven messages. I grabbed a pen and notepad to write down anything important.

Almost half of the messages were from reporters and writers, wanting to get an interview or just a statement. No idea how most of them had gotten my number. Some of them left really long, pleading messages, but I didn't listen longer than ten seconds to any particular message. I deleted them all without taking notes.

The remaining messages were from friends and various family members calling to check on me. Most of them I'd already seen or spoken to when I was still in the hospital, including Jessica, who had spent several hours in the room with me yesterday. She couldn't believe the way things had developed, and she had already told the cops everything she had told me about the Hanrahans and Brian Pierce. Best of all, at one point, she closed the door to the room and we made out like a couple of high schoolers. Then a nurse showed up and ruined everything.

The most recent message, which had come in just twenty minutes ago, was from Detective Ruelas.

"Hey, asshole. Call me back."

50

I'll give him this: At least he wasn't using that fake friendly cop routine he'd tried a few days earlier. Just being himself. A jerk. But, yeah, curiosity got the best of me and I called him back.

"Guess you're pretty proud of yourself," he said.

"I'm healing up nicely. Thanks for asking."

"Normally, I wouldn't share anything more important than the time of day with a needledick such as yourself, but after what you did the other night, I figure you deserve to know."

"Know what?"

He paused, deciding if he should tell me whatever was on his mind. "You'll keep it under your hat?"

"Oh, absolutely."

"Won't even tell your hot partner?"

"I'll tell her you're still a buffoon, but nothing more." I had no intention of keeping my word. I didn't know what he was about to tell me, but if it was important or intriguing, I'd call Mia the second I hung up with him.

He said, "Kathleen Hanrahan is finally talking again. She had some interesting stuff to say. And she finally let us interview Tracy.

Arrests are forthcoming."

"Forthcoming?"

"As in they are happening right now."

"Both Hanrahan and Erica Kerwick?" I said.

"Notice I said *arrests*, as in plural."

"How did Tracy do?"

"She was a champ. Sounded like she actually enjoyed the getaway, spending time with Aunt Erica, Uncle Sean, and Uncle Brian. Kid's so smart, she'd do great in front of a jury. But I'm guessing it won't come to that."

"What did Kathleen say?"

"What we already know — that she'd been threatening Patrick with divorce for quite awhile, because of his affair with Erica, but he threatened her right back, saying he'd claim she's an alcoholic and shouldn't have custody of a child. Probably right about that, from what I can tell. She's been in rehab twice, and he obviously never planned to stop cheating. Why two people like that stay together is beyond me. According to her, when things weren't bad, they were pretty good."

"But something important happened recently."

"Yep. Kathleen got drunk one night, they got in a huge argument, and she said she was going to claim he had been molesting Tracy."

And there it was. The one thing Kathleen wouldn't tell me when I interviewed her at her house. And I don't blame her. A claim like that — assuming it was false — was about as dirty as it got. Shameful. And yet, despite Kathleen's obvious character flaws, the authorities would be duty-bound to investigate her claim, and her sworn testimony, all by itself, might've been enough to win custody for her.

Ruelas said, "She says she was bluffing, just venting, but the next afternoon, while she was sleeping, that's when Tracy disappeared. Evidently, Patrick took it seriously enough to do something desperate. Probably just panicked, without really thinking things through. Actually, we think he had his brother do it. Sean Hanrahan flew down from Boston on the first nonstop that morning. Rented a car under his own name, too. Guy's a former cop and he does something that stupid."

Over the past several days, lying there in my hospital bed, I'd been pondering all the possible evidence the cops might have been able to find, and I'd come up with quite a lot — even if they hadn't had any testimony from Kathleen or Tracy. Evidence of Sean Hanrahan's travel plans was on my mental list. Nowadays, a man can't travel across the country without leaving tracks.

"What else you got?" I said.

"Plenty."

"Care to be more specific?"

"I can't get into that yet."

"How about the gun Sean Hanrahan shot me with? Same gun that was used on Brian Pierce?"

"You're a pretty smart guy." His way of saying *Yes*.

"You must've found all kinds of fingerprints at Pierce's place, no matter how much they wiped it down after they left. Sean's, Erica's, and Tracy's, but not Patrick's. Same at the Rollingwood place."

"You ever thought about being a cop?" Being sarcastic and condescending, but still saying *Yes*. I wondered why he was telling me any of this. Probably hoping I wouldn't badmouth him in the press. Fine by me.

"Phone records between Pierce and the rest of them?" I asked.

I figured the four members of the abduction team had to stay in touch somehow.

Ruelas sighed, like I was really putting him out — forcing him to cross ethical boundaries and reveal information. "Nothing there, but that's not a surprise. But we did find two cheap no-contract cell phones in the Rollingwood house. Pierce's prints were on one of them. Sean must have taken it after he killed Pierce. The records show dozens of calls between those phones and to two other cell phones, all four of them bought by Sean Hanrahan at the same time, the same day Tracy went missing. Smart money says those other two phones were Patrick's and Erica Kerwick's, at least temporarily, but I'm sure they're in a lake somewhere now."

"Get anything from Hanrahan's place? Or Erica Kerwick's?"

"Surprisingly little. They were smart enough to avoid using email. Only thing — she had recently applied for a passport. Went through one of those companies that rushes it through, for a price."

"When was this?"

"Two days after Tracy disappeared."

"Hanrahan already had one?"

"Yep, and the girl did too. They're big travelers, the Hanrahans."

I could picture it all. Patrick responded to Kathleen's threat by grabbing Tracy, without any kind of plan in place. Just a visceral reaction — wanting Tracy by his side, because he loved her like his own. He had to hide her, so he stashed her at Brian Pierce's place, offering so much cash that Pierce couldn't resist. Pierce worked with Kathleen way back when, so he probably knew about her problems with booze. Probably thought he was doing a good deed by helping Patrick out.

Meanwhile, Hanrahan slowly began to realize what a mistake he'd made. Should've owned up to it right away, as soon as Kathleen called the cops, but the longer he let it go on, the bigger price he'd have to pay if he got caught. Hanrahan's solution? Get out of the country. Take Tracy and Erica and relocate. Forever. He had plenty of money to start over somewhere. But he had to wait until the search for Tracy died down.

But then Pierce began to waver. Began to realize he'd put himself in major legal jeopardy. He probably started to panic. So Sean or Erica takes Tracy to the Rollingwood house. But even that's not enough, because the interview by Ruelas rattles Pierce even further. He wants to come clean. Maybe there's an argument with Sean that leads to violence, or maybe it was cold-blooded murder, but Sean kills him.

It all fit the facts almost perfectly. Almost. But there was still one piece that couldn't be explained. Maybe Ruelas had forgotten about it, or he was intentionally overlooking it, just as I was prepared to do. Because — if that unexplained piece meant what I thought it did — it wouldn't really change things. Patrick Hanrahan and Erica Kerwick were still guilty and deserved to be punished.

So I was prepared to leave everything alone and not worry about knowing the full truth.

Then Kathleen Hanrahan — who hadn't contacted me since I'd found Tracy — left a voicemail for me. She apologized for not reaching out sooner, but things had been hectic, as I might imagine. And now she wanted to say thanks.

51

She answered the door alone. Tracy wasn't in sight. I was surprised — you'd think she'd want the girl right there with her at all times — but then again, maybe she was afraid some unseen force would pull Tracy through the open door and take her away forever. Irrational, but that's the kind of thought that crosses your mind. I knew that for certain.

Mia was there with me, of course. No way was I going without my partner.

Kathleen glanced at Mia briefly, but then she focused on me again. She stepped out onto the porch and wrapped her arms around me. I carefully hugged her back.

"Easy, now," I said. "Stitches."

She relaxed her hold just a bit.

"Thank you so much," she said softly in my ear. "Thank you for my daughter."

I nodded. I could feel a lump forming in my throat, and I didn't expect that at all. I was elated that I wasn't smelling booze.

After a good half-minute, she let me go.

I said, "Kathleen, this is my partner, Mia Madison."

They shook hands, but Kathleen looked at Mia neutrally.

So I said, "You should know that Mia played a critical role in finding Tracy. We worked together. Without her, I would have gotten nowhere."

Kathleen looked at her again, reappraising her, and then she stepped forward and hugged Mia, too.

We went inside. Kathleen offered us coffee, which we declined, and then we ended up in the living area again, all of us sitting on the red L-shaped sofa. There was no glass of red wine on the coffee table. Just a large coffee mug.

"How are you feeling?" Kathleen asked me.

"Doing okay," I said. "Still a little pain, but not as bad as I thought it would be. Don't even need painkillers anymore. How are *you* doing?"

She shook her head, as if to say, *I truly don't know.* Just like the last time I'd been here, her face clouded with emotion, on the verge of crying, her eyes cast downward. "I've made so many mistakes. For years now."

After a beat, I said, "We all have. What's important is to learn from them and move forward."

Mia gave me a look, like, *Well, aren't you on top of your game this morning?*

Kathleen nodded and rubbed her nose.

"I'll be right back," I said.

I went to the bathroom down the hallway and returned with a box of Kleenex. Mia had moved next to Kathleen and had her arm over her shoulder. She pulled a couple of tissues from the box I offered and handed them to Kathleen, who looked like she was regaining her composure. She gave me an embarrassed smile.

"Seems like I'm always crying around you," she said.

"I have that effect. My mere presence tends to make people cry."

She laughed.

Sure, she was emotional, but I could see such a difference between this woman and the one I'd interviewed last week.

"These last few days," she said, "I've learned what you went through. I...I didn't know."

Normally I don't share details with people I hardly know — but Kathleen Hanrahan and I had a bond that was as undeniable as it was painful. "Hannah was missing for eight days," I said. "It seemed like eight months. I think I slept for an hour in that time. I still have nightmares about it."

Kathleen was looking at me with an expression of empathy unlike any I'd ever seen.

"We were incredibly lucky," I said. "A total stranger had taken her. Kids don't normally come back home from that. But there was this detective — tenacious as hell. Wouldn't give up. Smart. Checked every detail. He retired a few years ago and moved to San Diego. I think of that man, and what he did for me, almost every day. I think of him, even though my relationship with my daughter is almost nonexistent now. My wife — my ex-wife — well, she couldn't get past it. She grew so angry at me during those eight days that we never recovered from it. We tried, of course, or I did. But things were never the same."

I was surprised that I wasn't choking up. Just stating the facts, such as they were.

I shrugged, saying, "She divorced me, met a guy a year later, then moved with him to Canada. My daughter is up in Canada. That still seems so odd. Edmonton. More than two thousand miles away. She never seemed to suffer any lasting effects from spending eight days with a sicko. He never laid a hand on her, according to the experts, although he would have eventually. She's almost fourteen now, and I talk to her about twice a year. I call her more than that, but she doesn't call back very often. She's a teenager. Even if we were in the same room, I'd be way down on her list of priorities."

Kathleen gestured for me to move beside her on the sofa, and there we sat, the three of us in a row, Kathleen holding my hand, comforting me, while Mia comforted her.

There was still the one remaining question I needed to ask, because of that one unexplained piece of the puzzle.

Earlier this year, in February or March, Emma Webster had seen Brian Pierce with a little girl whose description perfectly matched Tracy Turner's. It would be easy enough to dismiss it — to assume Emma was mistaken. Just a confused old lady who wanted something to gossip about.

Or.

Or I could adjust my theory to accommodate my suspicions. Kathleen Hanrahan was a drinker. Maybe a former drug user, according to Jessica. A big-time party girl, in years past. Just how much did she sleep around? With whom? Would she have slept with a teenage dishwasher?

Was Brian Pierce Tracy's father?

That was the question, wasn't it? I could imagine a one-night stand. Then Kathleen discovers that she's pregnant. She works backward on the calendar to see who might be the dad, and realizes it's Pierce. She tells him. He's terrified. Eighteen years old, very little income, and not ready to be a dad.

She says, "Relax, kid. My husband doesn't need to know." So Tracy is born and, shortly thereafter, Kathleen starts sleeping with Patrick. She divorces her husband and becomes a Hanrahan.

But Brian's feelings change over the years. He matures. He wants a connection with his little girl. So he goes to Patrick and reveals the truth. Or he makes Kathleen do it. Or maybe Patrick knew all along. What does Brian want? He realizes he can't provide the advantages in life that Patrick Hanrahan can provide. That's okay. Brian just wants to spend some time with Tracy occasionally. To participate in her life. To be "Uncle Brian." Which could very well include the occasional afternoon, just him and Tracy. It wouldn't surprise me if Brian decided to show Tracy where he lived. But maybe that was outside the boundaries he'd established with Patrick and Kathleen, so when Emma Webster asked him about the little girl, he said, "What little girl?"

Of course, this was all conjecture. Without interrogating Kathleen, I'd never know for sure. Nobody would ever —

"Roy?"

It was Mia.

"Yeah?"

"Did you hear what Kathleen said?"

"I'm sorry, I was just thinking about something."

I turned to Kathleen, who had dried her tears and now looked positively content. Hopeful. Like someone who was ready to put the past behind her and start fresh.

She said, "Tracy is napping, but I think it's time for her to get up. Would you like to meet her?"

ABOUT THE AUTHOR

Edgar Award-nominated author Ben Rehder lives with his wife near Austin, Texas, where he was born and raised. *Gone The Next* is his ninth novel.

OTHER BOOKS BY BEN REHDER

Buck Fever

Bone Dry

Flat Crazy

Guilt Trip

Gun Shy

Holy Moly

The Chicken Hanger

The Driving Lesson

Made in the USA
Lexington, KY
27 June 2014